"*A* plane? Really?" I said as Cole led me up a ramp before opening the plane's door. "Is this where you take all the girls?"

But the Witty had come back out to play. She was growing on me.

Cole gave me a twisted little grin. "Only the girls that make me work really hard for it," he said. Before my mind could get carried away with what "*it*" entailed, Cole grabbed my hand and pulled me inside the plane.

I knew I shouldn't follow him inside. I knew what being in another dark, confined, quiet space would make me want to do with Cole. I knew the electricity shooting through my hand from his touch would only compound if we touched anywhere else.

I knew so many things.

But darn if my heart, or my soul, or that rebellious Elle inside of me, wasn't outwitting my mind at every turn tonight.

Also by
NICOLE WILLIAMS

CRASH

CLASH

And coming soon ... **CRUSH**

UP IN FLAMES

Nicole Williams

**SIMON &
SCHUSTER**

London · New York · Sydney · Toronto · New Delhi

A CBS COMPANY

First published in Great Britain in 2013 by Simon & Schuster UK Ltd
A CBS COMPANY

1 3 5 7 9 10 8 6 4 2

Simon & Schuster UK Ltd
1st Floor
222 Gray's Inn Road
London WC1X 8HB

Simon & Schuster Australia, Sydney
Simon & Schuster India, New Delhi

A CIP catalogue record for this book is available
from the British Library.

PB ISBN 978-1-4711-1846-3
eBook ISBN 978-1-4711-1845-6

This book is a work of fiction. Names, characters, places
and incidents are either the product of the author's imagination or are
used fictitiously. Any resemblance to actual people living or dead,
events or locales is entirely coincidental.

Printed and bound by CPI Group (UK) Ltd, Croydon, CR0 4YY

www.simonandschuster.co.uk
www.simonandschuster.com.au

Nicole loves to hear from her readers. You can connect with her on
Facebook: Nicole Williams (Official Author Page)
Twitter: @nwilliamsbooks
Blog: nicoleawilliams.blogspot.com

UP IN FLAMES

ONE

It was unseasonably hot for early June. The swimming hole I'd grown up jumping off tire swings into was already receding from the shoreline. High temperatures and low rainfall this early into fire season could only mean one thing—it was going to be a dangerous summer in the Methow Valley of Washington State.

If I hadn't been raised in the same house as two generations of Montgomerys before me, attended the same school I'd just graduated from with the exact same handful of kids I'd started kindergarten with, and worked as the night manager at the diner my parents had opened fifteen years back, I would have bailed the same day I woke up in Winthrop and realized I was going to die here. In fact, my plot at the cemetery just outside of town had already been picked out and paid for to ensure all of us Montgomerys could stick together. Even in death.

Morbid, I know.

Don't get me wrong, Winthrop, Washington was a beautiful little town: quaint, clean, virtually crime free, and abounding with more natural beauty than you could shake a stick at, but it was boring. And suffocating.

Every time I'd driven down State Route 20 this past year on my way to school, I reminded myself why this was a good place to live. Why it would be an ideal place to put down permanent roots and raise a family. The mental pictures of friends, hiking, swimming, baseball games, holiday dinners, so on and so forth, convinced me for a couple miles.

Every day though, by the time I pulled into the high school's parking lot, I couldn't breathe quite right. Like my lungs were only up to half capacity in Winthrop.

Speaking of putting down roots . . . Logan had started talking about marriage again, not even two days after we'd graduated high school. Logan Matthews had been my friend as a child and my boyfriend since I was allowed to go on my first official date at sixteen. The Matthews were almost as dug in deep in Winthrop as the Montgomerys, and I'd be willing to bet my life savings our families would consider forcing an arranged marriage if we didn't go about it the other way. Logan was a good boyfriend and an even better guy, but he was the companion equivalent to this town: safe, comfortable, and a tad boring.

However, this afternoon on my Grandma M's porch had been anything but boring. The big M word had come up before, and lord knew it wouldn't be the last time I'd hear it. You see, Logan loved four things in this world: his family, God, baseball, and me.

As far as he was concerned, he had three of those four in the bag. The fourth, that being yours truly, was being a bit evasive.

As soon as he'd dropped the M bomb, my stomach twisted and I broke out in a cold sweat in the middle of an eighty-five degree day. Some part of me knew it was the right thing to do, we'd grown up together and he was the only boy I'd ever kissed, but it just felt so wrong.

After basically leaping out of the porch swing and appeasing Logan with some story that I had something important to do, I hopped into my Jeep and bounced down a familiar dirt road until I could go no further.

I needed to let myself go. Feel wild and free for a few minutes, and since I lived in a small town where everyone was in everyone's business, I had to be careful when one of my free spirited bouts hit me. I couldn't go to one of the late night keggers in the woods because I wasn't that kind of girl. I couldn't make out with some random stranger because I had a promise ring on my finger from the town pastor's son. I couldn't get in my dad's old Mustang and play chicken with another car because my uncle was the town sheriff. I couldn't deface public property because my family was practically the unelected government in the Methow Valley. I couldn't do any of the things other teens did when the need to rebel struck them. But I had that need no matter how many times I tried to hide it away.

So what did I do?

I went down to the swimming hole that was smack in the middle of my Grandma M's hundred and twenty acres that her and Grandpa had purchased and built a log cabin on after hand-ing over the family house to my mom and dad before I'd been born. It had been over a decade since Grandpa had died, but Grandma M refused to move back to town. You would have thought she'd get lonely all by herself in the middle of nowhere, but she made it a point to stay active. If she was ever lonely, it was due to choice.

I parked my Jeep and hoofed it in about a quarter of a mile until the swimming hole came in view. Like the good rebel I wasn't, I surveyed the surrounding area to make sure today wasn't the day some random hiker had stopped to take an afternoon swim.

No one, nothing, nada.

Feeling that wild streak about to explode if I didn't loosen the stopper, I pulled my shift dress up and over my head before toss-ing it over a tree limb. On most days, this would appease the wild inside me enough, but not today.

Taking another scan of the area, I unfastened my bra and hung it next to my dress before I slid my panties down. They joined the clothing decorated tree branch.

There it was. I could breathe deeply again.

The wild I liked to pretend wasn't there was happy. Stripping down to my birthday suit in preparation for a cool dip had sati-ated its appetite for rebellion.

As soon as I stepped into the water, my skin bubbled with goose bumps. Another downside to the warm temperatures so early in the season? The lakes, rivers, and private little swimming holes hadn't had a chance to warm up yet.

By the time I was at knee level my skin still hadn't gone numb, so I decided it was time to abandon the whole ease-into-it-slowly idea and just dove straight in. The cold water assaulted my body. Just when I was sure I couldn't bear the cold anymore, it got better. My body adjusted to it just enough to make me comfortable enough to stay under, but it still knew this chilly world wasn't quite right either.

I kicked to the surface, rolled onto my back and floated for a couple minutes. I felt better. Not earth shatteringly better, but enough to make it count. Enough so I knew that when I got out and back to reality, I'd be able to resume smiling at all the right times and saying the right things.

The swimming hole was surrounded by a circle of giant oak, maple, and willow trees, which was part of the reason the water always stayed so cool. Hardly any direct sun could make it through the canopy of trees, but as I floated around the hole, I found a hand-sized patch of blue sky shining through the glossy green leaves. After staring at that ray of light for a while, I moved into deeper water.

Since the summer I turned twelve, I'd developed something of a swimming hole tradition. It was part competition with myself, part therapy, but it was all sacred.

Once I'd paddled over the deepest part of the hole, I exhaled, forcing all of the air out of my lungs. And then I started to sink. I always started with a couple warm-ups where I'd only sink a few feet beneath the water before resurfacing. But today wasn't just about warming up; today was about breaking the record I'd set two summers ago when Logan and I first started dating. I'd been underwater for a total of thirty-five seconds that year, far surpassing my previous record of twenty-seven seconds. Last summer I'd come within one second of breaking that record, but I was determined that this summer I'd annihilate that record.

After the day I'd had, I could really use that record breaker. I filled my lungs to capacity before slowly letting that breath out through my nose. As soon as I was below the surface, I started to count. The longer I counted, the blacker the water around me got. The farther my body fell below the surface, the colder the water got. Deeper and deeper I went until my lungs started to burn. The last of the oxygen was gone after ten seconds.

I pushed past the burn and ignored the fear that clawed at me when the black around me became opaque. I was three seconds away from tying the record. Four seconds away from breaking it.

Two more seconds down, two more to go. My lungs had gone from a burning feeling to hurting like raw open wounds. I felt myself go a little light headed when something grabbed a hold of me.

I jolted in surprise as a strong arm wound around my middle before I was towed to the surface. The instant my head broke through the water, I gulped in a mouthful of air. The arm around me didn't let me go, and as I took a second gulp of air, I felt a few emotions trickle into my veins: I'd been so close.

So close to breaking my record and this arm and its owner had ruined it.

"What do you think you're doing?" I gasped, shoving out of the arm's hold and swimming a few strokes away.

"You're welcome. Happy I could be of assistance and I'm even happier to have you show your utmost appreciation for saving your life." A male voice replied with a strong dose of sarcasm. It wasn't a familiar one.

When I'd put some distance between us, I twisted around. His face wasn't familiar either, but a girl wouldn't mind getting familiar with that kind of face.

That was, if a girl wasn't with another guy who was the town's unofficial crown prince.

"I wasn't drowning," I said, biting back the *you idiot* part. "I was swimming."

"You were under the surface for over thirty seconds," he said, swimming closer. I backed away until my feet hit the sandy loam. "I thought you were drowning. What was I supposed to do? Just let you go down without a fight?"

Sinking my feet into the sand, I stood up. "No. You're supposed to ask a person if they want saving before you go all hero on them."

Hero boy's mouth curved up when his eyes drifted south. "Thank God."

"No, not 'thank God' for you interrupting my efforts to break a sinking record," I snapped back.

"I'm thanking God for something else right now." The look on his face was one I'm sure God wouldn't approve of and, if it wasn't for the way it was making me breathe a little shorter, I wouldn't have approved either.

"What are you thanking Him for?" I said, ready to get out of the water and leave this stranger, who was both infuriating and appealing at the same time thanks to his own life-saving, God-thanking ways.

That was when I remembered I was swimsuit impaired in waist deep water. A fact that wouldn't have escaped my mind if it hadn't been so oxygen deprived.

"Right now,"—one brow arched—"I'm thanking him for cold water."

I glanced down, already mortified.

Yep. That dreamy look in his eyes and that twisted smile all made sense now. As if my bare boobs weren't enough, my nipples were on high beams for his viewing pleasure. I ducked beneath the surface so he had nothing but a neck up view. His expression didn't change as much as I thought it would.

"For someone who can stare like that at a girl's . . ." I stumbled for the right word to use. I fumbled even more trying to verbalize it.

"Rack?" the grinning boy suggested.

"*Chest*," I corrected with a tight smile. "For someone who can stare at an unsuspecting girl's chest for half a minute, I wouldn't take that person to be the thanking God, religious type."

"I'm not," he said with a one-shouldered shrug. "But after just witnessing that wonder of the world, I might change my mind."

I narrowed my eyes. "How long have you been here?"

He swam a little closer, and now I could make out the color of his eyes. A bright greenish-blue that, when paired with his dark hair, tan skin, and the appealing angles of his face, could make a girl weak in the knees even from ten yards back.

That sly smile of his went higher. "Long enough to know that your hair color is natural."

Despite the cold water, my face heated instantly.

"It's all right," he said immediately, lifting his hands above the water. "We were brought into the world naked and it's a damn shame somewhere along man's way he felt the need to cover up," those eyes of his sparkled, "because bodies like yours make clothing a real tragedy."

I knew in some sick, twisted way, he was trying to make me feel better, but I felt worse. My own boyfriend hadn't even seen me naked from the waist up, and this smiling stranger had gotten the whole shebang. Not only that, I was uncomfortable with the way he looked at me *and* the way I felt when he looked at me. Some part of me, and if I was a betting girl I'd put it all on that wild streak, liked the way he looked at me.

Liked it way too much.

I cleared my throat and tried to break eye contact. Tried unsuccessfully. "This is private property, you know."

"No, I didn't know," he said, looking around. "Besides, I adhere more to the land owns us, we don't own the land kind of philosophy."

"Most trespassers would I suppose," I said, wondering why, in all of the many lakes, streams, and swimming holes in the county, this guy who appealed to me on a primal level had to choose this one.

"As much fun as this flirty banter is, my balls are about to fall off if I don't get out of this cold ass water," he said, swimming towards me.

I told myself he was only trying to get closer to the shore, not to me, but his eyes told a different story.

"So who's getting out first? Me . . . or you?" His smile curved even higher over that last part.

My eyes went narrower still.

"I guess I am," he answered for me when my lips stayed sealed. I'd already given him the full show once; he wasn't getting it again.

Taking a few more long strokes, his feet hit the bottom and he started walking out of the water.

"Same time tomorrow?" he called back at me as his shoulders broke the surface. I'd seen wider ones, but I'd never seen more defined ones. This was so not helping the strange feeling I had coiling up inside of me. That face, those shoulders, that back, and that . . . butt.

I hadn't been the only one skinny dipping this afternoon.

Look away, look away right now, I told myself.

I didn't listen.

"My name's Cole," he said as he continued towards the shore.

"Don't care," I lied, not able to peel my eyes away from that long, tanned, muscled, dripping wet body.

"Last name's Carson."

"Care even less." Did I sound as unconvincing to him as I did to my own ears?

"What's your name?" he asked, pausing at knee level and glancing back at me.

"My first name's *Keep* and my last name's *Walking*."

What was I doing? I never talked like this to people. I'd come in second place as the senior class sweetheart. Second-place sweethearts didn't sass back to naked, hot strangers while they were naked themselves.

Suddenly, he turned around. *All* the way around.

My face went blank before I felt heat rush up my neck. It was the first time I'd seen a man's . . . *package*, and I'd be lying if I said it wasn't the first thing I zeroed in on. I'd be lying again if I said I looked away quickly. Instead my eyes lingered until I felt heat wind up my body, tightening around an area south of my navel.

Stretching his arms above his head, Cole cleared his throat. "I like that flustered look on your face," he said, and even though I wasn't looking at his face, I heard the smile in his voice. "See anything you like?"

"No," I snapped.

"Really? Because that flushed expression says otherwise," he said, his voice all tease. "I've got the whole afternoon open. I'd be happy to give you an in-depth, hands-on tutorial to Cole Carson."

I managed to close my eyes, and when I reopened them, I was finally able to look away from what I was fixed on earlier. "You have fun with your own hands," I said, cocking a brow.

He studied my face and that half smile of his moved into something a bit more genuine. "You gonna be all right out here if I go? Not going to drown?"

"Not today," I replied, my eyes automatically dropping as he turned his back to me again.

I didn't look away until he disappeared into the trees.

I couldn't stop thinking about Cole. His eyes, that cocky grin, and his backside.

And his frontside, too.

I was positively distracted and sufficiently flustered. That could have explained why three of my orders had gone out wrong tonight. One of the few perks to growing up in the same town with the same people? They let you off the hook easy when you delivered a savory crepe instead of the sweet crepe of the day they'd ordered. If ever there was a time to stiff a server, it would be when they brought you a smoked salmon and cream cheese crepe when you were expecting a crepe stuffed with bananas, chocolate sauce, and walnuts, but no one left me less than a fifteen percent tip all night.

Since it was a Friday night, the cafe had been hopping and I hadn't had a chance to pour myself a cup of coffee from the time I arrived until fifteen minutes before closing.

I'd worked at Le Crepe'erie most of my life in some capacity. That's the way it is with a family business. As a grade schooler, I used to sort and sharpen crayons into baskets for the guests that came to dine with kids. As a middle schooler, I'd helped plant flowers every spring in the overwhelming number of hanging baskets and window baskets. Le Crepe'erie had won "Best Floral Display" ten years running and my dad took almost as much pride in this as he did the quality products he put into each crepe. Since I'd turned sixteen, I'd been serving tables. I was even known to whip together a recipe or two when the chef was fresh out of new ideas.

You would have thought a crepe shop in the middle of small town USA wouldn't be likely to succeed, but Le Crepe'erie had been in business for over fifteen years and was an icon in Winthrop. Known for its basic menu that changed every day, there was rarely an empty table on the weekends or evenings on the weekdays. There were two options on any given day: sweet or savory. That was it. We didn't do pancakes, waffles, or French toast. We did crepes.

You couldn't get an egg over easy or a slab of ham on the side. I'll repeat. We did crepes.

But we made darn good ones.

Guests did have a selection of drinks, so long as it was coffee. We did drip, espresso, cappuccino, or the occasional latte if the customer was real nice.

Crepes and coffee were like a religion here at Le Crepe'erie and you didn't just come into someone's church and order hash-browns without it being considered a sacrilege.

"How'd you do tonight?" Dani asked me from two tables down where she was busy cleaning up.

The last guests were just leaving for the night, so I locked the door and flipped the closed sign over behind them. "Pretty good," I replied. "Fifty bucks or so."

"Day-um, girl!" she said, running back to the kitchen to crank on the radio. "My little Bs only pulled in just over thirty. I need to get myself over to Seattle, have a plastic surgeon hook me up, and start making fifty a shift." She came back out into the dining room, dancing to the song on the radio. "Do you think I could consider a boob job a business write-off if it helps me make more money?"

I took a long sip of my coffee before grabbing a bussing cart. There was a nice mess ahead of me. "Why don't you ask the working girls down at Dolly's Gentlemen's Club? I'm sure they'd know," I said, crumpling up a napkin and tossing it down at Dani where she twirled on a bar stool. "And mine are real, thank you very much."

"Yeah, a real waste of space since no one's having any fun with them," she said, tossing the napkin back at me. My mind flashed with the memory of Cole looking at me, gaping at me, and my stomach did another one of those coiling up things.

"Yours get enough action for both of us," I threw back as I sprayed down a few tables with disinfectant.

"Come on, though. Has Logan cupped, tweaked, squeezed, or hell, even grazed them yet?"

I grumbled as I started wiping down the tables. Dani had been my best friend since second grade. We weren't exactly an obvious best friend match. She was vivacious, cursed more than she talked, and had slept with most of Winthrop's male population that was under twenty . . . twice. She was short, blonde, and stylish. I was more your wallflower type that strived to stay inside our society's boundaries. A cuss word in my book was *crap* or *ass* if I was really worked up, and I still had my V card firmly in hand. I was tall, brunette, and wore what was comfortable.

I couldn't pinpoint what had brought us together and kept us together all these years, but I told everyone Dani was my kindred spirit. On the surface, we were nothing alike, but everything that couldn't be seen tied us together.

"He grazed them this past year at Winter Formal," I said, sounding defensive.

"Accidentally?"

"Does it matter?" I asked while I tossed coffee cups and plates onto the cart.

"Yes." Dani swung off of the bar stool and marched my way. "Yes, it most certainly does matter. You and Logan have been together for over two years and the only thing you've done is kiss. That is not normal." Dani was a few inches shorter than me, but she had a way of seeming taller when she looked at me the way she was now.

"Says the girl who lost her virginity when she was thirteen," I muttered.

She grabbed a dish rag and swatted my butt with it. "That's because I was the smart one. Why do you want to waste the most virile, wild years of your life keeping your knees closed?"

"We're waiting for marriage," I replied automatically, but that was Logan's reason, not mine.

I wouldn't have had a problem going all the way with a guy if we weren't married, but I had a few obstacles in my deflowering way. I was with Logan, and I probably always would be. He wanted to wait until we were married. I might have pushed the issue, but even the making out had gotten a little boring this past year. If Logan sliding his tongue into my mouth couldn't turn me on, why should I assume him sliding anything else inside me would?

"God. Don't even get me started on you two and your impending marriage and abstaining until that blessed day shit," she said, helping me clear off the next table.

"I didn't ask you to get started on any of it, Dani," I said. "So why don't you drop it?"

She made a face while she considered this before shrugging. "What are you doing tonight after work? Logan's out of town at a game, right?"

"Yeah, he left this afternoon and will be back on Sunday," I said. "And what do I always do on a Friday night?" It was a rhetorical question. As a general rule of thumb, Dad opened the restaurant and I closed it.

"Close this place down," she said, spraying a few more tables. I was confused as I watched her clean up. Dani was my best friend and all, but she wasn't scheduled to close tonight. Normally I'd be lucky if I could flip that closed sign before Dani was clocked out and running out of the place. "But what if I said I'd help you get this place cleaned and closed earlier than usual so you could go out and have a good time with me before your dad even knew you were late?"

"I'd say you're up to something," I said, rolling the cart of dirty dishes into the back.

"I am up to something," she hollered at me over the radio.

"Trying to show my best friend a good time this summer. Trying to show her what she's going to be missing out on if she gets married a few short months after graduating high school. Trying to show her the way a man *should* want to play with those fun bags."

I rolled my eyes as I loaded a tray for the dishwasher. Dani had invited me to plenty of parties in our years together and the only ones I'd said yes to were her birthday parties. I'd even started missing those over the past few years because they'd been more a study in hedonism than happy birthday.

I'd always said no. So why, tonight, did I feel like a yes was on the tip of my tongue?

I was pretty sure my answer had something to do with a certain Cole Carson and that stomach thing he made me feel whenever I thought about him.

"Where's the party at?" I said, not needing clarification as to what it was. Dani didn't do slumber parties or cosmic bowling on a Friday night. She danced on table tops and drank Smirnoff like it was going out of production.

Dani's head popped into the back, her brown eyes bugged out. So she was as shocked as I was that I was actually thinking about this.

"The clearing on old man Shanigan's property," she said, helping me load the next tray for the dishwasher. "It's the summer kick-off party and everyone's going to be there."

"Everyone?" I said sarcastically, sliding the first tray into the washer and closing the door. "I just graduated a few days ago with 'everyone'. I don't want to see them tapping kegs and dry humping against trees on old man Shanigan's."

"Not all the dip-shits we went to school with," she said. "I mean, sure they'll all be there, but when I say *everyone*, I mean everyone as in the smokejumpers."

How Dani could make the words smoke and jumper sound as filthy as she could was a true talent.

I groaned as I prepared to load the second tray. "Dani, the only thing that sounds like less of a good time than hanging out with all the same people we grew up with would be hanging out with a bunch of guys who think a local is something you put your penis in."

Dani's eyes bugged again. Given her eyes were already large for her face, the effect was rather funny. "I think that's the first time I've heard the word penis come from that sweet little mouth you've never had wrapped around one before," she giggled as she helped me stack the clean dishes. "This is as wild as I'll ever get you, Elle. I'm not taking a no tonight. You're coming. You'll drink a beer. Or two. You'll have a good time. Maybe even get felt up by one of those raving sexaholic smokejumper sinners." The glare I shot her only made her smile wider. "And then one day, when you're lying next to Logan in bed, wondering how he failed to pleasure you yet again with his cock or his tongue, you can have happy thoughts about that one night you let your hair down."

I cringed. "Two things. Don't ever mention Logan's . . ."

"Cock," Dani assisted, winking at me.

I nodded. "Logan's c-word or tongue again."

"Oh, hell, Elle. How can you and I be such good friends and you can't even manage to say the word cock?" she said, looking almost offended. "Cock has to be my second favorite four letter word."

"I wonder what the first is," I said, nudging her as I headed back into the dining room. Paul, the chef, was just finishing up his closing duties for the night, and thanks to Dani's help, we weren't far behind.

"Yeah, but it's my first favorite because of the action, not the descriptor."

"I'm all finished up here," Paul called from the kitchen. "I'll catch you ladies tomorrow night."

"Good night, Paul," I said, waving after him.

"And that's exactly the kind of night I have planned for you." Dani shouldered up beside me and nudged me.

I wasn't sure why, although I was sure I'd regret it later, but I nodded. "Let me grab my things and get closed up."

Dani clucked her tongue and grabbed one rogue dishcloth and gave my butt another smack. "The point of tonight is to get *opened* up, Elle."

TWO

I'd just told my dad a bold faced lie over the phone about staying late at the cafe to do inventory. I'd answered Logan's *What are you up to* text with *Not much besides missing you* and I was en route to a booze and bonfire party in the backwoods.

That streak of wild I tried to keep a lid on had officially burst free.

"So your dad bought your story?" Dani asked me as we headed for old man Shanigan's in my Jeep.

"Yeah. He bought it," I said with a sigh.

I felt lousy for lying to Dad, but even lousier because I knew he'd never doubt me. I'd never given him a reason to. I'd never stepped one toe out of line my whole life, at least as far as Dad knew. He'd probably feel differently if he knew about the summer skinny dipping breaks or the time I'd drunk a half bottle of fruity red wine from Dani's mom's liquor cabinet.

"You are so lucky you've only got one member of the gestapo to patrol you. Dad and mom finally gave up—mostly—when I turned eighteen, but it was a real bitch trying to sneak out with one patrolling the front door and the other at the back."

I kept my eyes focused on the road. "Yeah. I'm so lucky," I said.

The Jeep got really quiet for a few seconds.

"Oh, God," Dani said, grabbing my arm. "Elle, I'm sorry. I've got the biggest mouth and I don't think before I speak and . . . shit, I'm so, so sorry."

"It's okay, Dani," I said, keeping my voice flat. "I know you didn't mean anything by it." To distract myself, I fumbled with the stereo, changing stations until I found a good, thumping song that would make it hard to carry on a conversation.

I knew Dani hadn't meant to hurt me, but it had. My mom died when I was four, just a couple years after she and dad had turned their dream of being restaurant owners into a reality. I was young when mom died, so it was surprising how much I could remember of her. It wasn't so much play-by-play scenes, but images. Like my young mind had snapped photographs and seared them into my mind.

She was a vivacious, spirited woman who had smile lines before she'd turned thirty and the same hazel colored eyes as me. She was always up for an adventure and believed nature provided the terrain for the best kind of adventures. My dad had told me I'd spent more time in a hiking backpack than a stroller and learned to ski before I could ride a bike.

"Holy shit. I can see the bonfire from here," Dani said, pointing at a glowing orb up ahead. "This is going to be one epic party. I can feel it in my bones."

I lowered the volume on the radio. "I'm having second thoughts," I said. "Do you think if I drop you off someone would give you a ride home? Someone who isn't trashed? Because I really think I just need to go home and—"

"And what?" Dani interrupted. "Watch 'I Love Lucy' reruns while you stuff your face with marshmallows and try and fail to long for your safe, non-frisking boyfriend?"

Some days it was easy to remember why I loved Dani. This day wasn't one. "Okay, I don't even know where to start with that whole spiel, but—"

"So don't even try because nothing you can say will convince me otherwise. You're coming to the party and that's final," she said, pointing me up a potholed road. "I cannot allow you to go to your grave without at least one night you don't regret."

I parked my Jeep on the outskirts of dozens of cars. I could already hear the hooting and hollering. "And how many nights do you regret?" I shot her a look as I stepped out of the Jeep.

Dani came around front and weaved her arm through mine. "Not a single one," she said as she steered me in the opposite direction of where I wanted to run right now.

"This is a bad idea," I said, noticing all the familiar cars. The cars of people who would recognize me. Both Logan and my dad would know where I'd been tonight come tomorrow afternoon. "Every single person is going to recognize me and be more than happy to tell on the good girl going bad one night."

"Two things. One, everyone in this town loves you. Even the raging partiers up there. No one's going to say anything about you being here tonight. Besides, even if they didn't like you, there's a party code of conduct that you don't blab to anyone about who was and wasn't at a party," she said, continuing to tug me ahead. "And two, everyone's going to be so drunk no one will even remember you were here."

"Is that supposed to make me feel better?" I asked, zipping up my jacket before sliding on my gloves. The days might have been unseasonably warm, but the nights still required bundling up.

"Okay, since you're so worried about people recognizing you and actually caring you're living one night like an eighteen year old should,"—Dani weaved in front of me and stopped me in my tracks—"I've got an easy solution. Take your hair out of that damn ponytail," she said, tugging on my hair tie. Sheets of hair fell down my back as she wove her fingers through it, teasing and tousling until she was satisfied. "Put on a little makeup ..." Pulling out a few tubes from her coat pocket, Dani went to work on my face. She was finished before I knew what hit me. "And voila, you're my cousin from out-of-town who's here to spend a couple weeks partying it up in central Washington with me." Dani gave my hair a few last tweaks before grabbing a hold of my arm and steering me towards the party. "Oh, and your name's Savannah and you're from South Carolina."

"Shouldn't I have an accent if I'm from South Carolina?" This bad idea had just gone from marginally to entirely.

"Yep." She patted my arm as we stepped into the clearing. "Good luck with that."

Dani had been right; the bonfire was ginormous. It was easily as tall and wide as my Jeep and I could feel the heat rolling off of it from twenty feet back. Dozens of people milled around, red cup in hand, mainly congregating close to one of the six kegs stationed around the clearing. As expected, almost the entire high school student body was present and accounted for, although there was a group of young men whose faces weren't familiar.

I didn't need two guesses to know who they were. If the flock of girls batting their lashes around them didn't give it away, that wildness in their eyes did. All smokejumpers I'd come across had it. A wild, adventurous twinkle that never seemed to dim. They came every summer. Some were the same as the year before, but a handful were new faces. I suppose that was part of the appeal of the lifestyle: getting to roam from place to and see some of the most beautiful parts of the country from fifteen hundred feet up.

As if parachuting out of low flying aircraft wasn't extreme enough, the smokejumpers did it close to raging forest fires. If there was an award for most dangerous, deadly, and adrenaline pumping career, smokejumping would have won by a landslide.

"That can't be Elle Montgomery," a voice said from off to the side. "At a party? A party with alcohol on private property?"

I elbowed Dani as Derrick Davenport ambled our way.

Derrick had played football in high school and was heading to U of W in the fall. Derrick was friends with Logan, not best friends, but close enough to make me sweat.

"And here I thought I was Savannah from South Carolina," I said, totally hacking up a southern accent. "So much for everyone being too drunk to notice me." I shot Dani a glare as Derrick stopped in front of us.

"Where's the Mr.?" Derrick asked, peering over my shoulders.

"He's out of town for baseball," I said as another one of the guys who'd been on the football team showed up with two empty red cups in hand.

"Hey, Elle," he said, looking as surprised as Derrick had to see me here. "Hey, Dani. Pour yourselves a beer and drink up." He handed us the cups and pointed at the keg beside us. "This is a party, haven't you heard?"

Dani grabbed my cup and had our cups filled and properly frothed in record time. The girl knew how to work a keg. Handing me one, she tipped her cup and took a drink. If you call upending the entire cup a "drink".

"What did Logan say when you told him you were coming to the Summer Kick-Off Party at old man Shanigan's?" Derrick asked.

I took a swig of the beer to stall and made a face. I wasn't a connoisseur, but I'd had enough sips of beer to know this was the cheapest kind. "I didn't exactly tell Logan I was coming." Yeah, that sounded bad. "Yet," I added. "Dani convinced me to come after work and I didn't get a chance to talk to him."

Derrick's expression changed, like he was seeing me in a whole new light.

"Yeah, Logan doesn't know," Dani piped in, "so don't slip and say anything."

"It's not a secret," I said. "I'll tell him tomorrow when I talk with him. I'm sure he won't think it's a big deal."

"Yes, he will think it's a big deal and that's the reason for no, you won't tell Logan tomorrow."

I took another drink of my beer, but this wasn't a dainty sip.

"Damn, Elle Montgomery. At a party, tipping back a beer." Derrick shook his head, obviously amused. "If I knew you had this edgy side, I wouldn't have given in so easily when Logan said he was going to ask you to Homecoming our sophomore year. My loss." He smiled at me as his eyes wandered down my body in a way that made me squirm. "And don't worry. I'll take your secret to my grave."

"It's not a secret," I repeated as Dani grabbed my elbow and weaved me through the crowd.

"God," she said, making a disgusted face, "Derrick Davenport is such a horn-dog. I was going to need a shower if we hung around his filth any longer."

"I seem to recall you enjoying that horn-dog once or twice last summer," I teased as I nodded my head at a few familiar faces who called out my name.

"Eww. Please don't remind me of that. There's a reason I'm so big into repressing memories, you know?" She stopped in front of a huge tree stump and plopped down. She patted the space beside her. "Room for two."

"Remind me again why I'm here?" I said as I took a seat.

"Hmm," Dani said, staring at the group of smokejumpers and their groupies. "Let me get one of them to remind you." Her smile curved up as her eyes lingered on a few of the blond ones. Dani's weakness was men, but the blond ones would one day be the death of her.

"Come on, Dani," I said, waving my beer at them. "You can do so much better than some adrenaline junkie on an ego trip who wouldn't know commitment if it permanently attached itself to his pompous ass."

"Who's been telling on me again?"

I froze, and if it hadn't been for Dani's incessant nudging, I would have stayed that way. I didn't need to look to the side to know who was standing there. That voice was tattooed into my mind.

"You," I said, lucky I was able to get one word out. I turned towards him, and while I couldn't say Cole looked better now in his dark jeans and green jacket than he had earlier, because the wet hair and body thing really worked for him, he did still manage to make me feel things I shouldn't be feeling.

"Me," he replied, grinning at me. Even in the dark, those green-blue eyes of his glowed. Taking a couple steps closer, he motioned at me. "You."

I laughed a couple notes, but given I was nervous as all heck, I sounded more like a dying animal than a laughing girl. "Me."

Of course when Cole laughed, he sounded all swoony and sexy.

"Okay," Dani said, staring at Cole like someone had just decided to reincarnate a god and put him in a sinner's body. "Who is you? Or who is me?" she said. "I'm so damn confused."

"This is Cole," I said. "Cole Carson."

I saw a familiar gleam in Dani's eyes. The one that said *and I can get him into my bed how?*

"You were listening," Cole said. "I didn't think you were doing much else other than staring." His smile curved higher on one side.

"You know him?" From Dani's tone, I knew I'd just gotten twenty extra cool points.

"We met earlier today," I said.

"While we were both swimming at the same place," Cole added, stuffing his hand in his pocket. "Naked."

Dani's eyes popped. She was a worldly girl so it took something especially shocking to get those jaded eyes of hers to pop.

"What Cole forgot to mention was that he was on Grandma M's private property and I had no idea he was even there."

"Wait." Dani shook her head. "You swim naked?"

World views were being shifted.

"Oh, yes," Cole said, popping his brows, "Elle swims naked."

He'd seen me naked, but hearing him say my name was intimate in a way I hadn't anticipated. "How did you find out my name?"

"A bunch of people were talking about this Elle Montgomery

girl who didn't have a rebellious bone in her body showing up a few minutes ago. Of course, once I saw the girl all those fingers were pointing at, I knew they were wrong. How could a girl who swims naked and flirts with equally naked strangers not have a rebellious bone in that fine, fine body?"

"I was not flirting with you," I said, not really sure if I had or hadn't been. I wasn't even sure how to flirt in a calculated, alluring way, so if Cole was right, that meant it had all come naturally.

Which was possibly the most troubling piece of trivia I'd been made aware of all week.

Dani managed to peel her eyes off of Cole and studied me for a few seconds. She had always been able to see right through my lies, and it was obvious that that was what she was seeing through now.

"I'm going to go mingle," she said, standing up. "Let you two pick up where you left off."

"We don't need to pick anything up," I said.

Dani leaned close to whisper in my ear. "If you still feel that way in ten minutes, come get me. I'd be more than happy to pick up anything of his."

"You're disgusting," I hissed after her.

Her response was a wink as she beelined towards the growing group of smokejumpers and their entourage.

"So you really weren't flirting with me this afternoon?" Cole asked as he took a seat beside me. With him pressed up against me, the stump seemed a lot smaller than when Dani'd been next to me.

"I really wasn't," I replied, checking my nose to make sure it wasn't growing.

"Wow. I think my ego just took a serious nosedive," he said, making a hurt face.

Darn. Even when he was faking insult, Cole's face did things to my insides no face that wasn't my boyfriend's should do.

"From where I'm sitting, it looks like you've got plenty to spare," I said, smiling into my cup as I took a sip of beer. I liked this edgier, wittier Elle. I never talked this way to Logan.

Cole's eyes shifted to my mouth for one second before they flashed to mine. "And from where I was swimming, it looked like you've got plenty to spare, too."

If I wasn't already flushing from him glancing at my lips, now I was. Although flushing might have been understating it.

"Oh, shit," he said, as his eyebrows came together. "You're embarrassed. Actually, judging from that shade of red, I'd say you're more along the lines of mortified." I liked the way he studied my face, like he was really looking at me and *seeing* who I was. I hated the way he studied my face for the same reason. "I'm sorry, Elle. I assumed the girl who skinny dipped and tossed witty remarks at me this afternoon wouldn't be easily embarrassed." For the first time, Cole's face and words seemed genuine. "I'm a dick. Forgiven?"

Ah, crap. He said it, so now I was imagining his. Just when you think you've got nowhere else to go on the red scale. . .

"Okay, changing the subject before you pass out from red poisoning," he said, smirking at me just enough to let me know he knew what I was thinking. Or *picturing*. "So if the high class keggers in the backwoods aren't normally your scene, what is?"

"It's nowhere near as exciting as parachuting into forest fires," I said, liking the way Cole's arm felt against mine but knowing I shouldn't. "In fact, it's pretty much the opposite of daring, exciting, and adventurous."

"I find that hard to believe," Cole said. "Because it's no secret that girls who skinny dip are not in any way, on any planet, boring."

"Could you please, please, *please* stop talking about me and skinny dipping?" I said, because every time he brought it up, I thought about it. And every time I thought about it, that *zing* of heat rushed up my body. "And on this planet, this girl is considered painfully boring in every sense of the word."

Verbalizing it was depressing. It was somehow easier to accept when I kept it to myself.

Cole stared at me, his eyes amused and his mouth drawn in a serious line. Almost like he didn't believe me, but was smart enough to not push the topic.

I would have been good with him pushing the topic.

In the ten minutes we'd been talking, most of that exchanged in snarky banter, I felt more alive than I'd felt in. . .

Well, ever.

It was dangerous, feeling this way. And intoxicating.

"So what does Elle Montgomery have planned come fall when the scintillating backwoods parties come to an end?" he said. "You strike me as the kind of girl off to some top-notch college on the East Coast. Studying to become a doctor. Or a professional skinny—"

My glare snapped Cole's mouth shut, another point in his smarter-than-he-looks column.

"College would be nice, but my life's kind of taking a different direction."

"What direction?" Cole asked.

"A direction that doesn't leave a lot of room for majors and dorm rooms," I said around a sigh. Again, admitting this was about twice as depressing as keeping it to myself.

"And you're okay with that?"

"I don't know," I said, almost wishing we were talking about skinny dipping again because at least that kind of uncomfortable came along with the image of Cole's naked, wet body.

If I kept thinking those kinds of thoughts, I was going to have to unzip my coat and lose the gloves.

"If you don't take control of your life, Elle, someone else will," Cole said, his voice quiet, almost distant. Was that a glimmer of introspection that had just come from his mouth? Couldn't be. "That's a fact of life as guaranteed as death and taxes."

"Sounds like a lesson you've learned personally," I said. "And from the look on your face, I'm guessing you learned that lesson from a girl."

For the first time since he'd made his appearance, Cole looked away. "I'm not used to perceptive girls," he said, staring into the bonfire. He was in another world, but not for long. When his eyes latched back onto mine, I was able to exhale the breath I hadn't known I'd been holding. "I'll have to be more careful around you." His smile, that I'm sure had worked a handful of girls' clothes off, formed.

"What kind of girls are you used to then?" I asked, but only to hear him confirm the answer I'd arrived at.

"The kind that aren't exactly interested in getting down and dirty with my mind," he replied. "The kind that don't take a random piece of advice and turn it into a therapy session."

"So you're here beside me because?" I asked. I wasn't the kind of girl that got down and dirty with . . . *anything*.

Uh-oh. That sexy smirk of his hit the top of its range.

Leaning in, so I could almost feel his breath against my neck, Cole said, "Maybe I want to get used to something else."

I told myself that the chills running down my body were due to the cool night air.

"Until the summer's over?" I said, trying to ignore the heat rolling off his body onto mine. "I know how you smokejumpers operate. And since you were kind enough to give me a lesson, let me return the favor." I sat up higher and pretended Cole Carson was nothing that I wanted. "I'm not a summer fling girl."

Wow. What was coming over me? I didn't say these things or express this kind of emotion. I needed to find myself a muzzle or some strong duct tape before I said anything else I'd wake up regretting.

Cole didn't look phased, not even a bit. "Damn," he said, exaggerating a sigh. "There goes my whole summer."

"I'm sure you'll find more than enough distractions to get you by," I said, waving at the group that now had expanded so it was more of a four to one female to male ratio. "See? One girl for every night this summer."

"I'm more of a quality guy," he said. "Once I find that quality girl, then I like quantity. Lots and lots of quantity."

When Dani caught my attention, she jacked her eyebrows and made air kisses my direction. She already had some guy latched onto her and what looked to be another waiting in the wings if option number one wandered off to refill his beer.

"I don't know what you're talking about and I don't want an explanation," I said, looking back at Cole, needing to shift the conversation before he starting defining "lots and lots of quanity". "So what about Cole Carson? Is smokejumping the be-all-end-all for you?"

"It is for right now. As far as summer jobs go, nothing can beat it," he said with a shrug. "I'm not sure if it's what I'll be doing in five summers or even next summer, but I know it's what I want to do right now. I live in the present and figure the rest out as I go along."

I couldn't recall a time I'd thought like that, let alone done it.

"That sounds nice," I said a little wistfully.

"It is. You should try it sometime." He nudged me gently.

"I'd love to, but that's not in anyone's glass-ball for me."

"Why?" he asked.

"Because most days, I just feel like I'm going along with what everyone else but me wants for my life. And on the rare day I try and fight back, the battle is over before it even begins."

Why was I being so honest with Cole? For all intents and purposes, he was a total stranger who jumped out of perfectly good airplanes for a living. I shouldn't lay it all out and take his words of advice as the gold standard. I knew Cole wasn't the person I should confide in or take advice from, but it felt so darn right. My brain and heart had officially declared war on one another. I couldn't tell you which one I hoped would win.

"Each day kind of feels like a betrayal to myself, you know?" I added with a whisper.

Cole's hand dropped to my knee. The warmth from his skin bled through my jeans until it combined with the heat of my leg. "Then why don't you tell everyone to fuck off and start living your life day to day like me?"

I slid my hands into my coat pockets when I realized one of them had been moving towards his. "One, because I don't say the 'f' word, and two, because I don't have the luxury of day to day like some people."

"Everybody has that luxury," he said as his fingers curled into my leg. "Most people just choose to ignore it."

I knew if any one of the people absorbed in their own conversations glanced over and saw Cole's hand curled in my knee, all it would take was one quick photo or one call to Logan, and I could wave goodbye to the whole future I'd known to be mine for a while now. That was a paralyzing thought, but not as paralyzing as the thought of Cole's hand leaving me.

"So what are you saying?" I asked.

"Stop ignoring it. Live your life, Elle Montgomery," he said, his eyes glowing from his words. "I can tell from a couple of conversations with you that you're one hell of a woman. Imagine the woman you could be if you lived for no one else but yourself."

I considered that for a few moments. I loved the idea of it and hated the reality of it.

"That's exactly what I'll have to do," I said with a sigh. "Imagine."

"You sure about that?"

Simple question—I should have had a simple answer, but the responses firing off in my mind were complex. Was I sure about that? Did I have to accept what I'd assumed my future would be? Or was now the time, if ever there was, to shake everything up? Would I stay in Winthrop, take over the diner, and marry my high school sweetheart, or would I do the other things I wanted so badly to do?

So many questions and absolutely no solutions.

I guess Cole took my silence as my answer.

"Give me a call if that ever changes," he said, standing up.

His body no longer being beside mine shouldn't have affected me the way it did. Giving me a small smile, one that I mirrored, he headed back to his group of smokejumpers. I was mid heavy sigh when he spun around and jogged back.

His smile wasn't small anymore. "Never mind. I can't wait," he said, his eyes sparkling. "Let's say I just give you a call tomorrow night? Maybe we could go for another swim next week? Swimsuits not required."

He was asking me on a date. I hadn't misread his signals and I hadn't exactly discouraged him. This was my opportunity to tell him about Logan. The moment I should slide my glove off and flash my promise ring in front of his face. This was my time to prove that the life I was living was what I wanted to continue on with.

"Cole," I said, chewing the debate out on my lip.

"Elle," he said, and just the way he said the name and his face looked when he said it did things to me that I couldn't ignore.

The debate was over. "You don't have my number," I said, realizing I'd just tugged on the dangling string.

I wasn't sure if everything would unravel or I'd be able to stop it, but that was a distant thought when Cole dropped his mouth outside of my ear. His hand slid my hair behind my ear and I was fairly certain if he touched me again, I would burst into flames. The blue, hottest, burning kind.

I felt his breath against my jaw and I knew if I tilted my chin up a few inches, we would kiss. At least the ironclad willpower I'd honed through my teen years was paying off now. "Elle. I had your number before I came over to talk to you."

THREE

*C*ole really did have my number. In fact, he called it the next morning. And again the morning after that. He called every morning that week and left some sort of creative voicemail.

I never answered.

Dani had sworn an oath of secrecy to not mention a word about Cole and no one else had leaked the news to Logan that some smokejumper and I huddled rather close in conversation at a kegger.

Other than work and hanging out at Dani's house one night, I stayed home. I *cowered* at home. No more skinny dipping, even though it had been sunny and ninety all darn week. I took the long way to work to avoid the few hangouts the smokejumpers liked to frequent, and I definitely stayed away from the parties that seemed to crop up every night.

Cole was everything I needed to forget, and every thought I couldn't seem to.

It was another Friday night close at the diner, but I didn't have my persistent little helper. After Dani figured out there was either no dirt or none I would give her, she hadn't brought up the Cole topic again. She was headed to some other party tonight, this one high class since it was actually inside a building. A barn.

She hadn't even asked me if I wanted to join her at tonight's soiree before she high-tailed it out of here as soon as the doors were locked. Probably because I'd been in a funk all week, the kind of funk that would be a major buzzkill at a party.

Almost every table needed bussed and cleaned since tonight's florentine and triple berry crepes were a favorite, so I pulled my hair back into a ponytail and slid my promise ring off and put it into my pocket. Industrial strength chemical cleaners and scorching hot water weren't exactly jewelry friendly.

I was about to turn on the radio and get down to cleaning business when my phone rang. I was more disappointed than relieved when I saw it wasn't Cole's number. His calls had stopped that morning, and even though I hadn't answered a single one, I'd missed it today. For those few seconds, I knew Cole was thinking about me.

"Hey, Dad," I answered, carting the first batch of dishes back to the dishwasher.

"Hi, sweetheart. How was the night?"

"Crazy busy. Not an empty table all night." Like the queen of multi-tasking I was, I propped the phone up on top of the dishwasher and started loading a tray of dirty dishes. I was eager to get out of there. I hadn't had a night off yet that summer and I'd managed to convince dad to give me the whole weekend off. I didn't have plans, but that was kind of my favorite way to spend a day or weekend off. If I didn't have plans, I could do whatever I felt like when I woke up in the morning.

"Those florentine crepes are a crowd pleaser, that's for sure. Breakfast and lunch was hopping today, too," he said, sounding more tired than normal. "I'm heading to bed early tonight, Elle, so would you just wake me up and let me know when you get home? I think I'm catching that summer bug going around."

"Yeah. Sure," I said, trying to remember a time Dad hadn't been waiting up for me when I'd come home from work. I couldn't.

"Oh, and about this weekend,"—I started to grimace, already anticipating what was coming—"with the big baseball games going on and all the hotels being booked, I'm sure I underesti-mated the number of wait staff we'll need Saturday and Sunday night. I talked to Logan earlier and he said you two didn't have any set plans, so you'd be able to work," he continued as I felt my grimace work into a scowl. "I just wanted to let you know about the change in plans."

"Sounds like you and Logan have got it all worked out," I said, purposefully sounding overly sweet because I knew if I let my tone convey how I felt right now, Dad would wonder if I'd been lobotomized.

"Thanks so much, sweetheart," he said, clueless to my emo-tions. "I don't know what I'd do without you."

After saying goodbye, the line went quiet. I stared at my phone for a few seconds, contemplating when I'd let Dad and Logan start mapping out my life. I knew it wasn't done maliciously, but somewhere along the way, I'd handed them the reins.

Cole was right. If I didn't take control of my life, someone or someones would.

Right now, that was all I could think about. The electives Logan had chosen for me in school when I'd hmm'd and haw'd, the Jeep Dad had picked out for me when I couldn't decide, the earl grey tea Logan ordered for me every time we went out to breakfast when I couldn't decide on drip coffee or a cappuccino. The darn promise ring tucked into my pocket he'd gone out and purchased the same day I told him I needed some time to think about our future.

I'd become a backseat driver to my life years ago and I'd had enough. Dad's and Logan's intentions might have been good, but I was done with being steamrolled over at every turn.

At least for tonight I was.

The more I thought about it, the angrier I got. The anger was more self-directed than anything, but it was a powerful motivator. I had the diner clean in record time.

After turning off the lights, I locked the place up and headed to my car. I was halfway across the parking lot before I noticed the old Land Cruiser beside my Jeep, complete with the smiling face I'd been thinking about all week.

"Don't you know a young woman shouldn't walk into a dark parking lot alone at night?"

I really wished I would have freshened up before rushing out of the diner tonight, but it was dark and Cole was far enough away maybe he wouldn't smell the odd mix of tarragon and apple on my clothes.

"Since crime doesn't really happen here, unless you count a sketchy guy harassing a young woman in a parking lot, I think I'm going to live to see another day," I replied.

"Just because something's never happened doesn't mean it never will," he said, watching me with that intentional look. That look that said he both had me totally figured out and barely figured out at the same time. "You want to be ready for it when it does."

Stopping a few feet in front of him, I kept my expression in check. It was hard. Especially with the way he looked tonight. Like sex, seduction, and sin had decided to get it on and Cole Carson was the result. His dark hair was still damp from what I guessed was the shower, but what I liked to imagine was another round of skinny dipping, and his skin had darkened a couple of shades in the summer heat, making his eyes almost glow. Worn jeans and a dark tee that hugged his chest and arms topped off the triple S lovechild.

I told myself to breathe before replying.

"Was there some veiled, cryptic message in that warning?" Good. I sounded relatively unphased by the deity that was Cole Carson.

"Sorry. Subtlety isn't my strong suit. At least it isn't anymore."

I tried to ignore the way his gaze wandered over me, almost so imperceptibly I could have imagined it.

"What? You calling me every day and stalking me at work isn't subtle?" I teased.

"It's hard to be subtle when the girl you want to be subtle with won't take your calls." He shoved off his Land Cruiser and took a step my way.

Why hadn't I at least redone my limp, flyaway ponytail?

"So you used to be subtle," I said, glancing around the parking lot. It was empty. "But not anymore. Not right now."

He nodded. "Yep. Used to be. But not right now. Not with you."

He took another step closer, causing me to take one back. I wasn't sure if it was because I was more scared of him touching me or smelling me.

"What are you doing tonight?" he asked, the low notes gone.

"I worked the dinner shift and closed the restaurant tonight," I replied, knowing it was some time after ten and tonight was already over. At least if you were the good girl Elle Montgomery.

"What are you doing right now?" he clarified, moving closer. Now I could smell him and yes, his damp hair was thanks to a shower. He smelled like soap and shampoo. And some other s-word...

"I'm going home."

"It's a Friday night."

"It's late on a Friday night," I said, side-stepping my way to my Jeep.

Cole reached out and grabbed my wrist. His fingers wound around it gently, heating the skin all the way through. "You've got a couple of options here, Elle. I can either throw you over my shoulder and kidnap you, or I'll follow you to your place and hang with you there, or you can stop pretending like you're not dying to spend a couple hours with me and get in my car." Cole's expression was so darn confident I almost wanted to tell him to get lost.

But I didn't.

I couldn't.

"I don't have long," I said, checking the time on my phone. "My dad will call an Amber Alert on me if I'm not home by midnight."

"You're eighteen and officially out of school. Isn't it about time your dad eased up a bit?"

Of course it is, was my gut response, but if I gave him that one, Cole would turn that into one big carpe diem conversation I wasn't in the mood for. I didn't want to talk about life tonight. I didn't want to think about it either. I wanted to live it.

"I'm still his little girl," I said with a shrug.

"Daddy Montgomery sounds strict."

"Like you wouldn't believe," I replied.

"Why?"

That was a Pandora's box I didn't want to touch with a ten foot pole.

"It's his way of trying to keep me safe, I guess," I said. "My mom died when I was four in a river kayaking accident, and I think he believes if he puts a short leash on me, he won't have to worry about losing me like he lost her."

Cole didn't even flinch at my words, but I did. I never spoke about my mom or the way she'd died. Why was I now?

That was another Pandora's box I didn't want to be on the same planet as.

"So he's willing to risk your happiness to keep you safe? Or at least as safe as a person can pretend to keep another safe?"

"He doesn't know I'm not happy," I said, trying not to let the sadness I felt show. Dad never asked if I was happy and I never told him I wasn't. We both assumed what we wanted. "You're kind of the only one I let in on that little secret." I smiled sheepishly at Cole, feeling naked again.

"Why?" Cole asked his favorite one word question again. "Why haven't you told him you're not happy?"

"Because I don't want to rock the boat," I said, hoping he'd accept that tip of the iceberg answer and move on.

"Elle," he said, my name coming out of his mouth in a smooth caress, "you'd better start rocking that boat right now or else your life is going to pass you by before you even get started living it."

Those words hit me hard. Because they were true. And because they were what I'd been living in fear of for a while. My entire life passing me by while I offered conventional smiles and washed dishes at the sink.

A car whizzed by us on the road in front of the diner. Shaking the dreary thoughts loose for the time being, I squared my shoulders and approached Cole.

This time, when I looked into his eyes, I felt strength instead of the swoon I normally did. "I'm ready to rock that boat whenever you are."

*

"When you said you were planning on taking me on a grand adventure, I didn't exactly picture this," I whispered as Cole led me down the dark hall.

"You know what they say. Every great adventure begins and ends at a smokejumper camp," he replied back in a hushed voice.

I rolled my eyes. "Where is everybody?" I knew enough about the camp to know most of the smokejumpers lived, ate, and slept here, but I'd never actually been inside.

"It's a Friday night and it was a long winter," Cole whispered, his eyes gleaming when he glanced back at me. "If they're not on call, they're either at a bar or a party looking for a pretty girl with loose morals and looser standards."

I made a face. It was the same story every year. "Then why are we whispering?" I asked, as we entered a large kitchen and dining area.

Cole paused and turned to face me. "Because I like being able to make you whisper," he said, examining my mouth like it was something he wanted to taste. "Even if it isn't in the way I'd prefer to."

I might have been inexperienced and a prude-by-circumstance, but I didn't need to have slept with someone to know that look on Cole's face. The longer I looked at him, the more uncomfortable I became. The more uncomfortable I became, the more confident he became. When I was sure I was either going to slap him or kiss him, he spun around.

"You want something to drink?" he asked as he pulled the fridge door open.

From an intimacy that made me blush one moment to a casual question the next . . . I couldn't keep up with him.

Although I was enjoying the challenge.

"What do you have?" I came up behind him and peered inside.

Beer, beer, and beer. And an almost empty container of orange juice.

"I'll have some water," I said as Cole shuffled through the bottles.

"Yeah, me too." Ending his search, he shut the fridge door and wandered over to the sink.

"You can have a beer around me, you know. I'm not *that* straight-laced," I said, watching Cole fill two plastic cups from the tap. Even performing something as everyday as filling a cup of water, he intrigued me.

"I don't really drink anymore." Turning the water off, Cole handed me a glass.

"Why not?" In addition to being intriguing, Cole had perfected the art of surprising me.

"Because I'm that guy who doesn't do moderation too well," he said, chugging his entire glass of water. "The last time I had something to drink, the cops were en route when my buddies managed to wrestle me out of that bar."

"How long ago was that?" I asked and took a sip of my water.

"Right before I became a smokejumper three summers ago."

"Why did you become a smokejumper?" I looked around the dark room. It wasn't a glamorous life, nor did it pay all that well. It was dangerous, the hours were long at the height of fire season, and it made keeping a long-term relationship tough.

With all of these supposed downsides to the job, I'd never met a single smokejumper who didn't absolutely love his or her job. Cole was no exception.

"My grandma raised me and a couple of my cousins," he said. "My family was something of a dysfunctional mess, but Grandma took care of the responsibilities her daughters wouldn't." Cole had caught me, yet again, off guard. I hadn't arrived at any conclusions about his past, but I hadn't expected him to be so open about it over a glass of water in a dark kitchen. "My oldest cousin, Tommy, became a smokejumper a couple years out of high school. He loved the job and told me when and if I was ever ready for a change, I should give it a shot."

I scanned the room before scanning him. "Looks like you gave it a shot."

"I couldn't get out of Bend fast enough once I finally figured out the life I'd been living there wasn't the life I wanted. I was on the next bus out of town. Literally," Cole said, leaning his hip into the counter. "Sound familiar? Small town born and raised teenager, trying and failing to accept their small town future?"

When I didn't give him the satisfaction of an agreement, he grinned. "You and I are more alike than you think, Elle Montgomery."

I was starting to realize that. And it scared me. But it excited me just as much.

"So is your cousin Tommy stationed here too?" I asked. I wouldn't have known. The only interaction I'd ever had with the smokejumpers was taking their orders at the diner. I wasn't an SJ groupie like some best friends I knew.

Although the thoughts I had about Cole and the amount of time I'd spent with him might qualify me for that title now.

"Nah. He jumped out of Fairbanks." His voice got quiet again.

"Jumped as in he doesn't jump anymore?" I might not have known a lot about smokejumping, but I did know the profession was hard on the body and the burn out rate was high.

Cole gave one shake of his head.

"Why not?"

"He died," he said, staring at the floor unseeingly. "He was killed in action."

"Gosh, Cole," I said, automatically reaching for his hand. "I'm sorry."

He studied my hand, my fingers weaved through his, like they were an equation he was trying to solve. "Thanks, Elle." His hand tightened around mine. "Tommy was one hell of a guy and like a big brother to me, but he went out with his boots on. It was a good way to go."

My brows came together. "How was it a good way to go? He couldn't have been very old. Twenty-five? Thirty?"

The words were out before I could stop them. This was fast becoming my habit around Cole. I'd always been more of a think-before-you-speak person, but I was the opposite with him. I was all impulse and instinct, and I wasn't sure if this was a good thing.

"Tommy was twenty-three when he died," Cole said, not letting my hand go or even looking offended. "And it was a good way to go because one day, Elle, we're all going to die. We might not be able to change the day or the time, but we can at least control which way we get to leave this world. Tommy left it the same way he lived—with a bang." Cole was watching me in that way again, like he saw right through me. "It was a good way to go."

I tried not to think of my mom and the way she'd died. Would she feel the same way? That it was a good way to go? I know I certainly didn't feel that way.

"But he was so young. He had so much life ahead of him." I wasn't sure I was talking about Tommy anymore.

"I know for a fact that if Tommy had the choice between a short life that he got to live every day to its fullest or a long life of average, he'd choose the short life hands down."

"Huh," I said to myself, giving this some thought. I loved how Cole was confident and sure. How he was perfectly fine with living his life on a day-to-day basis. I loved that about him, but I was nothing like it. I lived by rules and made my decisions based on what might happen decades down the road.

"What would you choose?" Cole came closer, waiting for my answer.

I thought about it. I *really* thought about it. I didn't have one for him. At least not an honest one. On one hand, living carpe diem each and every day was appealing to that wild child within on a level that paralyzed me. On the other hand, I had firsthand knowledge of the void felt when someone you loved died young. My mom had barely made it to thirty. What I did remember of her, I do know she was happy, but was it worth it? Would I choose a few days of happy to thousands of so-so?

"I don't know," I whispered, gazing at our joined hands. I knew this wasn't right—holding another man's hand in a dark room when I had a boyfriend. When my stare went from our hands to his eyes, I almost gasped. The look in his eyes made me shiver. It was far too intimate for what Cole and I were.

We'd just climbed another rung on the inappropriate ladder.

"When you figure that out, let me know, okay?" His voice was low again, almost rough, and the darkness seemed to exaggerate the electricity flowing between us.

I needed to get out of this room and stop touching Cole before I did something I knew I'd regret. At least, I was pretty sure I'd regret.

"Why don't you give me a tour?" I said, moving towards the hall. My hand went icy cool the moment his left mine.

"What? You've never seen the inside of the camp before?" He was smirking at me again.

"Nope. I've never had the opportunity to experience a walk of shame from the bunks. Although I hear the bunks themselves are almost creak-free." I was smarting back at him again, but I was starting to like it. It felt like less of a vice and more of a virtue. I had wit. Deep down, it was there, and I shouldn't feel the need to hide it.

I'd kept it buried for too long.

"You've heard right," he said, coming up behind me. "You want to give them a test drive? You know, so you can have first-hand experience when the topic comes up on girls' night again?"

I felt a flush run all the way down my face, down into my neck. I could tell from Cole's tone he was only teasing; it wasn't him or his words that unsettled me.

It was my answer to his said-in-jest question. I was smart enough to not verbalize it.

"I think we can skip the bunk room," I said, thankful the hall was dark. If he saw the way he'd unsettled me, he'd never let me forget it. "I've been to camp before and I doubt it's much different."

"It isn't," he said, with a smile that suggested all the ways it was. "And it is."

Now that his smile had given me something to think about, I'm sure the smokejumper bunkhouse dominated mainly by young, single, impulsive men was vastly different from the bunkhouses I'd shared for a week in the summer with a bunch of girls at 4-H camp.

"So you don't want to see the bunks, you've already seen the kitchen, and I wouldn't let my worst enemy go into the communal bathroom the night before its weekly cleaning..." He tapped his temple as we continued down the hall. "What will I show you?"

I almost had to clap my hands over my mouth to keep from blurting out my immediate answer—*anything*.

He quirked a brow at me at the same time an easy smile slid into position. I was starting to believe he actually knew what I was thinking.

That idea was horrifying on so many levels.

"Okay," he said like he was answering my silent response. "I've got just the place." Without another word, he continued down the dark hall, and the only thing more disturbing than following a semi-stranger down a black hallway in an unfamiliar building was how willingly I did. I didn't feel threatened around Cole. I felt the opposite. It was irrational and I could have the survival instincts of a dodo bird, but I felt protected.

Cole did strange things to me and made me feel even stranger things.

"So . . . what schools did you apply to?" he asked me.

I came to a halt and, though I couldn't really see him, I knew Cole stopped too when I couldn't hear his footsteps anymore.

"What?" was my brilliant reply.

"Colleges? Universities?" I could hear that smirky smile in his voice. "Which ones did you send applications in to?"

"Who says I sent any in?" I said, crossing my arms, calculating what number this was on our uncomfortable conversations scale. I was pretty sure it was somewhere between fifty and one hundred.

"*You* said you sent some in," he said.

"No, I didn't say that. You did." I narrowed my eyes at him until I realized he couldn't see me.

"You might not have admitted it, Elle, but I know you well enough by now to say with absolute confidence that you applied to a good handful of schools. You do a good job of covering up that part of you you're ashamed of or scared of or whatever the hell it is, but you haven't let it die. I'm glad you're still fighting." He paused and I could both hear and feel him move closer. When he exhaled his next breath, I could feel it breaking across my face. "I'll repeat my question. What schools did you apply to?"

I sighed, just so he knew I was irritated. "U dub, Wazzu, and University of Oregon," I said. "Now that I've told you something, it's your turn. How did you know?" I hadn't told anyone about the applications I'd sent in last fall. Not even Dad, Logan, or Dani knew. *Especially* not Dad and Logan.

"You may have everyone else fooled, Elle Montgomery," Cole said, his voice vibrating through me. "But not me."

So it seemed.

Without another word, Cole grabbed my hand and pulled me down the remainder of the hall. I went with him not because it was what he wanted, but because of what I wanted. It was a foreign concept—acting on my own instincts.

It wasn't long before we burst through a door that led outside. Inside might have been dark, but the sky was clear, and one of the few things that made the prospect of spending the rest of my life here in Winthrop bearable was that I could stare up at a night sky like this at the end of every day. No clouds plus no city lights equated to a sky so bright with stars it was almost more light than dark.

Cole took in the sky for a couple moments with me before pulling me along again. I started laughing, for a hundred little reasons and one big one.

I felt free.

I *was* free.

I couldn't comprehend how running with Cole's hand wrapped around mine late at night could make me feel freer than I'd ever felt when, in truth, nothing had changed. I was still Elle Montgomery, promised to Logan Matthews, expected to manage and run the diner when Dad retired, the girl who would be born, die, and everything in between in this town.

But it did.

I was still laughing when Cole's jog slowed.

I'd been so busy staring at the sky and him I hadn't realized I was on a runway. Or about to run into a small plane.

"A plane? Really?" I said as Cole led me up a ramp before opening the plane's door. "Is this where you take all the girls?"

Elle the Witty had come back out to play. She was growing on me.

Cole gave me a twisted little grin. "Only the girls that make me work really hard for it," he said. Before my mind could get carried away with what "*it*" entailed, Cole grabbed my hand and pulled me inside the plane.

I knew I shouldn't follow him inside. I knew what being in another dark, confined, quiet space would make me want to do with Cole. I knew the electricity shooting through my hand from his touch would only compound if we touched anywhere else.

I knew so many things.

But darn if my heart, or my soul, or that rebellious Elle inside of me, wasn't outwitting my mind at every turn tonight.

"You jump out of this?" I asked, looking outside the tiny door. I felt sick at the thought and the plane wasn't even in the air.

"Well, the other guys jump," Cole said, stepping up behind me. "I fly out of it."

He was close, too close. I couldn't feel his body against my back yet, but I felt the heat coming from it. My eyes closed and I imagined Cole's chest pressing into my back, the rest of him sliding into position. Another flash of our first meeting went through my mind.

My breathing had just picked up when my body acted without my consent. No longer able to bear the line of distance between us, I stepped back until I felt his body hard against mine. I took one more step because now that I felt him, I wanted to feel more.

Cole inhaled sharply, but that was all the surprise he showed. His hands slid down over my hips, and when his fingers curled deep into me before he shoved me harder back into him, I gasped.

Apparently we could get closer and feel even more of each other.

I was breathing so hard I had to open my mouth to keep from passing out. Cole's hips pressed into my lower back and I felt something hard against my spine that both made me blush and moan.

My hands covered my mouth immediately. Where the heck had that come from? I didn't know I was capable of such a sexual sound.

Cole's mouth dropped to my neck. His breath was so hot against it, I felt the muscles relax.

Well, they relaxed until something wet and firm slid up the curve of my neck. I tensed for a moment, but then Cole's tongue played with the tip of my earlobe before he gently sucked on it.

I moaned again, louder and longer, but this time I didn't cover my mouth. I didn't want to fight anymore. I was done ignoring the way Cole made me feel with a simple look or a not-so-simple touch. I hadn't been exactly successfully ignoring him as right now—his hands gripping hard into my hips and his lips doing things to my earlobe I didn't know could be done—proved.

"That's it, Elle," he breathed as one hand slid up my body before forming around my cheek. "Don't fight it. I can see the person you are, the one you're fighting." He took my earlobe back into his mouth, but this time, his teeth sunk into it carefully. Of course, my only response was another porn-worthy moan. Or groan. Or sigh. I don't know how the heck you would classify the sounds I was making, but I did know they were the opposite of innocent. "And that girl makes me all kinds of crazy." Cole's hand guided my face closer to his. I couldn't decide what I wanted to stare at: his eyes or his mouth. Both were tempting on so many levels.

"I'm going to kiss you now. Unless you stop me," he said, lowering his mouth to mine. It was so close, I could taste his lips. But I wanted to feel them move over mine. I wanted to feel him suck at my lower lip the way he'd just done with my ear. I wanted. I wanted too much, and what was worse, I wanted what I couldn't have.

But tonight, I was going to finally have what I wanted.

"But if you stop me now," Cole said. His eyes had no degree of indecision; they stayed firmly on mine. "I'll try to kiss you again later. I'm persistent, Elle."

Those words, those eyes drilling into mine, those hands holding onto me so tightly I couldn't budge, and that certain something pressed hard into my back broke down any and all last reservations.

I lifted an arm and curled it around the back of Cole's neck. In this position, I felt totally vulnerable, totally not-in-control. But still, totally protected.

"And yet you're still talking," I whispered, lifting my brows suggestively.

When Cole's lips dropped to mine, I could feel the tilted smile on his mouth. I'd been right. Whatever voltage our combined hands could create was compounded to the hundredth power when our mouths moved against one another.

I felt clumsy at first, inexperienced in every way as I was, but what I lacked in experience Cole more than made up for for the both of us. The way his lips could both polish and suction to mine in the same heartbeat confirmed this man had been perfecting his craft for a while. I didn't want to even guess the number of women he'd been perfecting it with, so I tried to follow his lead and not make a kissing fool of myself.

I wasn't very conscious of his hands with his mouth doing what it was, but I did have enough remaining wits to realize they stayed where they were. I wasn't sure if I was more relieved or disappointed.

When Cole's tongue slid out, encouraging the seam of my lips to open, they didn't take much encouragement. In fact, his tongue hadn't even entered my mouth before mine met his. I think he was as surprised as I was because a sound that was deeper and more gravelly than the sounds I'd been making traveled up his throat.

Knowing I was responsible for that sound, despite feeling like I was all thumbs in the kissing department . . . all that knowledge made me want him more. Made me want him in ways I knew I couldn't, shouldn't, and absolutely wouldn't indulge.

So instead, I focused on our tongues winding around one another, our lips smoothing over each other, our bodies formed against each other so tightly I didn't doubt my back would be wearing a Cole-sized dent in it for a while.

My hand slid down to his hands kneading my hips. Our fingers curled together the way our mouths were. I'd never been kissed like this, never even close.

I'd kissed a total of one boy in my life: Logan.

Logan.

The name was familiar, it meant something, but Cole's mouth and body were making me forget what that name meant. Only when Cole's fingers started drifting lower, sliding into the front pocket of my shorts, did reality hit me head on. I felt the small, hard circle at the bottom of my pocket hard against my thigh.

I didn't know if I broke out of Cole's embrace because I was ashamed of what I'd just done or because I'd been scared of Cole finding the ring, but the pain of separation was instant.

"Elle?" Cole's face was as confused as his voice sounded. He had a right to be. One second ago I'd been a making out fiend and now I backed away from him like I was being chased by the devil.

"I've got to go," I said, more to myself than to him as I stumbled down the ramp. Apparently there were more ways to get drunk than from alcohol. Cole's body had done a number on mine and it wouldn't function properly.

"Did I do something wrong?" He stuck his head out the plane door and watched me.

"No," I said, having to look away. If I stared at him any longer, I was going to run back and pick up where we'd left off. "I did."

I had so much more to say. I had one big thing to *explain*, but I was either too cowardly or too confused to do any talking or explaining tonight. Without sparing another look or word Cole's way, I ran.

The tears fell when I realized this wasn't the first time I'd run away from something I wanted. My life was a snowball of regrets and dreams shoved to the side, and even though I ran in the opposite direction from him, I couldn't shake the feeling that Cole Carson would be the one to change all that. To change everything.

FOUR

I ignored Cole's calls again. He'd called every hour since I ran away last night. Lucky for me, the diner, where my Jeep was parked, hadn't been that far of a walk. Or a run.

When I'd heard a car approaching, I dodged into the dark tree line, guessing it would be Cole.

My guess was confirmed when an old Land Cruiser went by. It went slow, so I caught a glimpse of his face. It was a mixture of tortured and anxious. I stuck to the trees the last half mile back to the diner and didn't race to my Jeep until I was certain Cole wasn't lurking in the shadows waiting for me. I wasn't ready to face him, but I was even more not ready to tell him about Logan. I knew I had to tell him the very next time I saw him, but I also knew that would end everything we had.

I wasn't ready for The End.

Trying not to think about endings, or Cole, or Logan, or

anything at all the next morning, I headed up the bleachers towards where my dad sat. I had to squeeze and weave my way through a few bodies because I'd showed up an inning late. Reason for my tardiness? I wasn't ready to face Logan either.

I was convinced that Logan would know I'd been unfaithful. As soon as he took one look at me, he'd know another man's hands and lips had been on me.

So I avoided Logan.

And I avoided Cole.

And I wanted to avoid Dad too, but this was a small town baseball game and there was a total of one set of bleachers. It was kind of hard to get lost in the crowd.

"Hi, Dad," I said, sliding between a couple bodies before plopping down on the end of the bleacher. The row was so packed I practically hung off the end. "Thanks for saving me a seat."

"I was getting ready to call Bill," he said, tilting his bag of popcorn my way. I curled my nose and shook my head. My appetite had been next to non-existent lately.

"Why were you about to call Uncle Bill?" I asked. Dad's younger brother was the town sheriff. I wasn't exactly the kind of person that, if he wasn't my family, would be familiar with the town sheriff.

Correction, I didn't used to be that kind of person. Now I was the kind of person who made out with boys while her unsuspecting boyfriend was asleep. Cheating had to be on the list of gateway indiscretions that led to incarceration, right?

"Because the last time you were late to one of Logan's games, you had strep throat. Even then, you made it before the pitcher took the mound." Dad's voice was as light as a person as serious as him could be. I knew he was teasing, but it struck a sensitive chord.

"I had killer cramps this morning," I lied. "I could barely get out of bed."

That wasn't the first lie I'd told Dad, but after last night's lie and make-out session with Cole, I was starting to become a serial liar. This, I knew I wasn't okay with.

At least I could still be confident about something.

Dad shifted and cleared his throat. Girly business made any man uncomfortable, especially dads when it came to their daughters. "Well, I'm glad you're feeling better and could make it," he said, his face looking a shade redder.

Poor Dad. You would have thought being a single parent, the one who'd raised me the better part of my life, he'd be more comfortable talking about things of a female nature.

He was anything but comfortable.

So, not only had I lied to him, but I'd made him squirm. Maybe Cole was right: I wasn't the good girl everyone thought I was.

"I talked to Logan for a few minutes before the game," Dad said, shifting the conversation. "He said he feels like he's barely seen you this summer. Is everything all right with you two?"

I almost flinched. I knew Dad couldn't know about Cole and me, but that question couldn't have been posed at a better time to make me feel like the worst person ever.

Looking out at the field, I made sure to avoid the home team dugout. "He's been really busy with baseball, and I've been working a ton, too," I said. *I've also found myself wildly and inexplicably attracted to another guy who has the word HEARTACHE drawn in thick black Sharpie on his forehead.* "We're only a couple weeks into summer, Dad. Logan and I have plenty of time to hang out before . . ." I paused and tried again. "Before . . ." Nothing came. We weren't heading back to high school in the fall. In fact, in Dad and Logan's mind, the only place we were heading in the fall was to an altar. However, I couldn't let go of the hope of heading off to one of the universities I'd been accepted to.

It was a pipe dream, and I was a fool for clinging to it, but I just couldn't let go yet. I loved Logan and I loved my dad, but why did I have to give up what I wanted for them? I'd never ask them to do that for me.

Thankfully, my phone rang, saving me from stumbling over the "before, before, before" conundrum. I didn't really need to check it. Everyone who would call me, other than Dani, was here, but I did, and when I saw the number—the same number I'd missed a couple dozen calls from in the past week—I smiled.

Cole was one button away. At least his voice was. I was tempted, more than with any of his other calls, to answer. Whatever Cole had done, however he'd worked his way inside my defenses, I couldn't break free of him, and I most certainly couldn't forget the way that kiss had felt. If mouths could commit the act, his had made very hot, passionate love to mine last night.

As much as I wanted to answer, I knew I couldn't. For more

reasons that just being surrounded by my dad and my boyfriend. I might want Cole in ways I couldn't explain, but I knew I couldn't have him.

Sighing, I pushed ignore and pocketed the phone.

"Wow, so that confirms it. You really are ignoring me." A familiar voice came from beside me. "I was hoping you'd lost your phone or something."

I peeked over at my dad. He was focused on the game. So, leaning forward, I propped my elbows on my knees, trying to block Cole from him.

"What are you doing here?" I hissed over at him. He was standing to the side of the bleachers and, at this height, his head was right in line with mine.

"It certainly isn't for the warm welcome," he replied dryly while I did my best to focus on the patch of grass just beyond his left shoulder. I'd made the mistake of looking at him for too long, staring at his mouth and remembering the way it had played with mine.

I raised my eyebrows and waited for him to reply. Sans sarcasm.

"Since you seem to have some sort of vendetta against answering my phone calls, I got worried. I know we're in small town nowhere here, but a young, beautiful girl walking alone on dark roads is not smart, Elle."

I almost corrected him. I hadn't walked. Other than ducking into the trees when I saw his headlights approaching, I ran.

"I wanted to make sure you made it home and didn't run into any chainsaw murderers, rabid bears, or—"

"Too smooth for their own good smokejumpers who like to take advantage of girls in dark planes?" I smirked at him before I remembered my dad was barely a foot away. A quick peek revealed he was still engrossed in the game I had yet to watch a second of.

"If that was me taking advantage of you," Cole said, his eyes skimming down my face until they paused at my mouth. The corners of his mouth twitched. "I don't seem to remember you complaining."

I swallowed, pressing the heat of his voice and the glimmer in his eye out of my mind. "I was too busy trying to dodge your mouth to complain."

And chalk another lie up on the board for Elle Montgomery.

Cole leaned in closer, his eyes only glimmering brighter. "No, you weren't dodging me, Elle," he said. "If anything, you were too busy moaning in my mouth to complain." He made a small noise then, what I guessed was his imitation of the foreign noises I'd made last night.

I knew my skin was reddening, but I wasn't sure if it was due to embarrassment or anger. I wasn't an angry person by nature, but Cole seemed to bring out emotions I'd thought were non-existent, or dormant at the least.

When he made a similar noise, this one not so quiet, I slugged his arm.

Of course, this only made him laugh.

Casting another look back at Dad, I made sure my eyes were in full glare mode before looking back at Cole. "Those weren't moans," I half whispered, half hissed. "Those were groans of pure and utter disgust."

Cole's smirk didn't fade. He was apparently just as capable this morning as he had been last night of seeing right through my act. "If that was the way you show pure and utter disgust," he said, scrunching his face up dramatically before letting it iron out around another long moan. I was gearing up to slug him again when he dodged, his all-out smile in place. "Hit me up again."

I blew an annoyed rush of air through my nose. I hated being stuck to this bleacher. I wanted to leap off of it and either slap him or kiss him. I didn't want to care about what everyone else would think and just go with my instincts.

"I'm fine," I said, taking in another calming breath. "Obviously. Other than escaping a deranged man with an enhanced sense of self"—I made sure to outdo that smirk of his—"I made it home just fine last night."

His chuckle rocked his entire body. His whole body rocking reminded me of the way it had felt against mine. My next thought jumped right to the picture of how his body would feel bare, rocking into mine . . .

Excellent. I'd just become a hormone enraged thirteen-year-old boy with only one thing on my mind.

"Still fighting that girl I'm so smitten with?" Cole guessed, giving me a knowing look. Please, for the love of God, please don't say he really can read my mind. Especially not the last ten seconds of thoughts. "I thought we'd made some good progress in setting her free last night."

"She put up a good fight," I said, rolling my eyes and giving in to his teasing. "But so did I."

Talking about myself in both the first and third person should feel strange, but it didn't. I'd been ignoring it until Cole came along, but my life felt like I was living it in both first and third person most of the time.

"Obviously," Cole agreed, regarding me like I wasn't quite the same girl he'd been with last night.

I wasn't.

But when his eyes stayed on me, softening when they explored my face, I was, too. My life had literally gone from uncertain to downright confusing in one loaded look from Cole Carson.

Leaning into the side of the bleachers, he crossed his arms and watched the baseball game for a minute while I watched him. "Since I have the day off and this town's entertainment options give watching paint dry a run for its money, I think I'll hang around a while and see if that repressed Elle makes a reappearance."

At that moment, I kind of wished she'd show up too. "You like repressed Elle, don't you?"

The corner of his mouth lifted. "No," he said, "I *really* like her." He glanced at me through the corner of his eyes. His mouth curled higher. "But I kinda dig stick-in-the-mud Elle, too."

This admission made me happier than it should have. I shouldn't care what Cole thought of me and the other me. It shouldn't matter.

But it did. A lot.

For reasons I didn't understand, but for reasons that didn't really matter either. Cole liked me, all facets of me. He didn't choose one over the other or expect me to only let one side of me show. He might have preferred one side of me, but he didn't not like the other part.

"She kinda likes you, too," I said, almost whispering.

Cole turned to me, and I swear, I would have been content to live the rest of my life staring at the expression on his face. It was sexy as all heck—this was Cole we were talking about—but it was affectionate, almost adoring.

"Which one?" he said in that low voice.

Instinctually, I leaned closer to him. "Both of them."

I knew I was an inch or a word away from pressing my lips to his in the middle of my boyfriend's baseball game, in broad daylight, for all my friends, family, and lifelong acquaintances to witness.

"Logan's up, Elle." Dad's voice broke through my haze.

I might as well have been electrocuted for the way my body snapped upright, my head turning towards the game. I chanced a quick look my dad's way. He was totally oblivious to the man lingering beside me and the flushed expression on my face.

Logan was already squared up at home plate, his number twelve facing me. I was usually so focused on the game I knew when he was on deck, long before he went up to bat. Exchanging waves and smiles as he walked up to the plate had become something of a tradition.

I'd been so consumed by Cole, this was the first time I'd looked at Logan since arriving.

"Go, Logan!" Dad hollered beside me. "Hit a homer, son!"

I was usually the most vocal one in the stands when Logan was at bat, but now my vocal chords wouldn't work. Dad shot me an odd look as he continued to cheer with the rest of the spectators.

Logan was something of a hometown hero when it came to baseball. Well, when it came to just about anything really, but especially when it came to baseball. He was good. Always had been, too. I remember Logan dragging an old wooden bat around when most boys his age were playing video games. He was so good I was certain he could have received some athletic scholarships if he applied to some schools, but he didn't.

Logan's dad was the town's pastor, but he also ran a good-sized cattle ranch that Logan had been planning on taking over since the day he knew what taking over the family business entailed. It was eerie how similar Logan and I were at times, although I knew his reason for staying behind and working the family business had very little to do with the duty and obligation I felt for mine. He was staying because he wanted to. Playing minor league baseball was the cherry on top of his dream of running the cattle ranch and coming home to me and our little homestead every night.

Why did I feel like I was suffocating again?

"Who's Logan?" Cole asked, his eyes narrowing at Logan's back.

And there was the question. The one I'd been hoping to avoid by either A. explaining to Cole about Logan before we got to this point, or B. continuing to ignore Cole so I never had to explain who exactly Logan was, or C. waking up from this messed up dream.

"Logan?" I began, having no idea what I was going to say. "Logan's my . . ." I stopped and took a breath. Why was getting the last part out so hard? Logan was my boyfriend. Soon, if he had his way, to be my husband. When I glanced at Cole, who was studying me again, I knew why it was so hard. I knew when I told Cole I had a boyfriend, I'd never see him again.

I wanted to see him again.

Just then, a sharp crack sounded from the diamond. I looked just in time to see the end of Logan's swing as the baseball sailed high and long. The center fielder made a valiant run for it, but that ball landed a good ten yards past the fence. The stands erupted, chanting Logan's name. My dad was the loudest one of them all.

Cole caught that, studying my dad with the same intensity. Finally, as Logan rounded third base, Cole nodded. "Logan's your brother," he said with confidence.

I shifted in my seat. So he'd figured there was a closeness shared between Logan and my dad and me, but of course, he'd guessed wrong.

"Not exactly," I mumbled as Logan jogged over home plate.

The cheering went up a notch.

After high-fiving a few of his teammates, Logan turned around and jogged down the fence line until he was in front of me. He was grinning that boyish grin that had made me fall for him in the first place. Pointing his index finger at me, he winked. "That one was for you, baby!" he shouted for everyone to hear.

The crowd cheered even louder somehow. They loved their golden boy and his couldn't-care-less attitude towards showing his feelings for me.

I felt my shoulders hunching forward as I shot him a wave and a half-hearted smile. I wanted to fall in between the cracks of these old, rickety bleachers and die right now. Not because everyone in the stands was looking at me, giving me knowing smiles before turning back to the game, but because one person was looking at me with an intensity I was sure would set me on fire if he didn't blink soon.

"Baby?" he nearly spit the word. "*Baby?*" he repeated with as much disdain as one word could hold. "So I guess Logan isn't your brother."

I gave one shake of my head, checking the crowd to make sure no one was paying Cole and me much attention. After a quick pat on the back, the neighbor sitting on Dad's other side had gotten his attention and they were singing Logan's praises.

"Logan's your boyfriend," he said, the muscles of his jaw tightening. "I heard that the town sweetheart, Elle Montgomery, was with the hometown hero. I heard it . . . I just couldn't believe the Elle Montgomery I knew was a two-timer. I guess the rumor mill was more fact than false this time. You really do have a boyfriend." It wasn't a question, so it didn't require an answer, but I felt it needed clarification. If this was coming out, I might as well get everything out.

Lifting my left hand, I flashed it in front of his face to s how him my ring.

Cole nearly choked. "He's your fiancee?" He paled three shades before going red three seconds later.

"Not yet," I said, avoiding his eyes. "It's just a promise ring."

"Just?" Cole repeated, sounding disgusted. "*Just* a promise ring?"

I bit my lip and nodded.

Cole stared with disbelief and waited. This was the part where I explained myself. Explained my actions and what I'd been thinking.

I don't think I could have explained it if someone held a gun up to my head and demanded one. I'd been careless, reckless, impulsive, thoughtless, and never been so sure of anything when I'd been with Cole.

How did you explain something that felt just as right as it felt wrong?

Others might have been able to, but I couldn't.

"This explains a whole hell of a lot," Cole said loudly.

My eyes drifted to my dad. He was cheering for the next guy up to bat, none the wiser.

"Oh, I'm sorry," Cole said, his voice sarcastic. "Is that why we've been whispering? Why you've been all but shielding me with your body? You don't want your friends and family"— Cole's hand waved with agitation at the field—"your damn promise ring boyfriend to find out about your dirty little secret?" His face changed then. A small crack in his anger formed and what I saw in that crack broke my heart.

"Cole ..." I started, not knowing what I was going to say, but just needing to say something.

"Sorry, Elle. I'm out," he said, refusing to look my way. "I'm not going to be anyone's dirty little secret." He turned around, his shoulders tense, and walked away.

I leaped down the side of the bleachers before he'd made it to the parking lot. I knew dad would probably notice this not-so-covert-op, I knew Logan might too, but I didn't care right now.

Cole turning his back on me and walking away was what finally put me into action. I didn't check to see if anyone was watching, I just jogged after him.

"Cole!" I shouted, ignoring the way his body tensed even more when he heard me. He didn't stop.

"Cole, wait!" Knowing stopping wasn't his plan, I picked up my pace. I got to him just before he rounded his Land Cruiser. "Cole," I said, grabbing his arm.

I could have just slapped him for the way he flinched away from me. "What do you want, Elle?" he said, glaring at me in a way I'd never been glared at before. It was ... staggering.

"I'm sorry," I said, forcing myself to keep staring at him.

"You're sorry? You are sorry." Each word came out slowly, but each one was scalding with anger. "I suppose that makes everything all right now, right? Elle says she's sorry, so now we're good. Right?"

Shoot. He was really angry. So much so, his body was quivering. I couldn't recall a time I'd seen someone so angry.

"Cole . . ."

"Just . . ." He glared at me again before a flash of pain swept over him. "Just enough, okay? I'm done with whatever bullshit of a thing we had," he said, hopping into his Land Cruiser.

I stepped back when the engine roared to life. Cole rolled down the window and took one last look at me before sliding a pair of sunglasses on. If there was a contest for contempt, Cole would have just snagged the first place trophy.

"I guess you really had me fooled, too, Elle Montgomery," he said, gripping the steering wheel so hard it looked like he was about to rip it off.

I had so much to say. So much to apologize for and try to explain, but that would never happen because before I could get one word out, Cole peeled out of the parking lot like he couldn't get away from me fast enough.

I stood there for a few minutes, shedding a few tears for a boy I'd known a week. For a boy I was as wrong for as he was wrong for me.

Cole and I could never be. There was positively no future for us. I knew that. But my heart ached, and some part of me refused to accept it could be over.

FIVE

No one had noticed the event in the parking lot that had ripped my guts out. Not one person had witnessed what had surely been one of the most excruciating moments of my life. Strangely it reminded me of the saying about if no one's around to hear a tree fall in the forest, does it make a sound. If no one was around to witness what just went down between Cole and me, could I pretend it hadn't happened? Could I tell myself I hadn't just watched his face crumble into a hundred emotions? Could I imagine I'd have more missed calls from Cole Carson to look forward to?

Even I wasn't that naive.

After staring for a few minutes at the spot where Cole's car had been, I wandered back to the game. My dad assumed I'd been in the bathroom taking care of more girly business he wanted no part of, and Logan didn't even look my way again until he went up to bat a couple innings later.

I knew this might be a case of the grass being greener on the other side, but right now, I think I would have preferred being caught chasing after some guy than being totally ignored.

Other than Logan's mom asking me if I'd given any thought to what colors I'd like for Logan's and my wedding—I'd choked on the piece of popcorn I'd been munching on and told her I'd have to get back with her later on that ... *much* later—no one even spoke to me. Well, other than Dad, although I'm not sure if questions that required a one word reply constituted as conversation.

At the end of the ninth inning, my butt was numb, I was hot and sweaty from baking in the sun, and my mood was all over the place. It wasn't the best time for Logan to sneak attack me.

"Hey, baby." Logan's arms wound around me and he placed a chaste kiss on my cheek as I headed toward my Jeep. "Weren't you planning on waiting for me?" He sounded a little hurt, and when I turned in his arms, his expression revealed the same.

Whatever I was going through, Logan didn't deserve to be dragged into it. He wasn't perfect, and lord knows I was having a tough time with his old fashioned ways as of late, but he was a good guy. A really good guy. The kind of guy girls wait years to find, if they ever find that certain someone at all.

"Sorry, I just needed to grab something from the Jeep real quick. I wasn't leaving." The lies were becoming easier. "That was a great game. Two home-runs and one double in a single game? You better watch out or you're going to have colleges lining up to sign you to their teams."

Logan smiled. "Who needs college when I've got everything

I need right here? The ranch. Baseball." He motioned at the now empty field before tapping the tip of my nose. "And you."

It was a sweet thing to say, but it made my stomach squirm. Guidance counselors, family, or pop culture had seriously dropped the ball when it came to explaining to Logan we weren't living in the nineteenth century. People didn't get married and settle into home life at eighteen any more. They graduated high school, went to college, did a bunch of crazy stuff along the way, worked in their career field, and then, maybe then, did they decide to get married.

But Logan wasn't one of those people. And I wasn't going to be one of them either if I stayed with him.

"What time do you have to head into work tonight?" he asked, dropping his arms from my waist. Logan wasn't PDA self-conscious; he just didn't let himself touch me the way most teenage boys touch their girlfriends.

After experiencing what touching could be like, I wanted to be touched.

"Dad asked me to pop in around five," I answered, remembering why I was working tonight on what was supposed to be my weekend off. Logan had told Dad we didn't have plans so I could work if he needed me. No thought to clear it by me first. I felt a spark of anger flame.

"You want to hang out at my place until you have to go in?" he said, turning his baseball cap around. "I miss you, Elle. Here I thought we'd have tons of time to spend together this summer, and I don't think I've spent one uninterrupted hour with you yet."

I wasn't in the mood to be around Logan right now. Not just because of what I'd done with Cole, but because of Cole's and my fight and the prospect of never seeing him again. I wanted to cry, or sulk, or hit something until I'd eliminated even a tenth of the ache throbbing through me.

What I didn't want to do was be around my boyfriend who hadn't been the one I'd been making out with last night.

"Come on," Logan said, tucking my hand inside of his. "I'll make you a cup of tea and we can watch a movie or something. You look like you need a little time to relax." Logan's other hand lifted to my face, tracing over the creases lining it. He knew something was wrong, but I knew my trusting, optimist boyfriend didn't suspect anything remotely close to the truth. When his thumbs skimmed over the dark hollows under my eyes, he added, "You must have missed me as much as I missed you this past week."

Logan's blue eyes softened in concern. He was worried.

Another wheelbarrow full of guilt added to the mountain of it I already had.

Tugging on my hand, Logan led me around to the driver's side of my Jeep. "Come on. You look like you need some Logan therapy as much as I need some Elle therapy."

I needed therapy, that was obvious, but I wasn't sure if it was Logan Matthews kind. I gave an internal sigh before hopping into my Jeep and following him towards his place.

The Matthews' house was only a few miles out of town, so the drive didn't last long. It didn't seem possible I could feel even more guilty than I already did following Logan in his old truck, but when I pulled up in front of the house I'd been to at least a hundred times before, I discovered there was no limit on the guilt meter.

"Mom left a couple chicken salad sandwiches in the fridge," Logan said as we walked through the front door of his family's old farmhouse.

Logan's mom had spent the better part of her married life restoring it, and twenty-five years of hard work showed. The Matthews' place was as much my home as my own. I'd spent as many waking hours here as I had at mine.

"You want one?" Logan pulled a Saran wrapped plate of sandwiches from the fridge and placed it on the counter.

"No, thanks," I said, hovering in the doorway. I half expected the house to know what I'd done last night and who I'd been doing it with. I was almost holding my breath, waiting for it to reject me.

"Where are your dad and mom?" I asked. Usually one of them was always here, which made private time with my boyfriend hard to achieve. I guessed this had been part of their plan.

"Mom's setting up for the big church potluck tomorrow and Dad's getting a head start tagging the calves," Logan said, focused on piling a mound of chips around his sandwich. I swear Logan ate enough food to keep four men in working order. "Why don't you put a movie in? Girl's choice." He threw me a quick wink before heaping another handful of chips on his plate.

I studied Logan for a few moments, something I hadn't done in a long time. He was handsome in that classical, Kennedy kind of way. He was a bit taller, but not as built. His eyes were lighter in color and, when they gleamed, it wasn't with knowing or spine-tingling expectation. Logan's hair was blond, golden specifically. The irony was not lost on me. It was a good couple inches shorter, and his skin was a few shades paler than . . .

Cole.

I was comparing Logan to Cole. In his own house while he offered to make me some lunch. And Logan was losing this comparison.

It wasn't fair.

Pushing aside all thoughts of Cole, I made myself smile.

"You're going to regret that," I said, trying to sound playful. I wasn't quite up to that task.

Logan chuckled as he cracked open a soda. "Just please, I'm begging you, not *The Notebook*," he said. "I'll poke my eyes out for sure this time if I have to watch that girl get it on with two guys and complain about how terrible her life is." He drew his index finger across his neck.

He knew. I was going to puke.

No, wait. He was grinning now, stacking the leaning tower of potato chips. He didn't know anything; the movie reference was just a dagger-driving-into-my-heart coincidence.

"No. Definitely not *The Notebook*," I said as I headed into the living room. I loved the movie, or I *had* loved the movie, but I'd been on the same page with Logan. I could never feel sorry for poor little rich Allie, having to choose between two gorgeous men who worshipped her. Some people's lives must really suck.

My opinions on Allie Hamilton the two-timer had changed in just twenty-four hours. She had a tough time deciding between her first love and her fiancee; I had a tough time deciding between my boyfriend and a guy I'd known all of a week.

Not that I had a decision to make anyways. I'd probably never see Cole again, unless in passing. I didn't have a Noah Calhoun waiting for me if I broke it off with the man I was supposed to spend my life with.

I almost had to slap my cheeks to stop that train of thought.

Instead of plopping down on the couch in front of the TV, I headed up the stairs towards Logan's room. He had a small TV and movie collection in his room, and since his parents didn't let us hang out in there together when they were home, I walked right into his room and crashed down on his bed.

Logan's room was a lot like him: comfortable, warm, and a tad boring. He still had the same sports ball wallpaper border he'd gotten in grade school running along the ceiling, the same twin sized bed, and the same trophy shelves hanging above his dresser, though the number of trophies had grown over the years. Other than the few pictures of Logan and me at our senior year dances and his pair of work boots, I could have been walking into the eight year old Logan's room.

Change wasn't encouraged here in the Matthews family.

I was starting to suffocate again.

"Hey." Logan stood in the doorway, his overflowing plate in one hand and a steaming mug in the other. He looked uncomfortable.

He looked even more uncomfortable when I patted the space on the bed beside me.

I had to be with the only teenage guy in existence who didn't jump at the opportunity to crawl into bed with his girlfriend.

"I'm tired and wanted to put my feet up," I said, scooting over as Logan took a few tentative steps inside the room. "I might even pass out for a while before work, so I wanted to be comfortable. Do you mind?"

I could see from his face that he did, but he kept walking towards me. I didn't get any satisfaction out of making Logan uncomfortable, but the guy wanted to marry me and was uncomfortable lying next to me on his bed. Fully clothed, watching a movie, and maybe, *maybe*, a little hand holding.

"No, it's fine. Dad and Mom aren't going to be home until later anyways." He set his plate down on his nightstand before taking a seat on the edge of his bed. If he sat anymore on that edge, he was going to fall off. "It will be our little secret."

Little secret. *Dirty little secrets*. I couldn't seem to not think about Cole for longer than two minutes.

Scooting back, Logan leaned into the headboard and tried to get comfortable. He still wasn't quite there, but he got points for trying.

"I made some tea for you." He held out the steaming mug where I saw a familiar tag swinging from a string.

Every day I'd been here, I'd taken the tea and drank it down like a champ.

Every day until this one.

"Logan," I said, propping up on my elbows. "I don't like tea.

In fact, I hate it even. And if I could pick the kind I hated the most, it would be earl grey."

I watched Logan's face go through a few stages, from confusion to contemplation, before it ended on hurt. I could tell because he wouldn't look at me—that was always the dead giveaway that I'd hurt him.

"I'm sorry," I said as he set the mug down on his nightstand, looking dejected. "I could have said that in a nicer way."

"It's okay," Logan said, leaning his head back and staring at his ceiling where the glow in the dark stars we'd stuck up there in third grade still were.

"Then why won't you look at me?"

His gaze drifted down to mine. "I'm not upset because you just told me you don't like tea," he said. "I'm upset because you haven't told me until now. Why didn't you just tell me you didn't like it years ago?"

Because I was in need of some serious psychiatric help.

"Why didn't you ask?" I replied.

Logan's eyebrows came together. "I . . . well . . . I guess I just . . ." His eyes drifted from the cup of tea to me a few times before his face relaxed. "I'm sorry, Elle. I guess I just assumed you liked it."

I softened right away. "I didn't exactly give you any reason to assume I didn't."

"Yeah, but—"

"Really." I placed my hand over his. "It's all right. It might have taken us a couple years to figure it out, but now you know I. Don't. Like. Tea."

"Got it," he said, smiling as he tapped his temple. "What *do* you like then?"

I had to remind myself he was only asking about beverages.

"Coffee," I said, feeling weight fall off my shoulders. "With a little bit of milk and one raw sugar."

Logan nodded as he studied our entwined hands. He turned mine over, seeming to inspect every line and freckle, until he lifted it to his mouth. He pressed a gentle kiss into the backside of my hand, letting his mouth linger there for a bit longer than normal. So long, my heartbeat started to pick up.

"I'll be right back," he said, setting my hand down before hopping out of bed.

As soon as I heard Logan's footsteps thumping down the stairs, I lifted my hand above me. I turned it over and stared at the patch of skin Logan's mouth had just touched. My heart still pounded from that kiss. I hadn't expected that. The intimate kiss or the way my body had reacted to it.

I'd never felt the level of desire I'd experienced last night with Cole at any time in Logan's and my relationship and, even though it was only a fraction of what I'd felt when Cole's mouth had been on mine, it was of the same type of desire. That kind that never truly goes away and only explodes the instant the object of that desire comes within arm's reach. The kind of desire that is so appealing and all-consuming it leads girls to stray on their boyfriends.

So why, after months of Logan kissing me, had one gentle kiss to the hand done a number on me?

I thought about that question for a good minute before I decided it would have to be grouped into that cluster of questions I couldn't answer.

"I know this doesn't make up for pretty much forcing you to drink something you hate," Logan's voice broke me from my stewing as he reentered the room, "but think of it as a fresh start in the beverage making process."

Logan was carrying a new mug and had changed out of his baseball uniform. He had on his well-worn khaki shorts and an equally well worn-in tee that he must have snagged out of the laundry room downstairs. Topped off by the apology in his eyes and smile, I was reminded why so many girls at my high school had given me the cold shoulder the whole first month after Logan and I became an item. When you went to school with less than a couple hundred students, the pickings were slim. And Logan Matthews was the kind of guy who would even stick out at one of those huge schools in Seattle.

"What have you got there?" I asked, smiling at him.

"We didn't have any raw sugar, so I added a little regular," he began, holding the cup out for me, "but it's my way of apologizing and begging for forgiveness."

I took the mug from him and brought it to my lips. "Thank you," I said before taking a sip. It was the first cup of coffee I'd had at Logan's house, and while it was watered down and tongue scaldingly hot, it qualified as one of the best cups of coffee I'd ever had.

It embodied what could happen when I stood up to someone and they actually listened.

I took another sip and closed my eyes in satisfaction.

"So?" Logan said expectantly. "Am I forgiven?"

I settled the cup beside his plate on the nightstand and sat up on my knees so I was at eye level with him. "Not quite," I said, looping my arms around his neck and scooting to the edge of the bed. My chest formed against his and I felt his shoulders tense before they relaxed. I dropped my lips to his and gave him the soft, chaste kind of kiss that made up ninety-nine percent of Logan's and my physical intimacy.

"There," I said, leaning back. "You're forgiven."

Logan didn't smile his easy grin then. He didn't give me one final hug before picking out a movie and going to town on his sandwich. He was hungry, but in a way I wasn't familiar with. At least, not coming from Logan.

His pupils were fully dilated, his breathing coming in short bursts, and his hands weren't letting me go. They were pulling me closer.

Before I could wonder what had come over him, Logan's mouth was back on mine. His lips didn't move over mine in the soft, languid pulls I was used to. I almost started gasping from being unable to breathe.

His hands twisted into my shirt at my back as his thumbs polished over the skin just above my skirt. I didn't know what was happening, I barely recognized who I was kissing anymore, but I couldn't stop. When I slid my tongue inside Logan's mouth, teasing the tip of his, he let out a rough, low groan. It was so similar to the sound Cole had made last night in response to what I'd done to his body, it made me lose all abandon with Logan's.

Detaching my mouth from his, I grabbed the hem of his tee and tugged it over his head. It was on the floor behind him before he registered I'd been about to take it off. I saw him about to protest. I'd gotten his shirt off a total of once in two years and it lasted for a whole five seconds before he put it back on and made me sit on the opposite end of the couch.

I wasn't going to be so easy to order this time.

Before he could say anything, I slid my tank up and over my head and tossed it on top of his shirt.

Now me shirtless . . . that was a first. Sure, Logan had seen me in my swimsuit, the boring black racerback one I wore when he came to the swimming hole, but a swimsuit and a bra were a whole world of different.

As Logan's eyes that were unable to pry themselves from my pink cotton bra could attest to.

"Elle . . ." There was warning in his voice, but his entire expression was all want. Desire, even. And I needed this too. I had to know if a flame burned between Logan and me like the one that so obviously burned between Cole and me. I had to know if I married this man, my life wouldn't be punctuated by small sparks that fizzled into oblivion.

I needed fire. I wouldn't settle for less and I hadn't realized that until Cole had showed me.

With his eyes still taking in my chest, Logan wet his lips and took a step back. He obviously didn't trust himself to stay close to me, and I could see why as he continued to look at what was inside my bra like he wanted to see what they tasted like.

And then something Dani had teased me about popped to mind.

I grabbed Logan's hand before he was out of reach. Pulling him back in a way that wasn't quite gentle, I lifted his hand, splayed his fingers, and lowered it to my breast. I kept my hand over his and curled his fingers deep into me, to the point it was almost painful.

Logan shuddered before his fingers worked of their own accord, no longer needing my encouragement. They kneaded me almost frantically. It was so unexpected, so intense, my eyes closed as Logan's hand continued to work over me.

I recognized the noise that slipped from my mouth as the same kind I'd made last night, but Logan's mouth covered mine before it was finished. His tongue forced my mouth open, although it didn't require much force. Shoving me onto my back, his weight held me to the mattress while one hand fisted into my hair and the other one continued its torturous assault on my breast.

My mind went blank. All manner of reason flew out the window as my body felt things it never had before from the body pinning me down. I didn't acknowledge that my boyfriend, who hadn't so much as intentionally grazed me, was tugging on my nipple. I didn't acknowledge that should his parents have come home early and gotten an eye full of us going at it on his mattress, we'd be in a whole heap of trouble. I didn't even acknowledge that me making out with one man last night, only to be making out with a different one now, was wrong in every way wrong could be interpreted.

I just gave over to the need and the fire coursing through my body and hoped reason and consequences wouldn't be around when I resurfaced.

It was a foolish thing to hope for, of course.

When Logan's mouth left mine, I gasped when I felt where it had re-adhered to. My eyes were still shut, I couldn't seem to open them, but when Logan's tongue played with my nipple peaking through my bra, I tried opening them. I wanted to see his mouth on me, but my eyelids wouldn't cooperate.

The way we were aligned, I could feel Logan hard against my thigh. Pressing my thigh harder against him, he made another noise with my nipple in his mouth and I felt quite certain I might die if I didn't find some sort of release. After last night, and now this, I would lose it if I didn't let my body go.

Adjusting myself below him, I didn't stop moving until I felt his hips against mine. Pressing against him, I almost cried out when his hardness pressed into the thin material of my skirt, right between my legs.

"Yes," I breathed, moving against him slowly at first, but I was literally so close it didn't take long before I wasn't moving slowly anymore. His mouth still played an agonizing game with my nipple, sucking, flicking, and nipping at it. I probably could have found my release just from what he was doing with his mouth, but what was hard and pressed between my legs wasn't hurting either.

Before I knew my hands were going there, my fingers worked at his zipper. I had it down and was just moving for the button when the body and mouth covering mine were gone. Almost immediately, my body got cold and reason made its way back in. I could finally open my eyes. When I did, the first thing I noticed was Logan still breathing heavily as he paced in front of the bed with his hands on his hips. He wouldn't look at me, and I wasn't sure if that was because he was ashamed, or if he was afraid that if he did look at me, we'd pick up right where we'd left off.

I sat up, adjusted my skirt, and waited.

"Okay," Logan said to himself. "Okay." He ran his hands through his hair and kept them there. "I'm sorry about that, Elle."

"I'm not," I said, almost defiantly.

Well, I hadn't been. Right up until I opened my eyes.

Logan came to a stop and slowly let his eyes drift back to me. He was careful to keep them north of the neck. "I thought we were waiting until we were married."

I didn't like the way he was looking at me or the words that had just come out of his mouth. One minute ago Logan had been all but worshipping me, and now he was treating me like I was a hazard. That flame we'd lit a few minutes ago had just fizzled out.

All the way out.

"No. That was what *you* decided," I said, keeping my eyes on his. I wasn't backing down. I wasn't going to be the first to cave. I was done taking a backseat in my life.

His mouth opened, but no words came out. Clamping it shut,

he inhaled and tried again. "But we made it this far. We're so close to getting married," he said, his words almost a plea.

Glaring at him, I stood. "That's also something you decided on your own."

Logan's brows came together. I don't think he would have been more shocked if I'd just slapped him across the face.

"Never mind," I said, snatching my tank off the ground as I marched towards the door. "I've got to get to work."

"Elle?" Logan sounded a little lost and a lot confused.

"Give me some space, Logan," I barked back at him before jogging down the stairs.

I wasn't really expecting him to listen to me; ordering Logan around in any kind of way was a new thing for me. When he didn't chase me, I wasn't sure whether to be happy he'd listened or disappointed he hadn't thought me worthy of the chase.

SIX

I was being punished for my actions. After I'd dropped my third order of veggie and goat cheese crepes on the floor, I wanted to clock out for the night and be done with this whole mess of a day. Since the diner was bustling to the point of bursting, I didn't have that option. Or, as Cole would have said, I did have an option; I just chose not to acknowledge it.

After Logan's and my hot and heavy make-out session, followed by my speedy retreat, I hadn't heard from him. Not even a text to make sure I'd made it into work all right. Not even to check if *I* was all right.

Though I tried to assure myself I was checking my phone all night for Logan's call, it wasn't really his name I hoped would pop up. I knew Cole was done with me, I'd seen that guarantee in his eyes, but I didn't stop hoping for a miracle.

I wasn't ready to let him go, but what was more, it seemed I couldn't give him up even if I tried.

When I dropped a fourth order before I'd even made it from the kitchen, I eyed the back door. I even took a couple steps in its direction. Who knows how far I would have made it because by step three, Dani tossed a few paper towels at me before she kneeled down to help me clean up yet another mess I made today.

I had this making a mess of things down.

"Okay, Elle," she said when I kneeled beside her. Cherry and hazelnut crepes didn't look anywhere near as pretty on the floor as they did on a plate. "What the hell's going on?"

"Nothing," I muttered as I swiped up a heap of whipped cream.

"Oh, yeah?" Dani's voice had a sarcastic edge to it. "Is that why Liam told me that Cole was in one hell of a mood after he got back from a baseball game this afternoon? Is that why Cole almost tore his head off when Liam asked him if he wanted to come here tonight to grab a bite?"

I suddenly couldn't get this mess cleaned up fast enough. "I don't know what you're talking about," I said, keeping my eyes down. Dani could see through me about as well as Cole could. "And who's Liam and how do you know him?" Maybe diverting the conversation would get us off the Cole subject matter.

"Three things, Elle," she said. "First off, you most certainly do know what I'm talking about as those flighty little eyes of yours are a dead giveaway." I narrowed those "flighty little eyes" at her. "Second, Liam is one of the rookie smokejumpers I've been *seeing*."

"You've been *screwing*," I said under my breath, surprising us both. Dani gaped at me in the same way I would have gaped at myself if I could have. I didn't normally say things like that and knowing how easily it had slipped from my mouth unsettled me.

"Ignoring that last snarky comment and moving on . . ." Dani said as we finished cleaning up the crepe catastrophe. "Third and final point is not how I know Liam"—Dani's eyebrows danced as she smiled at me—"but how you know Cole. Or, more specifically, how well you know Cole."

I shot her another glare as I slid the broken plate pieces and soggy mess into a bussing bin.

"Oh my God," she said, gaping at me again. "There really is something going on between you two." She couldn't look more shocked if I'd just told her I was pregnant.

"No," I snapped, turning and heading back for the dining room. The rush was dying down, but there was never an end to coffee and water needing to be topped up, or extra napkins to be dropped, or bills to be totaled. "There's absolutely, positively nothing going on between us anymore." I tried not to imagine, for the thousandth time today, the way Cole's face had cracked a little when he found out about Logan and me.

"Anymore?" Dani said. "*Anymore?* Oh my God. Liam was right about you two."

I flinched at her words. I wanted to flog myself for mine. Who would have known the word "anymore" could give so much away?

I now had a keen understanding of the power of "anymore".

"No, rookie screw-buddy Liam is not right." I paused before heading into the dining room. "There never was, is, or will be anything between me and Cole. There's nothing." My voice was a whisper by the end.

Dani took a few steps towards me. "Then why does it look like you're about to cry?"

I couldn't answer her because if I did, I actually would. "Just leave it alone for now. Please, Dani?"

I didn't wait for her answer. Dani wasn't exactly one for sweeping things under the rug, but we were best friends. While I hadn't openly admitted what happened between Cole and me, I hadn't eased her suspicions either. I knew I'd have to talk with her soon, like I'd have to talk with so many others, but right now, the promise of the mundane chores of running a diner were ten times more appealing.

By the time I'd refilled the fifth cup of coffee, I'd calmed down and found my waitressing groove. Keeping my mind from drifting onto certain things or people that weren't of a diner nature took some discipline, but I sucked it up and did my best.

The remainder of the night, Dani delivered food and I poured drinks. We didn't need to make any more crepe offerings to the tile floor gods. Four was plenty.

A few minutes to closing, I finally got a chance to catch my breath and make my ritual end-of-shift cup of coffee.

"You want a refill, Grandma M?" I held up the coffee pot as I snagged another mug from below the counter.

"I'll be up all night if I do, but why not?" She smiled and slid the cup across the counter at me. "Life is short and who knows what kinds of adventures could await me tonight." She winked as her eyes filled with the gleam of possibilities.

"I'm kind of jealous my life is ten times more boring than an eighty-year-old widow," I said, filling her cup. I waved at the last table as they headed out the door and Dani flipped the closed sign.

"I'm kind of jealous for you," Grandma M said, taking a sip of her coffee. "I was really hoping one descendant of mine would be as free-spirited as me, but you were my last hope, Elle Belle."

I poured my coffee, added a splash of milk and packet of raw sugar, and leaned into the counter across from Grandma M. She came in every Saturday night and sat on the middle barstool. She always came alone, but she never stayed that way. By the end of the night, she'd made new friends, or caught up with old friends, or made amends with past friends. She was the social butterfly to my social cocoon.

"You had two sons. Two very serious sons who thought free-spirited was a dirty word, Grandma M. One had no children and the other had me." I arched a brow. "I'd say I was your *only* hope."

Grandma M chuckled that full-bodied one of hers. "Good point."

We sipped our coffee in a rare silence for a minute, nothing but the sound of Paul banging around back in the kitchen, occasionally yelling warnings at Dani to turn the radio down or else he was pitching it out the window. I was just about to get back to work when Grandma M reached across the counter and grabbed my hand.

"Honey, what's the matter?"

Talk about a loaded question. Pretty much every facet of my life was what was the matter right now.

However, when in doubt, claim ignorance.

"What do you mean?" I grabbed a handful of napkins and focused on fanning them.

"You're not playing the denial card with me, are you, Elle Belle? Because I might be old as dirt, but my mind's still sharp." Grandma M had this knack for being blunt in the nicest possible way.

I sighed. I needed to talk to someone, but how could I tell Grandma M what I'd done and ever look her in the eye again? She might be open-minded, but what I'd done was on a whole different level.

"I made a mistake," I admitted, setting the fanned stack of napkins aside.

"Good," Grandma M said firmly. "It's about darn time."

My mouth dropped a little. Maybe she hadn't heard me.

"It was a big one. A really big mistake."

"Good," she said again. "Those are the best kind to make."

My mouth fell open a bit farther. Something wasn't computing.

"Okay, Grandma M. Enough caffeine for you," I said, reaching for her cup.

She scooted her cup out of arm's reach. "Don't be scared of making mistakes," she said, waiting for me to look at her before continuing. "Be scared of making none. Because if you're not making a healthy number of mistakes along the way, you're not really living life to its fullest."

Whoa. Okay, Grandma M was on something stronger than caffeine.

"We live our lives afraid of change and if we were to just embrace it instead, it wouldn't seem like such a big deal when it hits us."

I had no response. On one hand, it made a whole heck of a lot of sense. On the other hand, I'd never once had an adult tell me to live it up by making as many big mistakes as I could. It sounded like a recipe for disaster.

It also sounded like a recipe for genius.

"I can see you need a little time to work all that out." Grandma M took one long drink of her coffee before rising out of her barstool. "When you're ready to talk, you know where to find me, Elle Belle."

I was so busy working all this new information out I couldn't seem to work up a response.

"Your father may only see black and white, but seeing a thousand shades of gray in between must skip a generation," Grandma M added as she headed towards the door. "Just look at me. Every morning I wake up and look in the mirror, I see at least ten different shades in my hair alone. I don't have any problem seeing any shade of gray you have for me, sweetie."

She was almost out the door when I spoke up. "Grandma M?" I waited for her warm eyes to meet mine. "Thank you," I said, smiling. Without admitting any of the details to her, I felt better. A lot better. "Hope your night's full of wild adventures." I glanced at her empty coffee cup.

When I looked back at her, she winked. "Yours, too."

Thanks to Dani helping me close up again, I locked the diner a half hour earlier than normal. I don't know if some generous streak had hit her or if it was her way of apologizing for pushing me on the Cole issue, but I appreciated it nonetheless.

When I got in the Jeep and headed down Main Street, I hadn't intended to take a left instead of a right. Or at least I hadn't planned on it.

I also didn't plan on veering off on that bumpy dirt road I'd been down so many times I could have driven it blindfolded. After I shut off the engine, I checked my phone. No missed calls. No new texts.

I should call my dad and let him know I would be home late. I should call someone to tell them where I was. I should call Logan and tell him what had happened. I should call Cole and apologize for deceiving him, too.

I should, I should, I *should*.

I was so sick of what I should do that I never wanted to do what was expected of me again. I was in a mood tonight—that repressed inner wild child had busted lose. All the way. I knew I should get back in the Jeep and go home. Call it quits on this epically awful day.

Too bad I kissed *should* goodbye.

The summer grass was getting long and it kissed my bare legs as I headed for the swimming hole. Sounds all around me told me even the animals felt the electricity in the air tonight. The light breeze was especially strong with the scent of the wild roses that grew on the outskirts of the water.

This is what I lost myself in when I felt responsibility and guilt knocking on my door. I turned off my brain and became all instinct, and when I did, the grass sliding over my skin became more stimulating. The howls, cries, and hoots became a crystal clear symphony around me. The smells became an aphrodisiac.

Shutting everything out was easier than I thought. The pain, guilt, and remorse were gone. I felt free again.

Even in a full moon, the swimming hole was dark. Not quite pitch black, but I couldn't make out anything on the opposite side. This wasn't the first time I'd visited the swimming hole at night, but I'd never come alone. Contrary to how some people might think it would feel, it wasn't scary at all.

It was peaceful. Serene.

Slipping out of my sandals, I dipped my toes into the water. The chill from the water shot up my spine. I was contemplating if tonight's swim would be done fully clothed or not when the charge in the air skyrocketed.

"I was wondering how long it would be before you showed up here."

I spun around, feeling goose bumps creep up my body. Was it from the water or from him?

"Cole," I breathed. "What are you doing here?" He was only

a few yards in front of me, but with his dark shirt and shorts, along with his tanned skin, he blended into the darkness well. The only thing that really stuck out was his eyes.

He smiled sheepishly. That stuck out in the dark, too.

"Waiting for you."

"How did you know I'd show up?" I hadn't even known I was going to.

"It was a lucky guess," he said with a gleam in his eyes that suggested guessing had very little to do with it. He knew I'd show up sometime tonight. I was starting to believe Cole Carson really did know me better than I knew myself.

"How long have you been here?" I wanted to approach him; I wanted to wrap my arms around him and feel his around me. My body ached when I wouldn't let it.

Cole's gaze dropped. Kicking something on the ground, he sighed. "Long enough to realize I owe you an apology."

I might have just experienced whiplash standing motionless. "*You* owe *me* an apology?" I said, wondering if I'd heard him wrong.

He nodded once.

"Cole," I said, "you don't have anything to apologize for. I was the one who lied to you about Logan. I was the one who let us get carried away with whatever this . . . *thing* is between us." One side of Cole's mouth pulled tight at my very specific term for our relationship. "I'm the one who owes you an apology. A huge, heartfelt one at that."

Cole's eyes met mine. "You might owe me an explanation, but

not an apology. You didn't lie to me, Elle. You omitted the truth, but you didn't bold face lie to me."

Okay, the way Cole was underemphasizing how wrong my keeping Logan from him was making me feel even guiltier.

"But what I said to you in the parking lot this afternoon . . ." He paused, his face grimacing. "That was cruel. And I'm sorry I said those things."

I was speechless. Was Cole apologizing to me for being upset when he found out I'd hidden a boyfriend from him?

"I deserved everything you said to me today," I said. "I'm sorry I lied to you." I swallowed because I felt tears wanting to work their way into position. "I'm sorry I lied about Logan."

Cole flinched at Logan's name, like I'd just slapped him across the face. "You didn't lie, Elle. I never asked if you had a boyfriend and you never told me you did. You omitted the truth," he repeated.

"Around here, omitting a truth is the same as telling a lie," I said, crossing my arms. I didn't want to be let off the hook on a technicality. I wanted Cole to be mad at me. I wanted him to yell and scream at me some more.

"We omit things all the time, Elle. Every day. In all walks of life," he said. "If we told every person we came in contact with every truth and fact about our lives, we'd all die alone."

"That's a pretty sad way to look at things."

Cole took a step towards me. I ordered myself to stay where I was. "Let's say you wake up tomorrow and your dad asks you how your night was. What would you tell him?"

I smirked at him. "I'd tell him it started out nice and ended with a lot of frustration and confusion."

"And if he asked you what you did?"

I knew where he was going with this and I didn't like it. "I'd say I went for a drive."

"Exactly," Cole said victoriously, "and that wouldn't be a lie, but it would be an omission of what else you'd done tonight."

I pinched the bridge of my nose. "Fine. I omit. What's your point?"

"I omit, too, Elle. We all do," he said, his voice low. "Don't beat yourself up over it. I could have just as easily asked you if you had a boyfriend, but you know why I didn't?"

I bit my lip, wondering what good any of these confessions would be.

"Because I didn't care." Cole took another step towards me and I knew if he took one more, my willpower would be a lost cause. "That first day I saw you, I didn't care if you were with someone else. That night at the bonfire I didn't care. And last night"—his eyes flashed with the reminders—"I *really* didn't care. I wanted you then, Elle. And I want you now. You might belong to someone else, but you kind of belong to me, too."

My heart was about to beat out of my chest. I'd never been talked to, or looked at, with the degree of intensity burning in Cole's eyes. To say it was intense would have described a fraction of it.

"So don't apologize to me. Explain." He took a breath. "Explain to me why you didn't tell me you had a boyfriend."

I could have answered so many ways. So many explanations for the reason I'd "omitted" it, but all answers boiled down to one.

One answer that I shouldn't admit to Cole, especially with the way he was looking at me now. Once I told him, there'd be no going back. There'd be no going back to the point where we could play innocent. Pretend consequences weren't a thing of our world. Pretend the guilt wouldn't eat us away.

This was perhaps the worst possible time for me to take a hiatus from *should*.

"Because when I was with you," I began, feeling my whole world about to change. "I didn't care either."

Cole exhaled, almost like he was relieved, before taking another step towards me. I was right. The moment he took that step, my willpower vanished. I don't know who was more surprised, Cole or me, when I crossed the last few feet between us before looping my arms around him.

I tucked my head beneath his chin and held onto him like he was all I had to keep me from drowning. I'd known Cole just over a week. I didn't know his middle name or the name of his first pet, but feeling his arms around me was like coming home.

It was so confusing and made no sense, but while I couldn't explain so many things when it came to Cole and me, I knew one thing for sure.

I was done fighting it.

"I'm sorry," I said into his shirt.

"I'm not," he replied. "I'll never be sorry for anything that lets me be with you, Elle. Right now, I'm happy to have whatever piece of you I can." He kissed my forehead and the warmth I felt morphed and heated into something deeper. His mouth on my skin created an instant fire that was next to impossible to resist.

But tonight, when I was all instinct, the moon was full, and *should* was on sabbatical, it wasn't just next to impossible to resist. It was positively impossible.

Lifting my head from his shirt, I slid my hand to his mouth. "I'm going to kiss you now, Cole," I said, not recognizing this girl saying these words and touching him this way. "And if you stop me, I'm going to wear you down. Because you might be persistent, but I've got the powers of persuasion on my side."

The lips I was tracing my fingers over lifted into a smile. "Not if I kiss you first."

The words barely were out before his mouth was on mine. I gasped and he took advantage of my parted mouth. His tongue slid inside, twisting against mine in a way that brought another one of those primal sounds from me.

My hands were at the hem of his shirt before I knew they'd moved there, and they'd successfully pulled it up and over his head before I could order them to stop. By the time my fingers traveled up the seam of his back, I didn't care. The feel of his skin against mine, hard, hot, and smooth, made everything okay.

"I'm not going to be the only one shirtless around here." His fingers played with the hem of my tank top before he slid it up and over my head. He tossed it behind him somewhere into the tall grass. His mouth was on mine again, his hands exploring the skin he'd just freed.

Our kissing was frantic, almost desperate, and I knew I would pass out from oxygen deprivation in another minute if we didn't slow it down. I had all night, or at least the instinctual part of me did. Deep down I knew Dad would call in another half hour if I didn't show up. I'd turned off my phone and left it back in my Jeep. It didn't matter when Cole was kissing me that way.

Splaying my hands over his chest, I pressed against it. Just enough so I could catch my breath before I passed out.

"Why are we stopping?" he said, not nearly as breathless as I would have hoped. "I was just getting warmed up."

Hoping I could find another way to make him as breathless as he'd made me, I wound my arms behind my back. "So was I," I said right before unclasping my bra.

That Cole managed to keep his eyes firmly on mine while I slid my arms, one by one, out of my bra was a testament to his restraint. Only when it had landed at our feet did he take a step back and lower his eyes.

"Damn," he breathed, gawking at me in a way that made my inner thighs clench. "They're even better to stare at the second time around." He sunk his teeth into his lower lip and grinned. "Do I get to touch them this time?"

Since he was giving me a hard time, I decided to return the favor. "No," I said, arching my back just to make it that much more torturous. "You don't. These are totally off limits tonight. You can touch me anywhere else." I was kind of impressed by this inner sex goddess breaking free, but I was also scared of her. How did a girl who hadn't even had sex with her boyfriend of two years wind up naked from the waist up, playing a game of no-touching-zone with a smokejumper?

"Anywhere else but there?" Cole said, partially wincing when his eyes inspected yet again what he couldn't touch tonight. Then they dropped lower, south of my navel, and my stomach coiled. "*Anywhere* else?"

Even if I wanted to take back my words, I couldn't speak with the way he looked at me. With the things he was imagining so explicit on his face, my nipples hardened in the warm night air.

Cole took a few steps back. Retrieving his crumpled up shirt, he spread it out over a smooth patch of earth. Then he came back and grabbed my hands. "Do you trust me?"

I barely knew him.

"Yes," I whispered.

"Are you scared?" He guided me over to where he'd laid out his shirt.

Terrified. And yet not.

"No."

Cole's eyes drifted to the ground, then back to me. They were expectant. "Are you sure?"

I'd never been so unsure and sure at the same time in my life.

"Yes," I answered.

His eyes never left mine as he guided me down, adjusting my back so his shirt was between my skin and the earth. By that point, my heartbeat could have registered on the Richter Scale. My breathing was treading the line between hyperventilation and asphyxiation.

When Cole lowered himself over me, I wasn't sure what his intentions were, but I knew mine. I wanted him. All of him. On me, around me, and inside of me. His mouth dropped to my neck, but he held his body above mine. I wanted to feel it crushing against mine, but the space between us did have its advantages.

My fingers had his zipper down before his sharp inhale vibrated over my neck.

Cole's hand stopped mine from continuing right before he rolled on to his side.

I was opening my mouth to protest when his dropped to my ear. "I'm not going to have sex with you tonight, Elle. God knows I want to so bad I'm about to lose it, but I won't take you until you're mine. All mine. I won't share you with another. I don't want to wonder if when I'm moving inside you at night, he was inside you that morning. I won't share you in that way."

If he stopped saying those kinds of things to me that left me all breathless, I could tell him he didn't have to worry about that. My virginity was his. All he had to do was ask for it. Or take it.

Right now, I didn't really care.

"Understood?" His breath was hot in my ear.

I was lucky to manage a nod.

Propping up on his elbow, Cole's hand left my mouth. It slid down my neck, took a detour at my chest, and finished the journey down my stomach. It stopped just above the hem of my skirt.

"Do you touch yourself?" Cole's finger dipped just under my hem while every nerve in my body went on high alert.

When I didn't answer, his fingers went lower until they teased the top of my panties. "Well?" His voice was low, gravelly. "Do you?"

As his fingers started to move away, my answer leapt out of me.

"Yes," I admitted, too far gone to even be embarrassed.

"Yes, what?" As a reward, or punishment, who knows, Cole's fingers dropped lower again.

"Yes," I agreed quickly. "I touch myself." My hips rocked against his hand, completely of their own accord. His response was a lazy smile and yet another lowering of his fingers.

"Has . . ." he stumbled for the next word, "does *he* touch you there?" His voice took on a hard, dark edge that would have terrified me if his body wasn't making mine feel things I wasn't familiar with.

Inhaling, I rocked my hips against his hand again. He was so darn close. From this torture, all it would take was the lightest graze and I'd be sent over the edge.

"No," I breathed. "He doesn't touch me there. Ever," I emphasized, hoping he'd take a clue and touch me already. This was a slow form of torture that my body couldn't take anymore.

Cole froze, his fingers along with him. "Never?" The low notes were gone, replaced by surprise.

I rolled my eyes, half in frustration and half in exasperation. "No, never," I said, not hiding my irritation. "Kind of hard to do when his hands follow some sort of Northern hemisphere rule."

Cole's body stayed frozen, but now it tensed. "Wait. Are you saying you're a . . ." He fumbled for words again. "You can't be a . . ."

"Virgin?" I said loudly, easing his suffering. "Yeah, I am. Don't rub it in, okay?"

Cole's eyes widened as they stared at me with disbelief. Then, before I could regret admitting it, he popped up, gave his body a full-on shake, and charged into the dark water. Cole dove into the water and was submerged for so long I was about to get up and go after him when his head bobbed above the surface. Just like that, he trudged out of the water, his entire body and his shorts dripping wet.

That didn't do anything to ease the throb coming from below my navel.

"What the heck was that about?" I asked as he dropped beside me again. I knew how cold that water was, I'd just had my toes in it, but when I skimmed my fingers down Cole's chest, he felt anything but cool to the touch.

"Because if I didn't calm my shit down," he said, molding his hand over my cheek. Droplets of water leaked from his face onto mine. "You wouldn't be a virgin in the morning."

I inhaled sharply. "That doesn't sound so bad to me," I said, wondering what the water clinging to his skin would taste like.

"Not to me either," he said. "But I already told you, Elle. I won't share you in that way. I don't care if you and him aren't doing it, I won't let myself be with you that way until you're done with him."

It felt like something of an ultimatum. You want sex, you have to break up with him. The way Cole's body felt against mine right now made the choice unnervingly easy. It was a good thing I'd left my phone in the Jeep.

"Understood?" His voice was silk on my skin when he moved his mouth down my neck. I tried to collect my breath. Or my wits.

"Understood," I breathed back.

His mouth sucked at the skin above my collar bone. I arched closer to him, wondering why I couldn't seem to get close enough.

"But that doesn't mean we can't enjoy each other in other ways." His words were muffled against my skin, but I heard him with crystal clear precision.

I didn't really know what he was talking about, but I agreed with a nod.

"There's the girl I love," he replied as his hand trailed down my side. It didn't stop trailing until it skimmed under my skirt.

I guess I did know what he was talking about.

His hand left my thigh, and when I thought a sigh of frustration would come, I gasped instead. At the same time Cole's fingers shoved my panties aside, his thumb dropped to a certain spot that had me feeling things I'd never been able to make myself feel when touching the same spot.

Applying just the right amount of pressure, Cole's thumb circled and stroked over me until I was quite certain I was about to become the female equivalent to a two-pump-chump.

My arms wound around his neck and my fingers fisted in his

long hair. All I could do was hold on while he touched me like he knew what my body craved better than I did.

As soon as I'd feel my body quickening, Cole backed off, slowing his strokes until I almost breathed normally again.

"What do you want?" Cole's voice was throaty and deep. That, combined with the pace of his thumb, was getting me to a point I wasn't going to be able to back away from. No matter what he did. Or didn't do.

"This," I said, pressing my hips into his hand.

He rewarded my answer with an increase in speed. "And?"

"Right now," I added, because I couldn't wait. If I had to, I was convinced I would have a heart attack.

This answer he punished by slowing his thumb.

I moaned in pain and pleasure.

"What do you want?" he said possessively just outside my ear.

I caught what he was getting at.

"You," I answered. "I want *you*."

My answer wasn't out before his mouth covered mine. His mouth kept pace with his hand and when I finally came, my screams were drowned in his mouth. Cole held me together as I fell apart and, even in my wrecked state of mind, the irony wasn't lost on me.

He held me tight long after the last trembles rolled from my body. His mouth didn't leave mine, gently tasting my lips with the tip of his tongue. My breath took a while to return to a somewhat normal rate, but I tried to time it to his. When his chest lifted, so did mine. When his fell, mine fell too. I'd never felt so in sync with another person. I'd never felt like I just opened myself up in the most vulnerable, intimate way, and the fact I'd not even known Cole two weeks didn't matter.

All that mattered was the way he held me and that his eyes told me how much he wanted me. I'm sure mine told the same story. Right now, it was less about wanting him to be mine. It was about me wanting to be his. The subtle nuance shouldn't change the thought as much as it did.

It wasn't about wanting to possess, it was about wanting to be claimed. I wanted Cole Carson to have a claim to me and that couldn't ever be while Logan held that distinction. I couldn't have them both, just as much as they couldn't both have me. I had to choose, and right then, the choice was easy.

"So?" Cole looked down at me, his face an entire gauntlet of emotions. Excitement, hunger, longing, but what was most evident was the smugness in his smile.

"So?" I repeated, rolling my eyes. "Like you're not absolutely gloating in what you did to me. You don't need a description from me to know that you . . ." I fumbled for the right word. I really needed to get over my prude talk complex and just spit those dirty words out. Cole wasn't the type who would mind. In fact, it would probably turn him on.

"That I rocked your world," he inserted, his smirk jacking up a couple of notches. "That I made you cry out so loudly I'm worried you might have woken half the town?"

I made a face, like I was considering these suggestions. Then I pushed my prude off to the side and wrapped one leg around his and tugged on it until he was on top of me. I adjusted my position below him until I could feel him hard between my legs. His body rocked gently against mine and I cried out again. I was going to fall apart all over again if he kept that up.

"I was thinking more along the lines that you made me come so hard I wished you could have been inside me to feel it."

I wasn't sure whose face looked more shocked: Cole's or mine. I guess when you removed the prude filter from Elle Montgomery, she had one dirty mind and mouth. Hitching my other leg around Cole, I rocked against him again. This time I slid my warmth down his entire length.

His body shook before his shoulders went rigid. "Fuck," he breathed, trying to break loose from my killer arm and leg holds.

"Where do you think you're going?" I said, smiling up at him. His face was as tortured as I knew mine had been minutes ago. Knowing I could make Cole feel the kinds of things he made me feel gave me a power I'd never known.

"I need to jump in that water and calm my shit down again," he said, squeezing his eyes together when I slid down him again. "Or else I'm going to tear those panties off and do you right here, right now."

I swallowed the heat coming up my throat from my stomach. "Why jump into that frigid water again when I'm right here?" I bucked my hips hard against his. His grimace deepened, like this was actually causing him physical pain. "Come on in," I breathed. "The water's great."

Who was this person and what had she done with sweet and innocent Elle Montgomery?

"Fuck, Elle," Cole hissed through his teeth. "Would you please stop humping me through our clothes before I rip off both our clothes and do the real thing to you? The way I am right now, there's no way I could be gentle with you. I'd want to do you so hard you'd be sore for a week and I'd never forgive myself if that was the way we did it our first time. I need to be careful with you. I *will* be careful with you." His eyes slowly opened. They looked less tortured, but just barely. "And I will not have sex with you when you belong to another man. That's not negotiable."

I was touched, and I was kind of irritated, too. I'd heard enough sleepover talk to know losing your virginity wasn't exactly a pleasurable experience, but right now, with the way my body was throbbing again for some kind of release, I didn't really care if it hurt or if he wasn't gentle with me. I wanted him to feel the same release he'd given me. I wanted to make him feel the things he'd made me feel.

The very non-prudish me came up with an idea. If he was adamant about not having sex tonight, there were other ways to help a guy out. Right? I knew there was, although I'd never actively participated in any. Logan would have blown a gasket if I even tried to graze the erection he tried to hide sometimes when we made out.

Sliding my hand around Cole's stomach, I lowered it to the button of his shorts. I tugged it free before lowering his zipper.

For only having one hand and being crushed beneath him, you would have thought I was an expert at what I was about to do.

"Elle..?"

Maybe he was going to say something else, but he was abruptly cut off when my hand dove into his shorts and grasped him firmly.

"Do you touch yourself?" I repeated his question back to him, bit my lip for him to watch, and slid my hand down the length of him.

He groaned so loudly outside my ear, it rang my eardrums.

"Do you?" I asked, finding a rhythm that he seemed to like best. More slow than fast, more firm than loose. This was the first time I'd ever felt a guy's ... *manhood* and it turned me on like I never thought touching one would. It was soft at the same time it was hard. Silky at the same time rough.

"Every damn day, Elle," he panted, flexing his hips into my hand, guiding me as I figured this whole hand-job thing out. It was much easier than I thought. "But from now on, it will be your face I imagine when I come."

His words and the speed his hips rocked into my hand had me sliding my other hand under my panties. Cole must have felt or seen what I was doing to myself because he cursed under his breath again before pumping against me even harder.

I had another question to ask him, the second one that he'd asked me, but I never got a chance to ask it.

We both came around each other, our cries lost to the quiet night.

SEVEN

*S*ometime after we'd both managed to catch our breaths, Cole folded me tight into his arms, whispered a few more sweet things—and a few more dirty ones, too—before he fell into quite possibly the deepest sleep known to a freshly satiated man.

I tried to keep the guilt at bay, to keep remorse from sabotaging me, but they were powerful opponents. Not even five minutes after Cole's chest was falling up and down evenly in sleep did I feel the guilt, or the remorse, or both, break through my defenses. When they did, they nearly crippled me.

All I could think about was how I'd betrayed Logan, my dad, the whole darn town if you really thought about it. The golden boy's girlfriend had cheated on him.

Yes, if we were getting technical, Cole and I hadn't done the exact deed that most constituted cheating, but what we'd just done wasn't exactly an innocent peck on the cheek either. I had cheated by some definition of the word and, as Cole's face nuzzled deeper into my neck, making me sigh with contentment despite the guilt, I knew I was still cheating on Logan. Cheating wasn't just physical. In fact, I'd say the most dangerous kind was emotional.

I might have just had Cole come around my hand, but that wasn't the only way I wanted him. I didn't just want him to be the boy I snuck off with to exchange naughty little deeds; I wanted him to be the boy who'd one day want to put that promise ring on my finger. I wanted Cole to be the one I got to walk around town with my hand in his. I wanted Cole to be the one my dad looked at like he could do no wrong. I wanted so much.

So much I could never have.

I had to think, to sort out ten million things that didn't want to be sorted. But I had to try. Just because I was with Logan today didn't mean I had to be with him tomorrow. If I decided Cole was the one I wanted to gamble on, then I had to place my bet and not cringe when the dice rolled to a stop.

Logan. Cole. Elle.

No equation worked when all of us were a part of it. I had to let one go. I knew who I wanted to let go, but I wasn't sure if that was impulse and abandon talking or if it was, without a doubt, my heart ordering me to choose the boy curled around me I'd known for a handful of days.

So I had a lot to think about and just as many decisions to make.

First things first though, I had to get home. It had to be getting close to, if it wasn't already, after midnight. Dad would be unleashing the bloodhounds soon, along with calling every resident in the phone book, if I didn't get home.

Only because I knew Cole wouldn't have noticed if I stuck my tongue in his ear, I pressed a light kiss into his forehead after I'd worked my way out of his arms. I retrieved my bra and tank from the ground and slid into them while I continued the search for my sandals. I finally found them close to the water, resting beside his sneakers.

I studied Cole's peaceful face for a few seconds before I made myself start heading for my Jeep. He was happy, even in sleep, and it made me smile to realize I'd been part of putting that happiness on his face.

The farther I got from Cole, the more my chest throbbed. I knew something was likely playing tricks on me, but by the time I'd made it inside the Jeep, I couldn't decide if my heart was closer to breaking or stopping. Either would have almost been preferred to the pain.

Before I ran back to him and nestled against his side, I started the Jeep and headed for home.

I could see the lights streaming out of every window before I was half a block away. Dad was awake. Waiting for me. Guaranteed to be angry beyond repair at me for coming in so late, shutting off my phone, and having no good explanation.

There was no way, if I wanted to live to see the dawn, I would admit to my dad who I'd been with and what I'd been doing with him. Even a chill dad wouldn't have been okay with that, and my dad couldn't have been any less "chill".

I paused outside the front door to put my hair back up into my standard ponytail and made sure my tank and skirt didn't look like they'd just been torn off, rumpled, or dirty. Other than a smear of dirt at the neckline of my tank, I was as put together as I could be.

My key hadn't clicked over in the lock before I heard Dad's booming footsteps coming towards the door. "No, she's home." Dad's voice was just as booming. I didn't hear any other voices, so he must have been on the phone. "Thanks, Logan."

Wonderful. He'd been on the phone with my boyfriend, no doubt wondering if Logan knew where I was. So much for having a little time to decide who I'd tell what. Logan might not come charging over tonight, but he'd be around first thing in the morning.

"Where have you been, Elle Marie Montgomery?" Dad was still clutching his phone when he swung the door open. His brow was set and his whole body was tense with anger, but his eyes were tired. Mom had died fourteen years ago, but dad had aged fifty years in that timeframe. He'd aged another ten tonight. "I expected you home almost two hours ago."

I hung my head a little as I stepped inside. Through all his overbearing faults, I loved my dad and I hadn't meant to send him over the worry cliff tonight.

"Sorry, Dad," I said. "I kind of lost track of time." *Because I was busy touching a man and having him touch me in a way that made me lose all sense of everything, time most of all.*

"Where is your phone?" he demanded.

"In my purse," I whispered.

"So why didn't you answer it when me, Logan, your Grandma M, and everyone else I called to see if they knew where you were called?" He wasn't shouting, but the telltale quiver in his voice gave away that he wanted to.

"I turned it off," I answered, still not able to look him in the eyes.

"Why in the world would you turn off your cell phone late at night when your family and friends thought you'd gone missing?"

Because I didn't want to be reminded of friends or family tonight. Because I wanted to live in a dream for two hours of my life. Because the reality I was living wasn't the one I wanted. Because . . . I was an eighteen-year-old woman who could do what she wanted without being treated and scolded like a child.

That last "because" was the one that got my blood close to boiling and the one that snapped back. "I turned off my cell phone because I wanted to. I wanted to have a couple hours to myself where I wouldn't get a darn phone call every two seconds if I wasn't doing what everyone expected me to do." I wasn't shouting either, but I had the same quiver in my voice. Like father, like daughter. "And where I was, I wasn't missing." I marched up the stairs, as ashamed as I was proud for standing up to my dad. Pausing at the top of the stairs, I looked back down at him. He was looking at me like he wasn't sure where his daughter was. "I wasn't missing out on anything."

After locking myself away inside my bedroom, I kept waiting

for my dad to come bursting through the door to announce I was grounded until the day I turned gray. He never did, though.

In fact, I'd crawled into bed and fallen asleep before I heard him climb the stairs to head to bed himself. I fell asleep that night picking up right where Cole and I had left off in my dreams.

I woke up late that next morning, thanks to the fact my phone was still off so my alarm wasn't there to help me rise and shine for my breakfast shift at the diner. I rarely worked breakfasts, especially Sunday breakfasts because I was expected to sit in the front row with Logan and his mom while his dad gave the sermon, but I filled in when needed.

Usually I dreaded going from closing to opening the next morning, but after Cole's and my "roll in the dirt" last night, I was quite certain I'd burst into flames if I even tried to enter through those church doors today. By some miracle, if the flames hadn't gotten me then, they would have when I sat next to Logan and he draped his arm over my shoulders after telling me how nice I looked.

At least the only heat I'd feel at the diner would come from the kitchen.

Thanks to waking up late, I had to shower in record time and slide into the first piece of clothing I laid my hands on in my closet. A sweetheart neckline summer dress. Maybe not ideal waitress wear, but it was light and comfortable . . . and fast.

I was dressed and down the stairs in under a minute. Dad wasn't anywhere around and I wasn't going to stop to look for him. I was late, but I was also not eager to see him after last night's not-so-constructive conversation.

By the time I pulled up to the diner, I had fifteen minutes to get the place ready. It was a good thing I had my comfy Keds on because I'd never moved so fast in my life. The breakfast cook, Sid, kept whistling at my impressive speed.

"If I didn't know better, I'd bet my paycheck someone got lucky last night," Sid called out as I went to unlock the front door. Thank goodness my back was to him so he couldn't see the red draining into my face. "Because you have got a spring in your step I've never seen before, Elle."

"It's called waking up without a hangover, Sid," I called back at him. "Unlike the way some people wake up every Saturday and Sunday morning."

"Oooh, sassy too," Sid replied. "You definitely got lucky."

After unlocking the door, I was just heading into the break room to grab my phone and finally turn it on so I could text Cole. I'd fallen asleep so quickly last night I hadn't had more than a few minutes to sort things out, but I still knew I cared for him. I liked him in a way that was shifting more from like to the other "l" word. I wanted him to know I was thinking about him this morning and my fleeing the scene last night wasn't because I never wanted to see or hear from him again.

"You better get your lucky butt out here, Elle!" Sid yelled back at me. "The tables are filling up. And filling up fast."

Of course they were. Sighing, I tightened my apron and headed back into the dining room. The first break I got, I'd call

Cole. Texting was kind of weak anyways after what happened last night, and I was pretty much dying to hear his voice.

Sunday breakfast went out of the gates with a bang. We really should have had two servers on today, but with a little energy surge from me and some extra patience from the customers, everyone got their apple and vanilla bean crepes or Andouille sausage and caramelized onion crepes in a timely manner without me dropping a single order.

That almost changed when the door whooshed open and the next set of customers came lumbering in.

"Careful," the first of the three young men in the front said with a smile my way. That was enough to snap me out of my stupor and right the tray of crepes before they toppled to the floor.

"Yeah," the guy at the end with a familiar face, but an unfamiliar tone said. "You wouldn't want to make an even bigger mess of things." Cole waited for me to look him in the eyes, and when I did, I wished I hadn't. Those green-blue eyes of his were dark and only darkened more as they stayed narrowed.

My stomach dropped. Cole was staring at me like he despised me, like what we'd shared last night meant nothing. It made me thankful I hadn't eaten any breakfast yet.

He didn't say anything else; he just moved by me and slid into the booth where the other two guys sat.

As I set the crepes down in front of a table of regulars, I racked my brain for what I could have done or said to make Cole so upset. Yeah, I'd snuck away from him last night, but that didn't seem like that huge of a deal. Especially not warranting that look he'd just given me. It wasn't like I snuck away because I never wanted to see him again. I needed to get home before life as I knew it came to an end.

There was Logan, of course. I knew Cole wasn't thrilled with that whole concept, but it hadn't seemed to stop him last night.

So what was it?

I mulled that over as I refilled coffee at the rest of my tables. I was stalling because I wasn't looking forward to walking up to Cole and his friends' table and acting like nothing had happened, pretending he hadn't had his hands on places no other guy had before him, and imagining that look didn't mean he would hate me until his dying breath.

Inhaling a dose of courage, I headed over to his table.

Cole wouldn't look at me. I wouldn't have thought he was even aware of me except his whole body went stiff when I spoke.

"Are you all ready to order?" Not exactly my friendliest greeting, but I was flustered.

"We don't even have menus yet," the guy sitting on the end of the booth said. He sat across from Cole and next to the other guy who . . . looked identical to him. Asking if they were twins would have been a wasted question.

"We don't have menus. We serve two different crepes every day. Today's sweet and savory are listed over there on the chalkboard." I pointed to the opposite wall and tried to focus on the guy seething in silence in front of me. I swear you would have thought he was getting his toenails pulled out with pliers from the twisted look on his face.

"Hold up," the other twin spoke up. "You're a restaurant that only serves two things that change every day?"

Wasn't that just what I'd said?

"Yep."

"And what the hell's a . . . crepe?" the first twin asked, studying the chalkboard with narrowed eyes.

"Like a thin French pancake that melts in your mouth," I rattled off, having said it a million times before. Any kind of cuisine even slightly out of the ordinary took a little getting used to around these parts. Complete with a layman's explanation.

The twin against the wall gave me a sly smile. "I've never heard food described in such a sexy ass way,"—he wagged his brows, as well—"coming from the mouth of a sexy ass waitress too."

"Matt," Cole finally spoke. "Shut the fuck up."

Matt's face pinched with confusion. "You just keep getting pissier by the minute, Carson. Why don't you find yourself a local to screw and get it out of your system?"

One corner of Cole's mouth twitched. "The screwing or almost-screwing of locals is what made me 'pissy' in the first place," he said, flicking a quick glance my way. It was all ice. "But I'm about to move from pissy to full-on pissed if you don't shut your trap."

"Forgive my friend . . ." Matt waved his hand, inspecting my dress. I assumed he was looking for a name tag, although his inspection wasn't brief.

"Elle," I said, crossing my arms. Matt continued to stare at my chest, making me every kind of uncomfortable.

Matt winked. "Forgive my friend, *Elle*," he repeated. "It's his time of the month. Just ignore him."

That was in no way possible. Ignoring Cole was like trying to ignore a firework going off six inches from your face.

"But me," his smile stretched, "I don't think I could let you ignore me even if you tried."

Cole made some sort of grunt under his breath. I had guests that needed refills, orders that needed run, and new orders to take. Every second I stayed here, I got ten seconds behind. Being near Cole when he was in this kind of a dark mood wasn't what I'd describe as pleasant, but it was better than being away from him. So I stayed and played along with Matt since the guy I wanted to talk to looked like he'd rather not speak to me for the rest of time.

"I don't know," I said. "I'm really good at ignoring people."

Matt chuckled, grinning wider that I'd taken the conversation bait.

"Yes. Yes, you are." I had to look to confirm that hard voice was coming from Cole. "Ignoring, avoiding, running away in the middle of the night . . ."

"Hey, Mr. PMS," Matt said, swatting the air in Cole's direction. "Stop interrupting with your mumbles. I'm trying to make an impression."

If looks could kill, Matt would be gone in his next life too.

"My name's Matt Johnson. And yes, the last name is an indicator of how impressive,"—his eyebrows filled in the blanks—"mine is. In case you're wondering which twin's better, let me break it down for you. I drive a nicer truck, I'm the better looking one,"—

he appraised his identical twin brother and curled his nose—"obviously, and my dick's bigger, too."

Matt's twin jabbed his elbow into his ribs. "That's not what your last girlfriend said."

Matt ignored his brother's come back. "Oh, yeah," he said, smiling like the devil, "and I jump out of fucking planes to save sweet baby Bambis from going up in flames."

This guy was entertaining. I gave him high marks for that, but he was in no way what I was attracted to.

As I glanced at who I was attracted to—glaring, clenched fists, anger rolling off of him in waves—I wondered if I needed to reevaluate what attracted me.

"Your point?" I asked, quirking my head to the side.

Matt tilted his head back at me. "You wanna fuck sometime? I'm free tonight."

Cole's arms flew across the table and grabbed Matt's collar before I could shriek in surprise. Cole's nose was all but billowing smoke, but Matt only looked marginally intimidated. This must have been a regular occurrence between these two.

"Dammit, Matt. Shut the hell up," Cole said, shoving Matt back against the booth hard. "Or else I'll slit your 'chute while you're asleep."

"Touchy," Matt muttered, adjusting his collar and tossing a sugar packet at Cole's chest. "What's got your jumpsuit in a bunch?"

Cole's eyes flicked to me and that was all Matt needed.

"Holy shit! Well done, Carson. Why didn't you just tell me

you've staked your claim?" Matt's meaty arm reached across the table and clapped down on Cole's shoulder.

Cole brushed Matt's hand away. "I haven't staked a claim on her," he said. "And I don't want one either. I don't want *anything* from her." Those darkened eyes swept back to me, and the look in them, combined with the hurtful words, had me stepping away.

"Hey, just ignore these two. This one's always an ass," the quiet twin finally spoke up, hitching his thumb in his brother's direction. "And this one's been in an insanely bad mood all morning." He smiled at me. Although he and Matt were twins, their faces looked totally different when they smiled. "Before you run away and don't come back because of the douche sitting to my right and dumbass in front of me, would you take our orders?"

I nodded, but refused to look in Cole's direction. The way he treated me was especially hurtful after last night.

"Could you bring us three coffees and three crepes? Whichever one you think's the best?"

I nodded again, taking another step back. I could see, from the corner of my eye, Cole's head turning my way.

"And I'm Liam, by the way. Dani said to tell you hi." This time, his smile was paired with the faintest coloring on his cheeks. I wasn't sure if that was because he was smitten with Dani or because of the nasty things she'd likely done to him, but I was impressed. For once, Dani had definitely chosen the better of two brothers.

"I'll bring your coffees right over," I said, heading towards the drink station.

"We won't hold our breaths," I heard Cole say after me.

I spun on my heels. Now this was getting to be too much. I didn't know what I'd done to deserve such disdain, but I was getting tired of it. Especially when it seemed he'd sought me out just so he could pour it on thick.

"You know, just in case you forget about us when you turn your back and walk away."

Whatever I was about to snap back was drowned in the wake of those words.

Trying to keep from wincing, I trudged over to pour three coffees. The spring in my step was long gone. None of us spoke when I dropped the coffee cups in front of them, other than Liam saying thanks for them all and Matt scoping out my cleavage when I leaned over to set his in front of him. Cole remained silent. At least verbally he did, but his body and eyes said so many harsh things I couldn't scurry away quickly enough.

After placing their order with Sid, I rushed through the dining room, trying to catch up. By the time Sid had the guys' order ready, most of the breakfast diners were gone or on their way out. I missed the distraction a full restaurant provided. Refusing to look anywhere but at the wall behind their table, I carried their crepes across the diner. After settling the plates into position, I asked, "Can I get you anything else?"

"It's been a few days since I've had a blowjob," Matt piped up, looking at me expectantly.

Another elbow to the ribs from Liam. "No, we're good. Thanks, Elle."

Shooting a quick glare at Matt, I turned and walked away. I didn't want to visit that table again. The bill was on me. Just eat, get out, and stop making me feel like I'd committed the worst crime known to man.

"I think you might have forgotten about me." Cole's voice carried through the almost empty diner. "Not the first time, I know, but still . . ."

Spinning back around, I glanced at the empty space on the table in front of him, then shrugged. "Didn't you just mention that you didn't want anything from me ever again?" I said, checking the diner to make sure no one was paying us any attention. "Looks like we're off to a good start then."

Liam had the decency to hide his smile, but Matt burst into laughter. "Whoa. Carson." He punched Cole's arm. "What the hell happened between you two because please, for the love of God, if and when you two get some wild make-up sex on, call me so I can get the video camera rollin'."

My small smile of vindication fell when Cole looked at me. He was smiling, but it wasn't the friendly, warm kind. "Nothing," he said, looking away from me like he never wanted to look at me again. "Nothing at all happened between Elle and me. A whole lot of nothing."

I rushed to the back room before the first tear fell and I stayed back there until long after the table in the back was empty.

EIGHT

Sunday nights in the summer were date night at the bowling alley. Logan and I had gone on our first date there, and over the past couple summers, the group had grown from two to about twenty. Most were Logan's friends from high school and baseball, but Dani usually tagged along too. If she didn't have anywhere else to be. Or anyone to do.

After my shift at the diner had ended, I'd driven as far as my Jeep would take me up some logging road, then I got out and hiked until my mind was empty. It took a while before I reached that empty feeling, but that wasn't much of a surprise after everything that had taken place today.

I'd managed to miss Dad after returning home to shower and change, and by the time I pulled into the parking lot of the bowling alley, the therapeutic benefits of that three mile hike had vanished. I tried not to dwell on Cole's looks and words from that morning, but I couldn't seem to focus on anything else.

My stomach hurt. My heart hurt. My head hurt. I could cure the stomach and head hurt easily enough, but didn't know of a quick way to fix a heart ache.

Telling myself to put on my big girl panties and suck it up, I went inside the bowling alley. As much as I wanted to curl up in my bed, I couldn't avoid Logan any longer. After the whole "Elle's Missing!" fiasco last night, I'd been lucky I could reassure him over the phone when he called after church. He had about a million and one questions for me, but after saying I was fine for the million and one'th time, he calmed down and let me off the phone when I said I had to get back to work. He wanted to get together after my shift, but I told him I had plans. He let it go and said he looked forward to seeing me tonight.

Logan was getting suspicious. While that irritated me, he was right to be. I'd let some man who hated me today touch me last night in ways Logan wouldn't even dream of.

I was almost convinced I never wanted to see Cole Carson's face again, but then I remembered the way it had looked that first day we met at the swimming hole and I knew I'd die a slow death if I never did see it again.

Logan, Dani, a handful of his teammates, and another handful of girls we'd either graduated or gone to school with were laughing and tying on their shoes, taking up half of the bowling alley.

I rolled my shoulders back and pretended life was great. I'd never been happier or more confident with the direction it was taking.

Yeah. That confidence booster fizzled flat.

Logan noticed me first as I made my way to the crowd. He patted the guy he'd been talking with on the arm and came towards me. His arms were already open before he'd made it halfway.

"Hey," he said, sounding concerned as he tucked me close. Those familiar arms, the ones I'd felt around me hundreds of times, didn't disappoint. I melted into him a little and pushed the differences in how Cole held me aside. That was all a moot point anyways. "You don't look so good," he whispered, rubbing the middle of my back.

"I don't feel so good," I replied, burrowing my head down deeper into his shirt. Inhaling that familiar smell of soap and leather. It didn't matter how many times Logan showered, he always smelled a bit like the leather of his baseball glove.

"You want to talk about it?"

I did. I didn't.

But I needed to.

"Yeah," I said. "How about afterwards?"

Logan nodded. "Okay. Whenever you want."

Might as well get it out in the open tonight. What I'd done with Cole, the fool I'd been to think there was this deep, earth-shattering thing between us. No matter if I wanted to marry Logan or call it off tomorrow, I needed to tell him. He deserved to know the truth.

I didn't let myself think about the repercussions of telling him. I would have been paralyzed if I did, so I just focused on one step at a time.

"I was so worried about you last night when your dad called."
His arms tightened around me.

"I'm sorry. I didn't mean to upset anyone." That was true.
However, my actions told a different story.

"Where were you?" he asked. "I searched all our normal
places. I was just heading towards the old swimming hole on your
Grandma M's land when your dad called and let me know you'd
made it back."

That would have been ideal in the worst possible way. Logan
stumbling on a half-naked, sleeping Cole, demanding to know if
he'd seen his girlfriend, Elle Montgomery. Cole smirking at him
with a sleepy smile and saying something about how he had seen
her recently. She'd just been curled around him moaning his name.

"I just needed to . . . get away," I answered him.

"From what?"

From you was my knee-jerk response, but it wasn't only from
him. I wanted to get away from myself, too. From the person I'd
become thanks to letting everyone else make the decisions in my
life.

The longer my thoughts went down this path, the closer I got
to tears. The heavier the guilt weighed down on my back. The
closer I got to telling him where I'd been last night and, more
importantly, what I'd been doing.

I was about to open my mouth when a finger poked my shoulder. "I'd tell you two to get a room if I actually thought you'd use
it the way it was meant to be used." Dani's voice was unmistakable. "And abused."

I heard the eyebrow pop in her voice, promptly followed by Logan's long sigh. He tolerated Dani because she was my best friend, but that was the only reason. He wouldn't have said two words to her if it wasn't for me, because Logan and Dani were about as opposite as two people could get. And no, the irony that my best friend and my boyfriend were polar opposites was not lost on me.

"Mind if I borrow your blushing bride for a minute?" Dani didn't wait for Logan's reply before she gave my arm a swift tug.

I went with her because I was too tired to fight. I gave Logan an apologetic shrug, but his attention was already being taken over by one of his teammates. Like that, I was forgotten.

Or at least that's the way it felt.

"Hey, friend," Dani said, cordoning us off to the side. "Or should I call you stupid, stupid girl?"

When Dani was on the rampage, it was best just to let her get it out of her system.

"Please, for the love of women everywhere, please tell me you weren't just about to tell Logan you've been playing with the fire hose of one of the new smokejumpers in town?"

My mouth dropped. Somewhere around the fire hose part.

"Please confirm you are not that stupid," she said, snapping her fingers in front of my face when I remained quiet. "Anytime now."

"What are you talking—"

"No," Dani snapped, looking insulted. "Don't you dare do

that to me. Don't play the innocent card with me. I know what's been going on and I'm hurt that you'd think by confessing your sins to me I'd tell someone or think any less of you."

"Liam," I muttered, not so sure I was such a fan of him anymore. "What did he tell you?"

"The things my best friend should have been the one to tell me," she said, shoving my arm. "What the hell, Elle? You start having some thing with a guy so damn hot he makes me come just by looking at him and I'm the last to know?" She shoved my arm again. "Not cool."

I sighed, glancing over at Logan laughing with his teammates. Oblivious. "Not the last to know . . ."

Dani sighed with me. "Damn, Elle. What are you going to do?"

I studied Logan's face. Really took him in. He was a good man, I knew that, but was he supposed to be *my* good man?

"I'm going to tell him. Soon."

"Good, it's about time you called it quits with zero-sex-appeal boy," she said, curling her nose. "But I was referring to Cole. What are you going to do about *him*?"

Hearing his name hurt my heart, too. Thinking about him, remembering him, longing for him, and now, hearing his name. Pain, pain, and more pain.

"After the way he acted towards me earlier?" I almost shivered remembering it. "I'm going to do my best to avoid him. He obviously hates me and wants nothing to do with me." I bit the side of my cheek to keep from welling up.

Dani's eyebrows went sky high. "You think Cole hates you?" she said, grabbing my elbows and giving me a little shake. "You think Cole hates you." This time, it wasn't a question. It was more a statement uttered to make me feel like an idiot.

"No. I know he does." I glanced over at the rest of the group longingly. I'd rather be heaving a ball down a lane than having this conversation with Dani right now.

"Well, that confirms it then," she said, patting my cheek.

"Confirms what?" I dodged away from her other hand when it moved to pat my other cheek.

"You really are a stupid, stupid girl." Without another word, she rolled her eyes at me and marched over to the ball rack. I glared at her while she took her time selecting a ball, rubbing a few in an inappropriate fashion when some of Logan's teammates stopped to check her out.

If the ball stroking didn't do it, her outfit did. Dani had showed up in her standard issue garb: tight shirt, short skirt, and loose standards. It wasn't that I was ashamed of Dani; that wasn't it at all. I was jealous of her. She knew who she was, was proud of it, and didn't let anyone push her around. If someone didn't like her, then forget 'em. Moving on.

I was envious of the way she'd molded and shaped her life to her liking, but happy for her at the same time as her best friend. I knew I could never express it to Logan. He'd have a coronary if I told him I wanted to be more like Dani, but it was true. I wanted to be more like Dani, in the Elle Montgomery way.

Whatever way that was.

The games were starting, so I headed over to pick out a ball. I was contemplating whether I wanted a pink, light ball or a heavy, dark blue one when the hairs on the back of my neck stood on end.

I felt that familiar energy in the air. I felt *him*.

My breath caught in my chest when I looked up and saw Cole saunter into the bowling alley with a few of his fellow smoke-jumpers. Complete with a flock of girls following them. Almost a three to one ratio, and Cole seemed to be the favorite, judging from the cluster of batting eyed floozies frolicking around him.

My stomach churned for what was possibly the hundredth time today.

Cole came to a sudden stop as the few other guys continued on towards a lane a couple down from ours. His harem skidded to a stop along with him. Meeting my gaze, his mouth curled up in a way that made me feel a little faint and not in the good kind of way. Extending both of his elbows, Cole glanced between the handful of girls around him and waited.

He didn't wait long.

Before I could narrow my eyes, two girls had glommed onto his elbows. He peaked a brow my way. That eyebrow said it all. *You were just an appetizer. Why should I settle for one when I can have five?*

I couldn't look away. Cole was a walking train wreck I couldn't turn away from.

"Hey." Dani popped in front of me and snapped her fingers. "Ignore the bastard. He wants to play games, you can too."

"I don't want to play games," I whispered.

"No one wants to play games," she said, grabbing the heavy, dark ball before winding her arm through mine and towing me back to our lanes. "But game playing is just part of the package. He's trying to make you jealous. Insanely jealous right now. What you're going to do is ignore him and throw that jealous shit back in his face." She hitched a hand on her hip and took a breath. She was riled up. She was fighting a war and wasn't taking prisoners.

I wanted to tell her Cole had no reason to want to make me feel jealous. He felt nothing for me, so why would he go out of his way to make me jealous? He wouldn't.

But it was working.

Especially when he reclined in one of the lane chairs and let a curvy redhead occupy his lap. Bile rose in my throat. I thought we were at a bowling alley, not a strip club, but she was clearly and unabashedly giving him a semi-lap dance.

"Show that bastard two can play this game," she said, getting her finger in my face. "And show him you play it better." Grabbing my shoulders, Dani spun me around and shoved me with such force I lurched into the arms of the person in front of me.

"I wasn't really in the mood for bowling anyways." Logan smiled down at me, wrapping his arms around me.

My mind melded with Dani's, as scary as that was, and I knew what she wanted me to do.

It was wrong, it wasn't what I'd do, but I was going to go with it.

"Me either," I whispered as I ran my hands up Logan's chest.

His face didn't have a chance to iron out with surprise before I popped up on my toes and crushed my mouth against his. I slid one hand behind his neck and the other fisted into the material of his shirt.

Logan tensed at first, he wasn't used to these kinds of public displays, but it took all of one second of my lips moving over his for him to relax and reciprocate. His hands gripped my face and he kissed me back. Harder than normal, almost frantically. A few of Logan's teammates gave a few hoots, but Logan didn't back away from the kiss. His tongue even slid across the seam of my lips before we pulled back from each other.

Logan was breathless and his eyes were excited. This was a side of him I wasn't used to seeing. I'd almost never seen it. But this kiss hadn't been about Logan, it had been about Cole. Winding my arms around Logan's neck, I looked over my shoulder.

Cole's eyes bored into mine and, if they were weapons, Logan would be dead at my feet right about now. I inhaled sharply and couldn't look away from him quickly enough.

Dani'd been right. That public makeup session had certainly gotten his attention. Although the attention it had gotten from him made me want to take the whole thing back.

"Wow," Logan said, tapping the tip of my nose. "I'm not sure what that was for . . . but thanks."

I doubted if I told him what that "was for" he'd still be smiling at me like I was the eighth wonder of the world.

"You're welcome," I said, using Logan's body as a shield from

Cole's continued glower. After that first flash of murder, I hadn't looked back at him, but I could intensely feel his eyes from my head to my toes.

"Do you want to stay and play or should we get out of here?"

I'd never heard words like those come out of Logan's mouth. Was he suggesting we ditch his teammates and friends? Was he hinting he wanted to pick up where we'd just left off a minute ago? Or yesterday afternoon?

The sideways smile on his face suggested that he was. I'd managed to waken the seemingly dormant sex drive in Logan Matthews after two years.

The timing couldn't have been worse.

"We should probably stay and show them how a proper gutter ball's done," I said, unable to look into his expectant face any longer.

"Yeah, you're probably right," he said. "It's a good thing one of us is totally selfless."

The dagger of guilt just drove deeper.

My smile fell flat.

"Maybe later, then?" he said, winking as he headed over to pick out his bowling ball.

I pretended like I hadn't heard that.

"Damn, that was perfect," Dani said, popping up behind me and smacking my backside. "You should have seen Cole's face. I didn't think that level of pissed could be reached by mere mortals."

"Remind me why I listen to you and actually take your suggestions?" I muttered.

"Because when it comes to the species that is man," she made a clicking sound with her mouth, "I'm the pro."

"And who's the judge of that?"

"Your sexy ass lover over there who hasn't taken his eyes off of you yet," she said, looking in Cole's direction and grinning.

Then she waved.

"Dani," I hissed.

"What?" she hissed back, waving again.

I didn't need to look to confirm Cole was not waving back. If anything, she was getting a different kind of hand gesture.

"I don't know," I sighed, feeling like this could be my life's current theme song. "I just don't know anymore."

"You can thank me when you do know again," Dani said, giving my backside another smack before going up to take her turn.

She got a strike on her first turn. I scored a nice gutter ball that had our whole group chuckling.

That was the way the rest of the evening went. Gutter ball after gutter ball after shameful gutter ball.

After yet another gutter ball, I plopped onto the back benches in a huff. We were in the eighth frame and a big fat zero sat beside my name.

The ironies just wouldn't quit.

"That was an impressive show." A low voice sounded behind me, making me almost jump out of my seat. I didn't need to look to confirm who it was, but I did. I missed having him close. "But you can cut the act out. If you keep that up, our poor old Logan is really going to have some prayers of forgiveness to make tomorrow morning after he rubs out that killer hard-on you've been giving him all evening."

I stiffened. Taking a quick look around to make sure no one was within earshot, I cleared my throat.

"But who knows? You're a wild little thing at the snap of a finger. Maybe you'll rub him out yourself like you did for me last night." Cole's face was so cold I could feel the ice. If I still had any doubts about how Cole felt about me, this confirmed it: he hated me.

"Me last night. Him tonight . . ." His eyes darkened even more. "I guess I'm up tomorrow night. Same place? Same time?"

I had this crazy urge to slap him. It was so intense, my hand was actually tingling. I wasn't sure if I was more sick about the expression on his face, or the words coming from his mouth, or the fact I'd thought we shared such a special thing that meant nothing to him.

"I'll let you get back to your . . . *game*." The word rolled bitterly from his mouth. "Just thought I'd let you know you can stop trying to make me jealous. It won't work."

Turning in my seat so I could face him straight on, I wouldn't let myself hold back the next words. "Is that because it would require an actual soul to feel an emotion like jealousy?"

Half of Cole's face flinched, like my words had hit their intended mark—hurt— but that was quick lived. That twisted smile that could knot my stomach every time formed. I'd seen that smile too many times today.

"In order to feel jealousy over someone, you have to actually care in the first place." Staying just long enough to witness the pain crease over my face, Cole turned and left just as suddenly as he'd appeared.

Just when you thought there wasn't a big enough chunk of your heart left to break . . .

After that, I did my best to ignore the increasingly loud group a few lanes down. I tried to pretend Cole was nothing to me, like he did with me.

He was much better at it than I was.

"Eww," Dani sneered, crashing down beside me after scoring yet another strike. "Why doesn't she drag him into the men's bathroom and blow him already? I'm getting sick of watching the bowling alley porn show."

Because I was a glutton for punishment, I followed Dani's gaze. I wished I hadn't.

Cole was reclining in a chair, his face lit up in a way I'd experienced last night, while the red head from earlier straddled him. She was leaning over him so far her boobs almost brushed his face and she gave him a suggestive smile that made me blush. Her hand moved over a certain zipper. She was practically giving him through his clothes what I had last night.

In public.

No one in their group seemed to care, and no one in ours other than Dani and me even noticed them, but now that I'd seen it, I knew it would be forever singed in my mind.

Cole's head dropped to the side, and his eyes glommed onto mine instantly.

"Don't look at that asshole, Elle," Dani instructed, flipping him off. "That's exactly what he wants while he lets Fire Crotch dry rub him in public."

I wanted to look away, I truly did. I just couldn't.

Tilting his head back to the girl straddling him, Cole motioned her closer with a curl of his finger. Whispering something that had her eyes lid like she was mid-orgasm, she dropped her mouth to his and those two kissed, sucked, and made out at each other so hard it made me wonder if a tongue could dislocate from their frantic efforts.

When I'd seen entirely too much of some strange girl's tongue inside the man's mouth mine had been in last night, Dani finally forced me to look away. Grabbing my head, she turned it until my stare landed on a familiar back. Logan had just rolled the ball down the lane, and when he turned around, his eyes met mine.

He smiled easily at me, like it was impossible not to.

I was out of my seat and heading for him before I knew what I was going to do.

He must have seen something in my eyes that scared, startled, or excited him because he tensed a little before I made it to him.

"Elle?" Okay, he was excited. I'd been friends with Logan for so long I could tell from one word just how he felt. It was so easy with him, and just as hard.

"Logan," I said, quirking a brow before stopping in front of him. I didn't pause until I was so tight against him I could feel the button of his jeans hard against my belly button. "You know that little kiss we just had?" In terms of what Logan and I had shared, it wasn't exactly *little*, but I was getting at something.

Logan's grin lifted higher on one side. "I think I'll know that kiss for a while."

I slid my hands up his chest until I grasped his shoulders. "Let's make our next one make the last one seem like a PG version," I whispered.

Logan's eyes widened for one moment before he recovered. "Sounds . . . *good*. When can I look forward to the next one?"

I flicked the quickest of glances Cole's way. He was watching, barely seeming to register the girl doing things to him in public that had been the reason "private" was created.

"How about right now?" I said, not waiting for Logan's agreement. I slowly lifted my mouth to his and left it there until Logan's newly tensed shoulders relaxed. It didn't take long for his arms to wind around my back and hold on like I could fly off with the wind. Just as our lips started their languorous assault, Logan did something totally unexpected. His hands slid south of my waist until they cupped my backside. Cupping wasn't the exact word; it was more like holding on for his dear life.

Logan's urgent hands, his lips sucking at mine softly, and his . . . *ahem* . . . growing against me made it easy. Too easy. With my eyes closed and my mind free, picturing Cole in Logan's place was simple. This person moving against me was more like Cole than the Logan I'd known anyways.

"Elle . . ." Logan sighed the word in between our mouths, and

I realized I was not with Cole. Their need and urgency might have been similar, but their voices weren't. Logan's went a few notes higher and clearer in the heat of the moment—Cole's went a few notes lower and rougher.

I was about to end the kiss and get my head examined when I felt his presence.

"Hey, am I interrupting?" He might have worn a fake smile, but Cole couldn't have sounded like he cared any less.

Logan's mouth left mine reluctantly, but his hands and arms stayed where they were. He studied Cole, looking a little irritated at being interrupted, but this was Logan. He wasn't a jerk for the sake of being a jerk. Especially to some stranger who'd just wandered up to him at the bowling alley.

If he knew who that stranger was, and exactly where and for how long he'd touched me, I doubt that conventional smile on Logan's face would have formed.

"Maybe just a little bit," Logan replied, winking down at me. "But she's not going anywhere. I won't let her."

Logan might have said it in a teasing way, but behind the teasing tone were truths that made me shift in place.

Cole saw through it, too.

"I'll let you get back to it,"—Cole crossed his arms and avoided meeting my gaze—"I just wanted to say you've got yourself one hell of a girl."

My breath caught in my lungs. What the heck was Cole doing? I didn't want to find out. All I wanted was for him to shut his mouth and march to the other side of the bowling alley. Then I saw Miss Lap Dance watching Cole like she was ready to devour him and I didn't want him going anywhere.

It was yet another cluster of confusion. Big surprise.

"Oh, yeah?" Logan said, nodding like he agreed.

Cole cocked his head to the side. "Man, she gave me something so damn delectable I about exploded all over the place. In fact, I think I might have." Leaning closer, Cole acted like he was about to divulge a secret. "It was so good I don't quite remember."

My mouth fell open. All the way open. I didn't care what the redhead had in mind for Cole, I wanted him to shut his trap and head the heck back.

I couldn't look Logan in the face—I was too ashamed and embarrassed that this was how he was going to find out.

I couldn't look Cole in the face—I was too furious with him.

So I wound up staring at the shiny wooden floor, wishing I could disappear into it.

"Yeah, those crepes are pretty amazing," Logan replied, one hundred and ten per cent oblivious.

I felt Cole's eyes shift to me because my whole body went a few degrees warmer. He inhaled slowly. "Fuck, yeah, they are."

Logan didn't flinch. He might not have used the word, or any even close, but he played with guys that thought it was the go-to adjective, verb, and noun for every conversation.

"I'm not sure what's better, though," Cole continued on, shifting a little closer. My heartbeat responded immediately. I checked Logan, half expecting him to notice. Nothing. He was still clueless, conversing with this guy thinking they were discussing crepes. From the way Cole's expression darkened in that sexy way when I peeked at him, I knew he heard, saw, and sensed exactly what his proximity was doing to me. "To be the giver of something that damn amazing or to be the receiver."

I wanted to die for Logan's sake. I wanted to live for Cole's and the things he was reminding me of with his innuendos.

Two words. Confusion. Cluster.

"So, what is it, Elle?" Cole's voice went a note lower, making me remember the things he sighed in my ear last night. My legs trembled. "Do you prefer giving"—his words lengthened, drawing the whole pleasure and pain of them out—"or do you prefer taking . . ." I inhaled, bit my lip, and waited for it. Waited for the whole world to explode around me. ". . . *crepes*?"

Logan made a face at him, like he was certifiable talking about crepes like they were to Cole what baseball was to Logan. I just gaped at him like he was crazy. Because he was.

My hand was twitching badly again. Since I wouldn't let myself slap him with my hands, I let my words do the slapping.

"I prefer giving *crepes*," I sneered the word. "Because at least if you don't like what someone else gives you, you don't have to fake anything." I took a breath because my body startled to tremble. "At least then you don't have to keep faking that you cared enough to either give or take crepes in the first place."

I might as well have slapped Cole across the cheek. The smug veneer cracked and I saw the shortest flash of pain.

"Touché," he said, recovering that hint of a dark smile before walking away as abruptly as he'd appeared.

"That was the weirdest conversation about crepes I've ever heard," Logan said, staring at Cole's back for a couple seconds. Shaking his head, his arms tightened around me. "There's a screw or twelve loose in that guy's head, Elle. I want you to stay away from him."

It was a heartfelt concern delivered in the wrong way. Where Logan likely heard protection in his words, I heard an order. Another rule. Another decision made for me. He'd done it dozens of times before and I'd thought nothing of it.

That pattern ended right now.

"And I want you to stop telling me what to do," I said, weaving out of his arms.

Logan's eyebrows came together.

"I need some air," I said, not able to watch the hurt settle into Logan's face. I'd been harsh. Yes, it was about time I stood up to him and told him I was done being a back seat driver in the journey that was my life, but I could have done it in a nicer way. Logan had never been cruel; he just hadn't known better and I hadn't taught him any better. "Play my turn, will you? I'll be back in a while."

I didn't wait for his answer. All I knew was that I needed to get out of the bowling alley. It was suffocating me, but it was only one of the many things that stifled me. The air in the bowling alley was a metaphor for my life.

Stifling.

Before Logan or Dani or anyone else could try to stop me, I rushed for the side exit. Fresh air was a mere three lunges away. I shoved the door open harder than necessary and it flew open right before it rammed into something.

A surprised huff came from the other side. "Shit!"

"Oh my gosh!" Grabbing the door handle, I pulled it back and hoped I hadn't just busted someone's nose open.

"Shit, shit, shit, shit!" was the pained response of the person I'd just inadvertently assaulted with a door.

So, yeah. I had busted someone's nose open. All I saw was the blood leaking through the fingers covering his nose. My gaze only stayed there so long, because that was when I felt it.

The electricity sparking to life in the air.

Cole's eyes skidded to mine at the exact same time.

It looked like I'd just nailed him with another door.

"Fuck," he cursed, but I guessed that had nothing to do with the blood dripping from his nose.

"Oh, shoot, Cole," I said, reaching for him.

Like that, everything was forgotten. The hurtful words, the girl grinding all over him, the stares of disgust . . . everything. He was hurt and my need to help him overrode all the rest. "I'm sorry."

He looked away from me. "I suppose I deserved that."

"I didn't know you were behind that door when I came charging through," I said, reaching out for him.

He flinched away and took a few steps back. "You might not have, but karma sure as shit did."

Shuffling through my purse, I found the small pack of tissues I kept for teary eyes, stuffy noses, or in this instance, a busted open nose. "Why do you think you deserved a whole heap of bad karma taken out on your poor face?"

"You and I both know you're not innocent or clueless enough to not know the answer to that," Cole said, taking the handful of tissue from me.

I felt some heat flood into my cheeks. Now that I knew he wasn't going to keel over and die, the emotions I'd battled today crept back to the front of the line. The attraction was the first thing I felt, then the confusion, and last the anger.

"You're going to need stitches for that," I said, grimacing when I caught a glimpse of the gash across the bridge of his nose.

"I'll survive," he said, packing the tissue on top of it.

Neither of us said anything for a few seconds, but neither of us made a move to leave the other behind. We were content in the mutual silence.

Then Cole heaved a sigh that was as heavy as it was long. "I'm sorry, Elle," he said, staring at the ground. "Shit. I'm so sorry."

The anger melted away. Just like that. *I'm sorry* was some powerful stuff.

"What for?" I asked just because it seemed like the next thing to say.

Cole kicked at the dirt with the toe of his shoe. "For everything," he said quietly. "From the second you met me to right now and everything in between. I'm sorry for it all."

That wasn't the answer I'd expected. He didn't have anything to be sorry for except for the way he'd been to me all day long.

"Why, Cole?" I took a step towards him. He took a step away. He seemed determined to keep a body's length distance between us. "Why have you acted like you hate me all day? Why have you been so . . . cruel?"

Hate. Cruelty. I would never have used those words to describe Cole until today. I wasn't sure who the real Cole was: the one that made my heart skip when I met him at the swimming hole or the one that made my heart break today.

"Why did you leave me, Elle? Why did you sneak away from me in the middle of the night while I was asleep like you were ashamed of me and what we'd done?" He kept his voice controlled, but I could hear the edge in it. "Why were *you* so cruel?"

I made a face and opened my mouth to reply. Nothing I'd done last night had been cruel, not even remotely, but as I studied the creases of Cole's face, I could see I'd cut him as badly as he'd cut me.

I might not have been as intentional about it, but I'd hurt him nonetheless.

"Is that what you think? That I left last night because I was ashamed?"

"Why else would you up and leave like that?" He was back to staring at everything but me. I didn't know why he found it so hard to look at me, but I missed the way he used to look at me.

Like he knew me better than I knew myself and was just waiting for me to figure it out.

I sighed, not proud of what I was about to admit. "Because I was scared, Cole. I was *scared*, not ashamed."

The skin between his brows creased. "You were scared?"

"Yes."

"Of what?" he said, adjusting the tissue packed against his nose.

Why did I have to remind myself to be honest with him?

It only took a moment before I had my answer: because I was even scared of admitting the truth.

The cowardly lion had nothing on me.

"I was scared of the way I felt about you . . ." This would have been so much easier if his arms were around me. Instead, a seemingly uncrossable distance lay between us. "Of the way I still feel about you." I looked away from him. I couldn't stand to stare as his tortured face grew more tortured with each word. "I was scared of what would be waiting for me in the morning if I stayed all night with you. I was scared of what my dad would think. I was scared of what Logan would say. I was scared of you waking up and leaving me behind." Now that I'd opened this can of scared, I couldn't seem to close it. "I was scared, Cole. I'm still so damn scared."

Cole looked as surprised as I felt that that baby curse slipped out. And now I was also scared of becoming a swearing sailor.

"So you left because you were scared, not ashamed," Cole said, summing it all up. "But are you going to have me believe you haven't felt any shame since last night?"

"No, I have felt it, Cole. I have." One side of his face twisted. "But only because this person I'd shared so much with acted like I was nothing to him. And treated me like I was nothing." I ran my hands down my dress. "I only felt shame because I was so sure there was something special between us that you so obviously never felt."

When Cole stayed silent after my heart wrenching confession, I knew I was going to cry. To break into huge, giant sobs right in front of him. The only other option I had was to turn around and head back through that door I'd just charged out of. I was going to cry either way, but at least it wouldn't have to be in front of him.

As soon as I took my first step towards the door, Cole cursed under his breath and sighed. "Come here," he said, crossing the space between us in two lunges before tucking me into his arms. I exhaled in surprise as he held me tight, and then I melted into him. It was as easy to do now, even after everything said and done today, as it had been before. "I'm sorry, Elle. I'm so goddamned sorry." His fingers wove through my hair and massaged my scalp. He was calming me—comforting me.

Cole had gone from a heartless monster to this caring creature in the span of ten minutes. His mood swings were impossible to keep up with, but right now, having him close and feeling the emotions I had for him charge back to life, it was worth it. As intimidating as violent mood swings were, feeling his gentle fingers tangle through my hair as his strong arms held me made it all right.

"I said those things and did those things because you'd hurt me," he continued, whispering just outside my ear. "And I wanted to hurt you. I wanted you to feel the same way I did when I woke up and found you gone. I wanted you to feel the anxiety I felt when I tried calling you and you wouldn't answer. I wanted you to feel the anger I felt when I showed up at the diner and watched you through the windows for a few minutes. Serving and talking to guests like it was just another day. Like you hadn't just broken my heart."

I wanted to interrupt him. To explain I hadn't taken any of his calls because my phone was shut off all morning. I'd never considered in my hopes of avoiding my dad's and Logan's calls, I'd also miss Cole's.

"I wanted you to feel the rage boil in my blood when I found out you were going on a date . . . with *him* tonight," he cursed the word, "after being with me last night. I wanted you to feel the same pain I did. The same goddamn debilitating pain."

I was silent. I couldn't speak even if I'd known what to say. Whether it was feeling Cole's arms around me or hearing his words, speech was impossible. Only when I felt him shift and adjust his arms did I find a few words.

"Mission accomplished. I couldn't quite find the way to describe it, but debilitating pain is just right."

Maybe they weren't the right words, but sarcasm seemed to be my default when I was around Cole.

He chuckled a few humorless notes. "I know it was a sick, messed up thing to do," he said, pulling me harder to him. "I'll never forgive myself for the things I did to you today, Elle."

I'd already forgiven him.

"So where does that leave us?" I asked, holding my breath.

He squeezed me tighter before his arms loosened. "An ocean apart, Elle," he breathed. "An ocean apart."

I shook my head against his chest. "No, Cole."

"Yes," he replied, running his hand up and down my spine. "You might care for me, but you chose him. You're here with him. That ring is still shining bright on your finger."

"I haven't chosen him," I said, fisting my hands into his shirt. I wasn't going to let him go. "I haven't chosen anyone. I just met you, Cole. I've known Logan since I was a little girl. I can't just figure this whole thing out and break someone's heart in a couple days. I need time."

"You don't need time to know what's in your heart," he replied, as calm as I was frantic. "You've chosen him and you were right to. I can't say if he is, but I do know I'm not the right guy for you."

The first tear I'd been holding back leaked out of the corner of my eye. It dissolved into his shirt.

"I might have only known you for a week, but it's long enough to know you're a special girl. You're the kind of girl that guys will still be mourning a couple decades from now. I know I'll be one of them."

I shook my head against him again. Out of the words and things Cole had done to me today, this was the most heart-breaking.

He cared for me. He wanted me.

But he was walking away.

"I need to let you go, Elle," he said, letting his arms fall away. "But you need to let me go, too." He looked at me now, but only to say goodbye. He took a step back, and then another.

My body went as cold as my thoughts. "No," I cried, stepping forward. "Don't do this, Cole. Stay with me."

I could make my choice. It was an obvious one now. Hearing him say goodbye and walk away from me kicked my decision making skills into high gear. I wanted him.

I was a breath away from admitting it, shouting my choice for all to hear, when he gave me the saddest smile I'd seen to date.

"Just let me go."

Watching Cole walk away brought me to my knees in a way that made it seem like I'd never be able to pull myself up again.

NINE

I wasn't really living. I was more like surviving.

After that fateful conversation with Cole, I felt like he'd taken a piece of me with him when he'd walked away that night. A large piece. He was true to his word—he let me go better than I thought "letting go" could be done.

He didn't take my calls, he never came back to the diner, he didn't show up at the swimming hole. Other than running into him once at the gas station and being stopped beside him once at the same traffic light, Cole had become a ghost.

A ghost that haunted me at every turn.

It didn't matter how hard I tried or how angry I got at myself for failing. I couldn't get him out of my mind. I couldn't get him out of my heart. I couldn't get him out of anything.

So I stopped trying.

Once I gave up trying to think about Cole, I felt better.

Marginally, but better. I accepted that he'd become a part of me and I had to learn to deal with it.

Last Monday, the whole crew had flown off to a particularly nasty fire on the edge of the Wenatchee National Forest. So Cole was gone, and now that we were in the heart of fire season, he'd be gone more days than he'd be here at camp. Especially since everyone was saying they couldn't remember such dry conditions this early in the summer.

Logan had also been gone. A few nights here, a couple nights there . . . baseball season kept him just as busy as fire season kept Cole.

So I was alone.

I suppose I could have used my newfound solitude to work out the fog of confusion that followed me everywhere, but instead, I used it to long for Cole and to let the guilt I had towards Logan consume my days and nights. Other than checking on Grandma M every morning and working double shifts at the diner, my life was as useless as I'd always feared it becoming.

Finishing up yet another long day at the diner, I said goodbye to the closing cook and server—I'd managed to get one night off from closing—grabbed my purse, and headed for my Jeep. It was almost eight, but still bright out, and I was half contemplating heading for the swimming hole and trying again for that sinking record when my phone rang.

I'd stopped hoping it would be Cole a week ago. Hope unrealized was poison in a person's bloodstream.

When I saw who it was, I almost let it go to voicemail, but I'd let her last two go there and a third would warrant concern. Mrs. Matthews had considered me like her own daughter since Logan and I started dating and she was in my business accordingly. The last thing I needed right now was for her to call my dad to try to track me down, or worse, Logan. Knowing him, he'd be on the first bus home from Yakima to make sure I was all right.

Logan knew something was up; he wasn't dumb. However, he didn't have the first clue as to what. He guessed it had to do with graduating high school and saying goodbye to that part of our lives. He'd also guessed my funk had something to do with him being gone so much.

I still hadn't had the heart, or the courage, to tell him the truth. Not that there'd been much opportunity anyways. Over the past week, I'd seen Logan all of three times. Once when I went to watch one of his night games. The second time when we'd gone out four-wheeling with a bunch of his friends, and the third time had been when he'd stopped by to have dinner with me at the diner before he left with his team on Friday.

My phone rang a fourth time and, this time, I answered it.

"Hi, Mrs. Matthews," I greeted, trying to sound as upbeat as I didn't feel.

"Oh, Elle. Thank goodness I finally got a hold of you," she said. I could hear a lot of voices in the background, not that that was a huge surprise, Mrs. Matthews was the social elite equivalent here in central Washington. She hosted more get togethers and headed up more charity drives than the last ten White House wives combined. "I'm just finishing up with the Women's Potluck here at church. We've got oodles of leftovers and I don't want to see this all go to waste. I have to go to the final planning meeting for next week's big Fourth of July Festival and I wanted to see if you'd be willing to drop all this food off for me."

Potlucks, planning meetings, shuttling back and forth frantically between this and that . . . It was a scary picture of what my life could become one day.

"Please, Elle?" she said when I stayed quiet. "I'd do it myself, but I'm already late."

I was a pushover. "Okay, sure," I said. "I'm just getting off work, so I'll be there in five."

"You're a lifesaver, sweetheart," she said, whispering a few quick words to someone. "Thank you so, so much."

"Don't mention it," I said, trying not to grumble. One of the last things I wanted to do tonight was run leftover potluck casseroles and pies around town. "Where am I delivering it to?"

"The smokejumper camp," she said.

I almost dropped the phone.

"They just got back in this afternoon after being gone all week fighting that fire over in Wenatchee. I can't imagine anyone who would appreciate a home cooked meal more than a bunch of smokejumpers who have been surviving on dehydrated meat and potatoes all week."

My heart trilled with excitement right before it dropped. I'd wanted to see Cole so badly these past couple weeks I was drowning in it, but knowing that I was less than a half hour from actually seeing him . . .

Well, it scared me to death.

I knew if I looked into his eyes and saw that he'd done what he promised me he would—let me go—I might curl up and die. I didn't want to be let go.

I sure as heck hadn't let him go.

"Mrs. Matthews?" I said, swallowing. "On second thought, I don't think I'll—"

"I've gotta go, Elle. The president of the Fourth of July planning committee is calling. Probably to yell at me for being late." I could hear her heels pick up speed as she clicked and clacked across the church parking lot. "Thank you again. You're an angel."

Yeah, if I was an angel, then mankind was screwed.

The phone went dead before I could beg and plead with her to find someone else to run a bunch of food over to the smoke-jumper camp.

Clenching my phone, I almost tossed it as far as I could. Instead, I took a deep breath to calm myself, got inside my Jeep, and tried to convince myself I would be in and out of that smoke-jumper building so quickly Cole would never even see me. He'd never have to know I'd been there.

Even after I'd made my way to the church, loaded the couple of cardboard boxes brimming with pyrex and ceramic dishes full of scalloped potatoes and green bean casserole into the back of the Jeep, and turned down the main road to the camp, I'd gotten nowhere in the convincing myself department.

It was starting to get dark by the time I turned the Jeep off. I sat there, staring at the building in front of me, and wondered if he was inside and what he was doing. The place seemed quiet, empty, but even from the parking lot, in the confines of my car, I could feel that energy sparking to life.

So he was here.

As if fate itself were confirming that assumption, a light flashed on in the dark building.

I took a breath, then another, before forcing myself out of the Jeep. After balancing one of the heavy boxes in my arms, I headed for the entrance. My palms were sweating; my stomach was a sea of nerves. I was a wreck, but I was doing it. I kept going forward. For the first time this summer, I was being brave and doing what was difficult instead of easy.

The door was unlocked, so I somehow managed to heave it open before hurrying inside. The box was getting heavy and cumbersome. Rushing into the dark kitchen, I dropped the box on the table and was considering if I should put the dishes in the refrigerator, since it appeared no one was here, when a sound caught my attention.

I followed the sound down the hall. Someone was inhaling and exhaling sharply. Repeatedly.

It was a sound I was familiar with, and the voice making it was just as familiar.

Knowing nothing good could come of this, I took the last few steps towards the room the hitched breathing came from. This room was just as dark as the rest of the building, but it wasn't as empty.

My whole body tensed.

Cole was lying on a bench, naked from the waist up, heaving a gleaming metal bar stacked with large weights on either end. He was alone and consumed by the battle he seemed to be waging with the heavy barbell.

Lowering it once more, he inhaled before exerting every last ounce of power he had left. His whole body, every muscle, flexed to the surface as he struggled to lift that weight. Just when I was sure it would come crashing back down on his chest, Cole let out a low roar and his body flexed even tighter. The bar went up easily after that, like it had figured out fighting against him was a wasted effort.

Cole racked the weight and dropped his arms.

I watched his chest rise and fall, feeling this huge sense of relief that he was here. That I was near him again. The ache that had gone everywhere with me these past couple weeks took a momentary hiatus. All was right in the world again as I watched him.

"I know you're here, you know."

My throat went dry. "I'm sorry," I said. "I didn't think you could see me."

Cole exhaled like he had just a few seconds ago, although this time he wasn't trying to lift a three hundred pound weight. "I couldn't." He sat up and his eyes landed on me in the same way they had before. It took my breath away like it had before, too.

"Hi," I said, giving a little wave before I crossed my arms. Being around Cole was still unsettling.

"What are you doing here?" he asked, rising from the bench.

What was I doing here? There were several answers to that and one big one. I wanted to see him. When he stayed frozen, not coming towards me with open arms, I went with one of the other answers.

"Mrs. Matthews asked me to swing by a bunch of potluck leftovers since she heard you all had just gotten back," I said, resisting the urge to go to him.

It was hard. If ever there'd be a time to want to run to a man, it would be now. As he stood shirtless, coated in a light sheen of sweat, in a dark room, in an empty building.

"Who's Mrs. Matthews?" Cole asked, crossing his arms. That did wonderful things to the muscles he'd just worked. "Besides the potluck leftover fairy?" A smile tugged on the corner of his mouth.

How could I answer that in a roundabout way?

"She's Logan's mom."

So much for roundabout'ing.

"Ah." Cole rolled his neck from side to side. "How is the other man?" He didn't wait for an answer. "Let me guess ... still in a state of ignorance is bliss. Right?"

He waited for me to respond.

I couldn't.

"You're too predictable. You might know what you want, but you won't do what it takes to have it."

I bristled. "What would be the point of that since it was made clear to me that I couldn't have what I wanted anymore?"

Cole's shoulders fell. "Good point," he said. "But you and I both know if push came to shove, I wouldn't be what you truly wanted. What you wanted was the idea of me. The dream. An escape from the life you're living. You wanted freedom. Not me."

Disillusioned was the word that came to mind when I heard his words. I didn't want the idea of him. I wanted him.

"I don't care who would have pushed or shoved, I would have chosen you."

"Says the woman who never had to make that choice in real life," he snapped back.

I didn't flinch. "I guess we'll never know."

Cole took a few steps backwards until his back was against the wall. I wasn't sure if his way of putting as much space between us as the room would allow was intentional, but it certainly felt that way. "I guess not."

I gave myself a few seconds to calm down before speaking again. "Where is everyone?"

He shrugged as he leaned deeper into the wall. "Out. It's Saturday night and we've been fighting a forest fire for close to a week. They're getting drunk and laid tonight. They've earned it."

"And you?" Cole had never struck me as the one to hang back when everyone else was en route to a good time.

"I already told you. I don't drink anymore."

"And what about the getting laid part?"

Why did I ask questions I didn't want to hear the answers to? It was a riddle.

Cole answered me with a cool look.

"How was the fire?" I asked, taking a step inside the weight room. When Cole flinched, I stopped.

"Hot," he said dryly.

He wasn't making this easy. "Did anyone get hurt?"

"Chase sprained his ankle and I took a little tumble." Cole lifted up the right leg of his shorts.

"Oh my gosh," I said, covering my mouth. A bright purple bruise covered the entire front of Cole's upper leg.

"It's no big deal," he said, dropping the short leg back over the monster sized bruise. "I've sustained worse injuries this summer."

I doubted it was the main one he was referring to, but my gaze jumped to his nose. Nothing but a small scab remained of the damage I'd done to him that night at the bowling alley. It was nearly healed.

"Cole . . ." I began, not sure what words would come out of my mouth next, but going with it. "I'm sorry for hurting you. I'm sorry for leaving you. I'm sorry for not going after you that night at the bowling alley and telling you I cho—"

"You need to get going," Cole interrupted, lifting his hand. "I'd walk you to the door if I was certain you wouldn't smash it into my face again."

My eyes welled. He was saying goodbye. Again.

"Cole," I said, taking a few more steps his way. "I miss you. I don't want to let you go." There it was. My heart couldn't be any more vulnerable.

His gaze didn't shift when he opened his mouth. "You should really let me go. It's just getting pathetic now." He shoved off the wall. "Besides, I let you go so long ago, I barely remember your name."

He was just saying those things to hurt me. That was his self-defense mechanism. When he was hurt, he lashed back. I wasn't going to let him off so easy.

"Cole—" I started before his eyes narrowed into slits.

"I'm over you," he hissed.

"Obviously," a new voice came from behind me. A half-naked woman sauntered into the room.

Cole sighed.

The redhead from the bowling alley wore nothing but an over-sized white undershirt and a triumphant smile.

The room started to spin.

"Are you coming back to bed?" she asked, appraising Cole in a way that made me feel all kinds of territorial. The room spun a bit more when I realized I had no right to claim any kind of territory to Cole Carson.

"No, Kayla," he said. "I'm not."

He didn't have any problem remembering her name.

I remembered the way he'd breathed my name when I had my hand around him, and I knew then that none of what we'd shared had meant anything to him. He'd breathed my name, he'd breathed her name, he'd breathed dozens of others along the way too, I was certain.

"And now," I said, biting the inside of my cheek as I glared at him, "I'm over you, too."

I couldn't get out of that room fast enough. As I sprinted down the hall, I heard what sounded like Kayla laughing and Cole cursing, but none of that mattered. At least I wanted to pretend like none of it mattered.

I shoved the door open and ran for my Jeep. Only once I had it started and was peeling out of the parking lot did I let a tear drop. As soon as one was free, the rest poured out like I'd been repressing a lifetime of tears. Maybe I had, but one thing I was certain of was that, after tonight, I would never cry another tear for Cole Carson.

I wasn't driving anywhere in particular as I sped down the dark road. Just away. I was so sick and tired of feeling this way, all I wanted to do was wake up tomorrow and not remember anything of Cole. I wanted my mind erased of him.

Yet no matter how fast I drove or how far out of town I got—there was no forgetting about Cole. A half-lit sign flashed ahead, giving me an idea. If I couldn't force Cole out of my mind, maybe I could drink him out.

Biggie's was a backwoods bar that had always been around. No one could quite remember when it had opened since it had changed hands and names so many times, but it was the kind of place you guessed would thrive even in the middle of a zombie apocalypse. I'd never been inside; it wasn't exactly the kind of place a girl like me hung out. I'd been in the parking lot once to rescue Dani when her date had left with another girl, but other than that, I never thought I'd step foot inside the place. Funny how life can change in the blink of an eye.

It was a Saturday night and the parking lot was full. So full I had to park on the side of the road. I didn't worry that my Jeep could be easily recognized if any one of my friends or family were driving this road tonight. I didn't worry about who was inside who could recognize me. I didn't worry about the repercussions of my actions tomorrow. I didn't worry about anything but the next ten minutes and my need to drown it all out with as many shots as I could get the bartender to pour me before I got cut off.

Then I remembered I was at Biggie's. It wasn't known as a place that cut people off. It was known for cheap beer, cheaper whiskey, and easy women.

I was hoping to take advantage of two of those three things tonight.

It was also a place that didn't check IDs, so I didn't need to worry about that either.

The music the live band played tonight was so loud it thumped my eardrums halfway across the parking lot. It really should have been a crime to play any song from the Rolling Stones that poorly.

I ignored the man heaving a few feet from the entrance. I pretended the man and woman I passed as soon as I walked inside weren't having sex, but gauging by the screwed up expressions on their faces and the easy access skirt the woman was wearing, it was quite plausible.

The music was ten times as horrifying inside as it was in the parking lot, and the place was so busy it looked like ten people had arrived per vehicle. But it was dark, and everyone was so busy paying attention to someone else that I disappeared into the crowd. My cutoffs might have been longer, my camisole looser, and my eyes clearer than the rest of the women, but barring these minor differences, I blended in.

As I made my way to the bar, I scanned the room to make sure there wasn't anyone who would recognize me. At least easily recognize me. This was Winthrop we were talking about, and everyone knew everyone to a certain degree. Other than a few regulars from the diner, I didn't think anyone would be able to place me. Elle Montgomery at Biggie's wasn't quite a connect the dots scenario.

I had to shoulder through a couple of broad shouldered guys sporting flannel shirts with cut off sleeves and a pair of mullets that were obviously their pride and joy. They shot me irritated looks until their glossy eyes adjusted.

"Hey, sweetheart," the one on my right said, leering at me in a way that made my skin crawl. "I don't recall seeing you around these parts." He burped and the alcohol fumes that came at me could have singed my nose hair if I had any.

I motioned at the bartender. The sooner I got my drink, the sooner I could get away from Backwoods and Trailer Park.

"I've obviously been missing out," I said, not even trying to mask my sarcasm. These two were too drunk to pick up on tone and subtle nuances anyways.

The other one grabbed his hubcap sized belt buckle and nudged me. "You want to see just exactly what you've been missing out on, honey?"

I wrinkled my nose. "From where I'm standing," I said, doing a quick scan of flannel, mullet dude, "it doesn't look like I've been missing out on much."

Walking into this place had bolstered my bravery. Or stupidity. Knowing I was seconds away from drowning everything gave me an edge I'd never had before.

"I like a girl with a smart mouth," the guy said, staring at my mouth before licking his lips. "Especially when that smart mouth is sucking on my—"

"You two assholes aren't giving this girl a hard time are you?" the bartender interrupted, eyeing the men on either side of me. He was about my dad's age, but he was bigger, broader, and just had this kick-butt vibe.

"You don't know how hard of a time we'd love to give her, Biggie," the mullet on the right said, wagging his eyebrows at the bartender.

"And you are about to know how hard of a time my shotgun will give you when I shove it up both your asses if you don't get the hell out of my bar."

All I'd wanted was a drink or two and to forget myself for a few hours. That was all I wanted.

Why did everything have to be so darn difficult lately?

Without another word at Biggie or another look my way, the mullet twins shoved off the bar and headed for the exit. Just like that. Two guys that looked like they ate two dozen eggs a day for breakfast, who were drunk as a pair of skunks, just up and left the party with one threat from one guy.

What kind of person intimidated those kinds of guys? I was scared to find out.

I met Biggie's gaze and tried on a smile that I was sure didn't do anything to make me look any less scared of him.

His eyes suddenly widened. "Laurel?" he said, his face blanching a few shades.

The name caught me off guard. I was sure my own face blanched at hearing my mother's name in this scuzzy place.

"No . . . I'm Elle," I said. "Laurel was—"

"Your mom," Biggie said, exhaling like he could have been relieved or disappointed.

I nodded. How did this guy know my mom?

"God knows I love this bar, but it's such a seedy place even Satan stays out, so why in the whole world of bars does sweet Laurel Sheehan's daughter have to walk into mine?"

He'd used my mom's maiden name. No one used that. Everywhere I went, she was known as Laurel Montgomery. She might have grown up here and been a Sheehan until she was nineteen, but this whole town only knew her as a Montgomery.

Except for Biggie.

"How did you know my mom?"

He paused a few moments before answering, almost like he was having an internal debate. Then, clearing his throat, he said, "I was in love with her."

So not what I'd expected.

"You were in love with her?" I almost whispered, taking another look at him. He was still big, broad, and badass.

"Crazy in love with her," Biggie replied.

"When?" I asked, leaning into the bar.

"The better part of my teenage years," he said, shaking his head. "The best years of my life."

"Did she know . . . you were in love with her?"

Mom had been with Dad almost their entire high school lives. They'd gotten married a few short months after graduating high school.

"Of course she did," he said, looking a bit insulted. "And she loved me right back."

Whoa. This was a mind trip. This whole entire night. This whole entire summer.

"Did my dad know?"

He'd obviously wound up with the girl, but I couldn't see him being the understanding type once he found out his girlfriend was in love with another guy at the same time.

Biggie and my dad couldn't have been more different. Both in the looks department and the everything-else-department.

"I don't know why the hell I'm telling you any of this. Nothing good can come of raising the ghosts of the past . . ."

"Please," I said a bit too eagerly. "Please tell me. There will never be a better time for me to hear about you . . . and my mom . . . and my dad."

Biggie took another minute, studying me, before letting out a long, resolved sigh. "Yeah, she wound up telling your dad," Biggie said. "Laurel never meant to fall in love with me, and I sure as shit tried to steer clear of her, but nature kind of just drew us together. I never loved anyone like I fell for her. I had it bad. And I still haven't loved a woman the way I loved her. What we had was . . ." He paused, searching for the right word.

But I had it.

"Special," I said sadly.

"Exactly. Special." Biggie nodded. "Of course I screwed things up the way I was born to do, and Laurel realized that your dad was the better man, which as much as I hate to admit it, he was." Biggie's forehead lined as he continued, "Laurel got married, I married this shitty bar, and the rest is history." He studied my face again, and I could tell from the glimpse of intimacy that flashed in his eyes he was seeing my mom. "But I still think about her every day. Even after she and your dad were married, she helped me out when I hit some low times."

My brows went sky high.

"No, no," Biggie guessed at what I was thinking, "our relationship after she and your father got married was strictly on a friend to friend basis. But that woman saved me in about every way a person can be saved." Biggie ran his hand through his short dark hair and stared at the floor. "You know, I might be all alone and have some pathetic what-could-have-been story about the time the most perfect woman in the world loved me, but every day, I'm able to get out of bed because I know if someone like her could see something in me to fall in love with . . . I must have one or two redeeming qualities." After a few moments of reflection, Biggie's face ironed out into the intimidating, chew 'em up, spit 'em out bartender who'd sent grown men running with a few words.

I was speechless. It had become a habit as of late. When I'd slid into this dark joint, I had not been expecting to be harassed by a couple of flannel wearing mullet heads, only to be saved by my mom's dirty little secret named Biggie. A man who was obviously still in love with her. In love with a ghost.

This story hit far too close to home for comfort. I needed that drink STAT.

"So, Elle. You know my story now—what's yours?" Biggie leaned across the bar and stared at me without blinking.

My mom had stared into these same eyes and probably gone a little weak in the knees. My mom had loved this man while loving my dad. My mom was me, or more like, I was my mom.

I really wished she was still around because I could have used her advice right about now.

"I know you can't be any older than eighteen or nineteen, you're the glorified good girl all set to marry the prince of Winthrop anytime now, so what could have brought you to the bad side of humanity late on a Saturday night?" There wasn't anything antagonistic in his voice, just genuine curiosity.

I almost told him.

I almost admitted I was following in my mom's footsteps and had fallen in love with the dangerous bad boy while I was the good boy's girlfriend. I knew he wouldn't judge me and could probably offer me some reasonably sound advice. I was so close to telling him, then Cole's face flashed into my mind and my whole body ached.

"I needed a drink," I replied, staring at the wall of bottles I couldn't have named if he'd held a gun up to my head. "A *strong* drink."

Biggie studied me for a few seconds, grimacing when he met my eyes again. "Because you're Laurel's daughter, I'll pour you a drink," he said, reaching back to grab a bottle from the top shelf as he snatched a shot glass with his other hand. "But because you're Laurel's daughter ..." his smile turned sad, "I'm only pouring you one."

Of course. Out of all the bars I could have stumbled into, I had to be in the one that would put me on a one drink limit tonight. I didn't need any more limits. I needed to forget about limits for a few hours.

"I might not be the guy Laurel chose, but I sure as hell am not going to let her daughter lower herself to this level."

I would have put up an argument if I thought it would work.

"So we're clear?" Biggie poured the clear liquid to the top of the shot glass and waited for my response.

"We're clear."

Biggie slid the glass in front of me. "You look so much like you're mom I just about shit myself when I saw you standing in front of me," he said, shaking his head. "But you're a bit like your dad, too. He's a good man, kiddo, damned as I tried not to believe it for the better part of my life. Whatever this is you're going through, whatever brought you here tonight ... you should talk with him about it. He loves you and only wants the best for you. I'm sure he'll understand whatever it is." Dropping his large hand over both of mine that were reaching for the shot in front of me, he squeezed them. "It's an honor to meet you, Elle."

He'd already wandered down to the other end of the bar by the time I lifted the glass to my lips. The fumes alone were making my eyes tear up.

The instant Cole's face popped into my head, my mouth dropped open and I upended that shot in one fell swoop.

It burned my throat like it was actually searing off the top layer of flesh as it made its way down into my belly. I'd never had a shot before. I'd had beer, wine, and even a few jello shooters, but never a hardcore, honest-to-goodness shot of alcohol.

I almost immediately felt the effects. My head went a little light, woozy even, and I relaxed. Instead of trying to blend into the crowd, I wanted to become a part of it. The band even sounded better somehow, so I shoved off the counter and made my way towards the dance floor.

The shot hadn't completely removed my memory of Cole, but it had at least made me care less. I might be able to picture his face and remember what his hands felt like, but not enough to ache for him. Not enough to give a darn if I ever saw or felt him again.

I understood why this alcohol thing was so addictive.

I was having a little dance party with myself in the center of the dance floor when a familiar face appeared in front of me. Another point for the alcohol? I didn't even care anymore about being recognized in a place like this.

"Elle Montgomery." The guy in front of me grinned wide.

I grinned back. I hadn't seen him since the bonfire. "Derrick Davenport."

"What's a girl like you doing in a place like this?" he shouted above the band who was now murdering an Aerosmith song.

"What's a guy like *you* doing in a place like this?" I swayed a little then, like the dance floor was spinning, although I wasn't so drunk I didn't realize it was the alcohol spinning me, not the actual room.

Derrick grabbed my arms and steadied me. He stepped closer until my chest brushed against his. "Looking for a girl like you."

I was fairly certain what that gleam in Derrick's eyes was, but I ignored it. "Looks like it's your lucky night then."

He dropped his mouth outside my ear. I told myself it was so he didn't have to shout over the band. "Looks like it is," he said, his voice sending a tingle down my back. Not the good kind of tingle, either. Leaning back, he examined my face. "How many drinks are you into the night?"

"One," I said, sticking out my lower lip. "The bartender cut me off at uno."

One of Derrick's eyebrows lifted. "I can help you out with that," he said, sliding his wallet out of his back pocket. "Whatcha drinking?"

I had no idea what Biggie had poured me and I was sure if I told Derrick to order me something that was strong and clear, he'd roll his eyes. "Anything that will get me drunk."

One side of Derrick's mouth lifted. "I believe I can manage

that," he said before cutting through the crowd and heading for the bar.

By the time Derrick made it back, I'd almost forgotten he was here. It was sad how one shot could undo a girl so quickly, but I didn't care because my heart hadn't ached once for Cole. In fact, I couldn't even feel my heart anymore.

"As ordered," Derrick said, appearing in front of me and extending another shot of clear liquid. This glass was twice the size of the one Biggie gave me and just as full. "Bottom's up."

Derrick tilted his own equally large and full glass at me before draining it in one large sip. He dropped the glass on the nearest table, then looked at me expectantly.

What was one more drink? I'd come here for the stumbling drunk experience, right? I was going to be the best stumbling drunk I could.

Tilting my drink at Derrick, I closed my eyes and opened my mouth. I was careful not to inhale while I downed the entire shot. This one didn't sting my throat as badly as the last one, but the effects were almost as immediate. The room wasn't only moving now, it was spinning. Fast.

My stomach almost instantly spasmed. What sucked about that last shot was that my body was affected, but my mind was just as sharp. That wasn't the plan. I didn't care if I did or didn't have control of my body, I just didn't want control of my mind. I wanted it lost and emptied of all memory.

Then Derrick stepped close again and all of his body shoved against mine. His hands dropped to my hips and latched on. "I knew you were a wild one, Elle," Derrick whispered in my ear. "Glad I could be around when that woman decided to bust free."

Derrick had been my friend almost as long as Logan had. I couldn't have picked a better night to get plastered. Knowing Derrick was here to look after me and make sure I didn't do anything too stupid made me let go a little more. Allowed me to let go of the girl everyone expected me to be and behave like.

Winding out of Derrick's embrace, I leapt up onto the closest table. I knocked over a couple beers and my feet grazed the head of one of the guys scattered around it, but no one seemed to mind.

In fact, when I started to move to the beat of the music, people started cheering. My body moved in ways it had never moved before, in ways I'd never known it could move—bending, flexing, and shaking like I was trying to make up for eighteen years' worth of inhibitions.

One song ended, and then another one, and I still hadn't stopped shaking my stuff up on some rickety table in some dive bar, but I was long past caring about what I was doing and where I was doing it. All I felt was this heady sense of freedom and I was chasing that feeling wherever it led me.

I vaguely remembered Derrick handing me yet another tall glass of clear liquid at the start of the third song I'd spent up on the table and, by the end of it, I was no longer dancing. I was teetering. Lucky for me, when I fell over, Derrick was there to catch me.

The entire bar exploded into a roar of hollering and clapping at the conclusion of my fully clothed rendition of a strip club quality dance.

"Shit, Elle," Derrick said, righting me before guiding me back onto the dance floor. "Now that you're off that table, I sure wouldn't mind you moving against me like that."

The entire room was a blur. Derrick's voice sounded like an echo in my ears. I was drunk, long past it.

Keeping my arm firmly locked around Derrick's back, I nudged him. "Only if you say please."

"Please?" Derrick said, his voice low as he stopped in front of me. "Pretty please, Elle?"

"O—kay," I said, draping both arms around his neck. It was difficult. Every limb felt like I'd lost most of my control of it.

This time, when Derrick's arms wrapped around me, his hands slid around my backside. His hands dug into my butt before he thrust up against me. I was drunk, but there was no mistaking the bulge in his pants I felt pressed against me. "Later on it will be your turn to beg, you know." His hips flinched against me. "You'll be screaming my name and begging me before I'm done with you tonight."

My breath caught in my lungs. Derrick was a friend. A friend who was crossing a line and I knew that had everything to do with the amount of alcohol he'd had and the amount I'd had.

I pushed him away.

It didn't work.

"The only thing I'll be begging you for is to let me go," I said, shoving him again. Derrick only held me tighter.

"No one would have to know, Elle," he said just outside my ear. "Logan would never have to know I was the first one to fuck his virgin wife."

It didn't matter how much I had to drink, I could never get drunk enough to wind up with Derrick between my legs. Not in this lifetime or the next.

"The only virgin you'll be screwing tonight is your left hand," I hissed, shoving his chest. The alcohol hadn't only made me dizzy, it had made me feisty. "Let me go!" I pushed him again.

Nothing. He only laughed, and what was worse, no one around us knew what was going on. No one realized I could really have used a helping hand about now.

Derrick laughed. "I'm not letting you go until I get you naked and horizontal."

So Derrick might have been a friend before, but he certainly wouldn't be after tonight. Alcohol or not, I could never forget the things he'd said.

Suddenly, a finger tapped Derrick's shoulders.

"Change of plans," a familiar voice said, sounding like murder was on his mind.

Derrick glanced back, huffed, and replied, "Get lost, man. Find your own chick."

"I'm giving you one chance to let her go and step away." Cole came around the side of us, and if I thought his eyes were dark at the bowling alley, that was nothing in comparison to the color they were now.

Derrick's grip strengthened. "Get lost."

Cole's mouth turned up as his fists balled. "Bad call."

Cole threw his first punch before Derrick knew what was coming. That powerful fist to the jaw was enough to loosen Derrick's grip on me.

"Let her go," Cole seethed, shoving his way in between Derrick and me.

"What the hell, man?" Derrick shouted as he reached for his jaw.

Cole's other arm drove towards Derrick and landed square in the hollow of his cheek. "And step away."

If Derrick hadn't expected the first, he certainly didn't expect the second. The punch sent him back into the crowd before he stumbled to the floor.

My breathing had picked up, watching this whole testosterone fused ordeal, but the alcohol numbed me of any other response. That was, until Cole turned around and his anxious eyes fell on me. Those eyes managed to illicit the same kinds of responses as when I was sober.

When he came towards me and wrapped both arms around me before tucking me close and guiding me through the crowd, I wasn't quite sure if I was dreaming.

"Cole?" I reached out and touched his face. He felt real enough.

"Elle." He sounded real enough, too.

"What are you doing here?" I couldn't quite remember what *I* was doing here, but I was pretty sure it had had something to do with him.

"Protecting too-innocent-for-their-own-damn-good girls from guys who would have no qualms taking advantage of that innocence," he replied tightly.

"I can handle Derrick Davenport all on my own, thank you very much." I didn't like knowing he was here because I was like a responsibility to him.

"Fine," he said, shoving a guy away who drunkenly stumbled in front of us. "I'm here to hold your hair back while you puke your guts out."

"I've got a ponytail holder for that," I grumbled.

Cole groaned as we approached the bar. "Why are you so damn difficult?"

I huffed. "Why are you?"

"I wasn't until you came into my life," he replied, waving at Biggie.

"Good thing I'm not in your life any more then," I snapped back, reaching for my head. It already hurt. That was not a good sign for tomorrow morning.

"Then why am I here right now with you?"

Even if I had an answer for that, I wouldn't have been able to give it right then because Biggie stopped in front of us, clutching my purse.

"It's a good thing you left this thing on the bar before you started table dancing," he said. Cole grimaced at the words table and dancing while Biggie looked down on me in such a way he could have been my dad right then.

"Why's that?" I said, grabbing for my purse, but my depth

perception was drunk like the rest of me and all I did was fall forward. Cole caught me and, after righting me, clutched me tighter. So tight the only part of my body I'd be able to move would be my legs. "Did you need to borrow some chapstick?"

Biggie shook his head. "No. I needed to call someone who wasn't your dad who I could trust to get you out of here before that other shithead tried to."

"So why did you call this shithead?" Nice. I didn't only drink like a sailor, I cursed like one.

Biggie held my phone up before dropping it back into my purse. "This shithead's phone number was the first number that showed up under your missed calls. That showed up about a dozen times. I figured if a guy was calling a girl that many times in one night, he must care a hell of a lot for her."

Cole had called me tonight? Multiple times? After weeks of ignoring me, why was he suddenly blowing up my phone? Then a nearly naked redhead and a weight room flashed to mind. I squirmed against Cole, but got nowhere.

"Then when this guy answered . . ." Biggie and Cole exchanged a look. "Well, I knew you'd be in good hands."

"Unlikely," I mumbled as the room took a very violent spin.

"See you around, Biggie," Cole said, taking my purse from him and moving for the exit. "Thanks for the call. You did the right thing."

"I hope so," Biggie said, watching the two of us with a hint of nostalgia and sadness on his face. "It was nice meeting you, Elle, but I don't want to ever see your face in my bar again. Or I will call your dad next time. You got it?"

I figured after tonight, I'd never drink another drop of alcohol, let alone step into this place. I answered him with a thumbs-up before Cole led me through the crowd.

The minute we were outside, I took in gulps of the cool night air. It cleared my mind just barely and made it easier to believe I wasn't about to vomit in the next instant, but then a wave of tiredness overcame me and the exhaustion made my head loll onto Cole's shoulders and my feet wouldn't cooperate.

"Shit, Elle. How much did you have to drink?" Cole sighed before shifting around me and before I knew how I'd wound up there, I was in his arms being carried across the parking lot.

I hated the way every part of me melted into him. I'd come here as an escape from Cole and I was leaving here wrapped up in his arms. In the same arms he'd held that other girl close with tonight.

My stomach churned and I came dangerously close to heaving.

"Obviously not enough," I said, adjusting myself so I could get down.

"Oh, I think you had more than enough," he said, cinching his arms tighter.

"You're here and I'm not drunk enough to not remember who you are anymore," I said, the words like venom. "I clearly didn't drink enough."

Cole stopped outside of the passenger side door of my Jeep. "So there's not only a wild girl you like to keep hidden inside, there's a mean one, too." He set me down and started rifling through my purse, no doubt looking for the keys.

I wavered in place. I really had had too much to drink. "It's not mean if it's the truth."

Cole's jaw set as he heaved the door open. "Fine. You hate me. I get it," he said in a voice so controlled I knew he felt anything but in control. "Now would you just get in the damn car already?"

"I'm not going anywhere with you," I said, stepping away from him. It was more of a stagger. "So stop wasting your time. Go get back in your car and get back to what you were . . . *doing*."

Cole lunged at me. Ringing his hands around my wrists, he pulled me back to the Jeep and pressed me firmly up against it. Throwing my wrists above my head, he held them tight as his body pressed into mine. I wriggled against his grip, but gave up after it was clear Cole's grip was unbreakable. His eyes blazed into mine, with unmistakable anger and . . . desire.

That was probably the alcohol speaking.

"Let's not pretend that I couldn't get you to do whatever I asked of you," he hissed, shoving harder against me when I tried breaking free again. The impact and firmness of his body against mine made me moan. "Let's not pretend that, even though you might hate me, you wouldn't let me do anything to you I wanted." His head dropped to my neck, and the next thing I felt was his mouth warming the skin at the base of it. His mouth never touched me, just his warm breath, and even with that small intimacy, my eyes closed, my head rolled back, and I moaned again.

I wanted to cry. I couldn't control my body around him. I couldn't control my mind much better. I was totally and irreversibly out of control when I was in Cole's presence. I was going up in flames at just the thought of his touch.

"You might hate me, Elle," he said roughly. "But your body doesn't."

Leaning back, his body left mine, but his hands stayed glued to my wrists.

"If I let you go, are you going to get in the car or am I going to have to make you? Because really, I'm kind of hoping you don't go willingly."

"It won't be willingly, but if it means you taking your filthy hands off of me, then I'll get in the car myself."

Cole smirked at me as he slowly removed his hands. "And here I'd been under the impression that you couldn't get enough of my filthy hands all over you."

Twisting away from him, I crawled into the Jeep. In my drunken state, it was a formidable obstacle.

"You've been under a lot of wrong impressions," I snapped, regretting the words instantly. I regretted them even more when I saw the smirk fall right off Cole's face.

"I know," he said quietly, before shutting the door behind me.

This night had been doomed from the outset. That should have been clear when Mrs. Matthews said the words "potluck", "smokejumper camp", and "pretty please" in the same sentence. Stumbling on Cole, the woman he'd just got it on with, my mom's old flame, downing so many drinks they started to taste like water, Derrick Davenport's hands all over me, and now this. Hurting Cole with my false words.

It was time to put this day to rest.

When Cole leapt into the driver's seat, he was stone-faced. The pit in my stomach grew. "Where do you want me to take you?" he asked, his voice just as stone cold.

"Um . . ."

Where could I go? There was no way I could show up this late at night, rip-roaring drunk, at home. Nothing good would come of that. I couldn't go to the Matthews' because that would be even worse than showing up at home. Dani was gone on some camping trip this weekend. Grandma M's was the only option, but I didn't want to bring her into this mess. I didn't want her to have to keep my secrets for me.

I had nowhere to go. When I wasn't maintaining that veneer of perfection everyone expected, I had no one to lean on. When I made a mistake and needed someone to fall back on, I had nobody. Everyone in my life, save for a couple, loved the idea of Elle Montgomery. Not the real me—not the warts and all version.

How a revelation of this magnitude was able to break through the haze of alcohol, I don't know, but it felt like the most depressing thought I'd ever had.

"I don't know," I whispered, staring down into my lap. "There's nowhere really." I hated being this transparent with Cole, he'd already seen so much vulnerability from me that had clearly not impressed him, but there was no one else.

I felt Cole's eyes on me for a long time. I wasn't sure what he was seeing or looking for, but at least a minute must have gone by before he sighed. "Okay. You can stay at the camp," he said, and then something unexpected happened. Cole's hand rested on mine for a moment before his fingers wove through mine. "I'll take care of you and then we'll figure out what to do tomorrow morning, when you're not up to your ears in cheap vodka."

Relief flooded me. At least for tonight, Cole would take care of me. He'd help me with this mistake when no one else in my life would. "Thank you," I breathed, dropping my head back onto the headrest and holding onto his hand like it was a lifeline.

"You're welcome." Cole started the Jeep and pulled out onto the road. "It's the least I can do given I was pretty much the one to blame for what happened tonight." The motion of the car made me queasy, so I cracked the window, closed my eyes, and took long, slow breaths. "I'm sorry you saw that, Elle."

My stomach heaved, but not from the alcohol. From the image of that girl wearing Cole's undershirt.

"Will she still be there . . . when we show up?" I asked as unemotionally as I was could. Cole wasn't mine, he had the right to bring a girl into his bed, but at the same time, he felt like he was mine and had no right to sleep with any girl that wasn't me.

"Highly unlikely since the only person that peeled out of that parking lot in more of a rage than you was her two minutes later."

My brows came together. "Why's that?"

"It might have had something to do with me telling her to get the hell out and give me my shirt back," he answered.

"Do you think you'll see her again?"

"No."

"Do you want to?"

"Hell no."

"Did you sleep with her?" Wonderful. The alcohol was making me ask questions I didn't want answered.

Cole exhaled. "God knows I tried," he said, "but I just couldn't do it. No matter how damn hard I tried."

I opened my eyes and peered over at him. If ever a man could brood, Cole was doing it now.

"Why not?"

His hands tightened over the steering wheel. "Because I couldn't get the face of another girl out of my head," he said. "I don't know if I'll ever be able to get her face out of my head."

My heartbeat quickened. Was he saying what I thought he was?

"Me?" My voice was a whisper.

Cole nodded once. "You," he admitted, like it was a sin.

I stared at his hand in mine and I let myself pretend everything could work out between us. I let myself play "make believe" that Cole and Elle would get to live happily ever after. That was one of the benefits to the alcohol—it skewed reality and make believe enough that they almost melded into one.

We just pulled into the smokejumper camp when Cole broke the silence. "Will you promise me something, Elle?" he asked as he parked and turned off the engine. "Promise me you won't do something like this again. If Biggie hadn't called me ... Who knows what ..." Cole's face lined. "There's no shortage of Derrick Davenports out there, Elle, and as much as I wish I could promise that I'll always be here to swoop in and save you, I think we both know that would be an empty promise."

Not in my world of make believe.

"So I need you to promise me you won't do this again. Please," he said, almost begging.

Even if I hadn't already made that promise to myself, I couldn't deny Cole when he looked at me that way.

"I promise," I said, giving his hand a squeeze. It hadn't left mine the entire drive, and when it finally did as Cole hopped out of the driver's side door, my hand went a little limp.

Cole jogged around the front of the Jeep and opened my door. He helped me out, and before I knew how I got there, I was in his arms.

"Cole?" I said after I'd nuzzled my head under his chin.

"Elle," he said, his tone all tease.

I nudged him. I was trying to be serious here. "I don't hate you."

He took a few moments before he replied. "I know," he said as we went through the front door. "But sometimes I wish you did. Leaving you alone would be so much easier if I knew you hated me."

The building was still dark. Everyone must have still been out having a good time.

"Why do you want to leave me alone?"

Cole's body went a little rigid. "Because I can't have you the way I want you. I know I told you at first that I was fine with any piece of you, but that changed when I—" he cut himself off abruptly. Clearing his throat, he carried me into a large dark room filled with a handful of bunk beds lining the walls. "I tried being content having a piece of you, but then that changed, and I wanted all of you. I needed all of you. But since I can't have all of you, I'll just have to figure out how to live without you."

I didn't know which was sadder: his voice or the way my heart felt after hearing those words. It was all or nothing of me with Cole. He wouldn't settle for less. Those were the two options he could live with, but I could really only live with one.

That was my answer. I couldn't live without him. I'd tried and failed miserably.

"Come on," he said, walking across the room. "Let's get you into bed."

"Let's do," I said, raising my voice in expectation.

Cole chuckled softly. Stopping at the bunk on the far end of the back wall, he set me down. When he'd steadied me and seemed mostly convinced I wasn't going to fall over, he jogged across the room again. "I'll be right back. Try not to fall over or hurt yourself."

Once Cole had left the room, I fumbled with the button and zipper of my cutoffs. My fingers weren't quite themselves, but were at least working better than they had fifteen minutes ago.

As I let my shorts drop, all I could think about was crawling into Cole's bed and falling asleep. This entire day from start to finish was exhausting, and eight hours of sleep in between Cole's sheets sounded like just the way to end the day.

Winding my arms back, I unclasped my bra and worked each arm out of it before sliding it out of my camisole. Wasn't exactly my every night kind of pajamas, but this wasn't exactly the way I spent every night either.

"You need to drink both of these and take three pain relievers before you crawl into bed unless you want to wake ..." Cole charged back into the room shaking a pill bottle into his hand. It took him a few seconds to look up, and when he did, his mouth fell open a little.

I glanced down at myself. Maybe I should have crawled into bed before he came back into the room because my lace underwear and thin cami, my nipples were presently poking through, were more lingerie than sleepwear.

Cole's eyes wandered down me, taking their time, and had made a return journey before he unfroze himself from the floor. His eyes darted away from me as he came closer.

"I'm the top one," he said, motioning at the bunks behind me. "Take these and drink these." He held out his hand and waited for me to open mine. When I did, he dropped three white pills into it before unscrewing the cap off one of the bottles of water.

He wouldn't look at me, but that apparently took a significant amount of restraint. He wanted me. I could see it in his face, I could tell from the way his chest lifted harder, I could see it under the zipper of his shorts.

Knowing Cole was ready for me in every way a man could be made me respond in every way a women could. I wanted to throw myself on him, but I forced myself to drop the pills into my mouth. Cole handed me the bottle and I lifted it to my lips. I could feel his eyes on me again as I kept the bottle tilted until I'd drank all of it.

When I tilted my head back down, my assumptions were confirmed. His eyes were on me again, staring at the area just south of my belly button. My inner thighs clenched.

"Cole," I whispered, stepping towards him.

His eyes clamped shut and he took a few steps back. "No," he replied. "I can't, Elle. I want you so damn much, but not if you're not mine. All mine."

I almost whimpered in dismay. I'd wanted Cole before, wanted him bad, but this was different. This was so all consuming it was all I could think about. I had to have him inside me. I wanted him to be the first man I felt like this. But that wasn't all . . . I wanted him to be the last, too.

It was a lot for a young woman to take in, especially when she'd had about three too many drinks, but I could already feel the liter of water making its way through my system, clearing out some of the alcohol haze.

"Let's get some sleep and sort out whatever needs sorting in the morning." Cole hung his hands on his hips and nodded at the top bunk. The bulge in his shorts had only grown, but so had his resolve it seemed.

Disappointed, I turned and threw myself up on top of the

bunk. It was a safer bet than climbing a couple rungs up the ladder on the side.

Cole chuckled. "That was graceful."

"At least I made it," I replied, getting comfortable. Cole's sheets smelled like him. Usually his scent made me sigh; right now though, it served as more of an aphrodisiac.

I heard the telltale sound of a zipper lowering and turned over onto my side to watch. Cole was stepping out of his shorts and tugging off his shirt. My throat went dry. When I was sure he was about to dig through the dresser behind him for a pair of pajama bottoms or something, he went to the end of the bunk and started climbing up.

Okay, this was too much. There was no way I'd be able to sleep next to a nearly naked Cole while I was just as nearly naked and . . . *sleep*. Since sleep would be impossible, the only other way to share a bed with Cole tonight would have to work.

I wasn't taking anymore nos from him. I wanted him, I'd chosen him. If what he said was true and he wanted me as much as I wanted him . . . things were about to get interesting.

I sat up on my knees and waited for Cole's head to crest the top of the bunk. As soon as it did, his gaze dropped on me with a bit of confusion. Likely stemming from what I was doing sitting up in his bed, playing with the hem of my camisole. The confusion faded the second I started pulling it over my head.

"Elle . . ." he warned.

I smiled at him before tossing the cami at his face. "Cole."

Grabbing my cami before it fell on the bed, Cole's eyes

widened. With his eyes on them, my nipples hardened even more. They got so hard they ached. "I want you, Cole," I said.

His forehead creased as his breath came in shallow gasps. "I want you, Elle, but I can't . . ."

My fingers slid under the hem of my panties and I tugged them down to my knees. I skimmed my thumb over the part of me that throbbed and made a low moan.

Cole groaned. "Fuck," he breathed, clamping his eyes shut, but it only lasted a moment before they opened again. He could fight it, I'd tried to as well, but neither of us would win.

What we were about to do had been inevitable from the first smile we'd shared that day at the swimming hole. It was inescapable.

"I want you, Cole," I repeated, rubbing my thumb over myself again.

"Elle . . ." He sounded as undecided as his expression read.

"I want you to be my first, Cole," I said, lying back on his mattress. I adjusted my knees out from beneath me, slid my panties the rest of the way off, and spread my knees until I could see his anguished face staring at me. I spread them farther apart before dropping my knees to the side. My body was so turned on and ready for him, I could feel my wetness dampening the sheet beneath me. "I choose you, Cole. I. Choose. You."

He sucked a sudden breath through his teeth, and after a few moments, the tortured lines of his face faded. The only creases there now were of pure, primal desire.

"You don't know how bad I've wanted to hear those words," Cole said, before climbing the rest of the way onto the bunk. My breathing was coming so hard I felt like I could have a heart attack and I guessed that the adrenaline did a heck of a job burning off the remaining alcohol in my system.

I was glad. I wanted to feel every last touch. Every last caress.

"Say it again," he instructed as he crawled over me.

"I choose you, Cole. I want you," I whispered as his face hovered above mine, along with the rest of his body.

He groaned when I repeated those words, almost like he was coming inside of me right now. "I want you, Elle," he said, lowering his mouth to my ear. "And now that you're mine, I'm going to take you." His teeth sunk into my earlobe and he whispered, "I'm going to take all of you."

I rolled my head back and arched my neck to him. His mouth moved there and as his tongue started gliding up it, my hands moved down him. My thumbs hooked under his boxers and I slid them down until everything I wanted freed was nestled hard into my stomach.

My fingers curled around his length and stroked all the way down him. His tongue stopped its journey and his mouth suctioned to my neck instead, sucking at the sensitive skin with the same degree of speed as my hand moving up and down him.

"I want you inside of me," I said, guiding him closer. "I can't wait any longer."

I lifted my hips to meet him, and just as his tip slid against my wetness, he shoved away from me.

I sat up on my elbows and pleaded with my eyes. He kneeled between my legs, breathing heavily. "What's wrong?"

"You're a virgin, Elle," he said, wincing when he looked at the space between my legs. "This isn't going to be a pleasurable experience for you and I don't want to cause you any pain."

"You don't want me?" I guessed, trying not to sound as insecure as I felt.

Cole shot me a look. "I want to fuck you so bad I'm about to come just thinking about my cock being inside of you."

Heat raged through me as yet another surge of wetness trailed down my legs. "God, Cole," I breathed, touching myself if he wasn't going to do it. "Do me. Please."

He licked his lips as he watched me touch myself. "Shit," he breathed, before dropping his hand to where my finger continued to play with myself. His finger tangled with mine as it lazily stroked all around.

I sighed his name and flexed my hips into his hand.

"I don't want to come that way," I said, gently pushing his hand away. "I want to come with you deep inside of me."

Cole's hand lowered and I felt his finger circling my opening. His brows came together. "You're so damn wet," he said, and then his finger slipped inside of me.

I inhaled sharply as he slid it in deeper. "You really are a virgin," he said, his whole face creasing. "You're so tight, Elle. I don't think I can get a second finger inside of you, let alone my cock."

Hearing him talk about it made me think about it. I moaned and relaxed around him. Another finger slid inside.

"Yes, Elle," he said as I started rocking up and down against his fingers. "Hell, yes, baby."

He was right, I felt a little bit of pain, but it was next to nothing compared to the pleasure of feeling his fingers touching places deep inside of me.

"I want to feel you, Cole," I said, sliding far enough back that his fingers slid out. "I want to feel you inside of me."

He growled roughly when I said that. "I'm going to give it to you so damn good, Elle," he said, lowering himself over me again. "I'm going to make you come so hard you won't be able to stop screaming my name."

"Sounds like one heck of a first time," I said, smiling up at his face hovering a few inches above mine.

His hand slid under the mattress, fumbling around before pulling out a square plastic package. I arched a brow as he tore it open.

"I like to live on every dangerous side except when it comes to birth control," he said, rolling the condom into place.

"Cole Carson," I said, as he moved into place between my legs. "Responsible condom user. Just when I thought you couldn't get any sexier."

He smirked down at me before kissing me softly, like he was tasting the flavor of my mouth. "I'm going to try really hard not to hurt you. I'm going to do my best not to screw you the way I've been jacking off to lately. Okay?" I felt the tip of him press against me. My head tilted back; it felt so good. "You just let me know if I'm hurting you and I'll ease off."

I flinched my hips against him. "I don't want it easy, Cole," I said, wrapping my arms and legs around him. "I want it hard."

Cole groaned and then his hips rocked into mine. He stretched me wide as he slowly slid inside.

I whimpered and dug my nails into his back.

"Does it hurt?" Cole's voice was low and his hips stopped pushing into me immediately.

"No," I breathed. "It feels so damn good." Since he wasn't moving fast enough, I slid my hands down to his backside.

Grabbing hold of his butt, I pressed him hard against me. He slid the rest of the way inside me.

I cried out in pain. In pleasure. In pure ecstasy. Cole was buried all the way inside me now; he could go no deeper. He'd been my first and, with any luck, he would be my last.

I felt myself stretch and relax around him, wishing there was more of him I could take deeper inside of me. I couldn't get enough and my release was so close.

Cole was breathing as hard as I'd heard him yet. I could feel him swelling inside of me.

"Make me come, Cole," I breathed, wanting him to move inside me like his fingers just had.

"A moment," he panted just outside my ear. "I'm trying to keep myself from coming right now. I want this to be perfect for you. I want to feel you come around me before I do."

"I'm so close to coming right now," I said, sinking my teeth into his shoulder. He groaned loudly. "If you move inside me for just a few seconds, you're going to get your wish."

"Shit, you talk dirty in bed, Elle," he said, sliding out of me to the point I moaned in protest.

"Again," I begged, pressing my hips into him. Trying to take him back inside. "Harder."

Cole growled and then thrust hard and deep inside.

"Yes!" I cried, digging hard into his backside, encouraging him in his pace. "Oh, my God," I breathed.

Cole started moving fast and hard then and he looked as capable of holding back as I was. "You're so tight," Cole breathed, before ramming back inside of me. "It feels so fucking good."

I felt the spiraling out of control feeling fast approaching. "I'm yours, Cole . . . take me." All I could do was hold on as he rocketed harder inside of me. The whole bed shook and I could feel my orgasm about to roll through me.

"Say it again," he ordered, pulling out of me.

I winced from the separation. "I'm yours," I repeated, lifting my hips higher, wanting him so badly I could feel myself pulsing with desire. "Take me."

Cole's eyes blazed down into mine. "You are mine," he said slowly, right before he thrust deep inside of me again.

"Oh, yes, oh yes, oh my God," I panted as Cole recommenced his rhythm.

"You," he growled, ramming deep inside. "Are," he breathed, sliding back. "Mine," he moaned, thrusting so deep inside of me it sent me over the edge. My entire body pulsed around him as I screamed his name so many times it became a prayer on my lips.

Cole came a second after me and pumped inside me so fast I almost came a second time. His body fell down on me and relaxed, except his cock, which stayed hard and deep inside of me.

"You are mine now," he breathed outside my ear. "Mine forever."

There was nothing quite like waking up to a tangle of sheets that smelt like Cole while his fingers tickled down my spine.

"Good morning," I greeted, opening my eyes.

"Why, yes. Yes, it is," Cole replied, grinning at me. He was on his side, propped up on his elbow and still naked. Or at least I guessed he was—his sheet covered the area south of his navel.

"When did you wake up?" I should have been worried about morning breath, bed head, and the few still sleeping bedmates in the bunkhouse. Not to mention the storm waiting for me this morning after never showing up at home last night. I had plenty to worry about, but I just wasn't up to it when I was so close to Cole and still feeling the heady after effects of that beyond mind-blowing sex we'd shared.

I had all day to worry. Right now, this morning, I was just going to be in the moment and enjoy it.

"Just a few minutes ago," Cole said, sliding a chunk of my hair behind my ear. "I haven't slept that good in I can't remember how long."

I lifted a brow. "I wonder why . . ."

Cole chuckled. "Well, yes. There's certainly *that*, but I swear I could feel you next to me even in my sleep." His mouth dropped to my forehead and kissed it lightly. "You stayed."

There was nowhere else I could have gone. Or wanted to go.

"I stayed," I said, sliding closer to him until my shoulder pressed into his chest. His fingers went back to stroking my back. "Why were you so upset when I left that night at the swimming hole? I mean, I get it was a cowardly thing to do, but the way you reacted . . . It was like you'd never been so hurt before."

Cole didn't reply right away; he just continued to skim my back and seemed deep in thought. "I told you about being raised by my grandma," he began, his eyes wandering off. "Well, the whole reason I ended up with Grandma was because my mom up and left me one night. I was only two and don't remember much of her or her leaving, but that nighttime exit set the stage for my life. Next it was my cousin Tommy. He didn't say good-bye, I didn't even know he was leaving, but the day he turned eighteen, he left Grandma and me at night. I didn't hear from him for two years, when he first joined the smokejumpers up in Fairbanks."

I draped my hand over the side of Cole's neck. I couldn't hear these dark histories and not touch him.

"Next it was Grandma. Although she didn't leave willingly. She died in her sleep in the middle of my senior year of high school. I was eighteen by then, so I didn't have to go into foster care or anything, but sometimes I thought I would have preferred it when I went to sleep in that dark, quiet house."

Cole's voice didn't waver, his face never creased, but I could tell he wore this pain inside of him. He held it close and didn't let anyone share it.

"And then there was that summer night four years ago." Cole paused, and now his face creased. "The night my fiancee crawled out of our bed and left me for another man while I was asleep."

I must have heard him wrong. "Fiancee?"

Cole nodded. "Fiancee."

My stomach churned a bit. "You were engaged?"

"To my high school sweetheart. The girl I was positively certain I was meant to spend my life with. Unfortunately for me at the time, she didn't feel the same way." Cole's eyes didn't leave mine, and they steadied me in the midst of finding out this kind of thing.

"How long were you engaged?"

"A few months. You know, I remember waking up and reading her note and, after feeling like I'd just been run over by a train, I felt . . . relieved."

"Relieved?" I rolled onto my side and tucked my elbow under my head.

"I loved her, don't get me wrong, but it felt like I was marrying her because that was the next thing to do. I'd fallen into the trap of letting others' expectations and hopes for my life take it over. When she left me, I had no ties to anything else in Bend. I was free to be who I wanted and, even though I didn't know right then, I had the freedom to figure it out." His hand molded over my cheek while his thumb skimmed the seam of my lips. "After the pain and rejection faded, I was thankful to her for calling it quits when I wouldn't. She wanted something else, I wanted something else, but duty and fear of the unknown kept us together."

"You were thankful she left you?" I knew if Cole up and left me for some other chick, thankful wouldn't be on the list of things I'd feel afterwards.

Cole shifted closer. "If she hadn't left me, I wouldn't be here, with you, right now. Would I?"

When he put it that way . . .

Now I was thankful to Cole's ex-fiancee for ditching him for another man in the middle of the night.

"So that's why you were so upset with me," I said as it all made sense. "Me leaving you reminded you of everyone else who'd left you before. You thought I left for good and was never coming back?"

The skin between his brows creased and he nodded. "Wasn't that your plan? To stay away from me?"

I gave him a *Really* look and stared pointedly down at our naked-save-for-a-thin-sheet bodies. "Obviously not."

He smirked at me just before his arm slid over my back and drew me close. The entire length of my body running down the length of his sent heat into every last nerve, muscle, and vein.

From Cole's expression, he was experiencing the same thing. Just as I was about to lift my lips to his, his expression went a shade worried. "How are you feeling this morning?"

"Great," I said. "That whole pain reliever and water chugging thing works miracles to prevent a hangover."

"I'm glad to know your head isn't throbbing, but what about your . . ." His eyes lowered to that spot between my legs.

"I tried to be gentle with you, I tried to be careful, but I'm afraid I lost all and total control the second I got inside you. I'm sorry," he said, looking truly pained that he might have caused me any. "Are you sore?"

I did a quick check. Nope, no soreness there.

"Cole," I said, tugging on the ends of his hair. "Last night was amazing. You weren't gentle with me. I didn't want gentle. I wanted it just the way we did it." Thinking and talking about it made me want it again. "And I'm not sore, not even a little bit, so maybe we could . . ." I filled in the blanks by lifting my brows.

Cole's smile curved wickedly. "I'm all for that brilliant idea, but I want to make sure you know that we're not alone anymore." Cole scanned the room where about half the bunks were occupied by his fellow smokejumpers. "I can assure you they don't mind, but I'm guessing you might."

I thought about that for a moment. I'd just had sex for the first time less than eight hours ago, I probably wasn't ready to do it again in a room full of sleeping or near waking guys, but then Cole's body shifted beside me and all reservations went up in flames.

"Maybe if we're really quiet," I said, running my fingers down his stomach.

Cole grunted softly, then his eyes cleared. My hand froze.

"I have to clarify something first, Elle. Something I realize now you might have said only in a sex and alcohol hazed mind last night." He sighed and looked down. "Something you might regret saying this morning, and something I need to know." His eyes flicked back to mine and if eyes could, his were wincing.

Even before he'd asked his question. "Am I still the one that you've chosen? Are you still as much mine this morning as you were last night?" Joining his eyes, the rest of Cole's face braced itself for my answer.

My heart broke a little bit again, but this time for a different reason. For knowing I'd done and said things that made Cole doubt himself and us. I was done with it. I was done with doubt, both in his and my life.

"I chose you last night, Cole. And I choose this morning." I lifted my hand from his stomach and formed it over his cheek. "And just to save you the suspense . . . I'll choose you tomorrow morning, too."

The worry was draining from his face with each of my words.

"And, if anything, I'm even more yours this morning than I was last night," I said, pressing a soft kiss to his mouth. "Now, any other questions you're dying to run by me before we . . ." Man, I was perfecting the art of insinuation, both with my voice and my face.

"When are you going to tell him?" Cole's face flashed with something. Jealousy? Anger?

Logan. What was I going to tell Logan? I didn't quite know how I'd explain any of this to him, but I'd figure out a way. Good thing I had a few days to figure it out.

"Logan's at a baseball tournament this week," I began. "He won't be back until next weekend for the big Fourth of July Festival. I'll tell him then." I wasn't looking forward to it, breaking the heart of the guy I'd loved for two years, but I had to set him free. I couldn't pretend to give him my heart when someone else had it.

"Why don't you call and tell him today?" Cole said. "Otherwise, I won't be able to see you until you've called it quits with him because I won't be able to control myself around you."

"I'm not going to tell Logan I'm calling off the whole future he planned we'd have together over the phone. I'm sorry, Cole, but I'm just not," I said, trying to ignore the way Cole's face fell a little with each word. "I'll tell him as soon as he gets home, in person. He deserves that. And why in the heck won't you be able to see me until I tell him?" I made a face. After last night, I would go insane if he kept his hands off of me all week. I'd go even more insane if I didn't even get to see him.

"Elle, please don't take this the wrong way because last night was amazing, I don't and I won't ever regret it, but . . ." I held my breath. "I can't be with you again like that, or in any way, until you're totally mine. It's like what I told you before. I can't share you, Elle. Other men might be all right with it, but I'm not one of those men. I want you totally and wholly to myself."

I groaned out loud until I remembered the sleeping bodies around us. "Did you miss that part where I told you I CHOSE you?"

"No, I definitely didn't miss that part." A small smile played at his mouth. "But I also didn't miss the part where you said you're not going to call it off with Logan until next weekend."

"Cole," I groaned again, this time more quietly, "I chose you."

His eyebrow peaked. "But he doesn't know that. He still thinks you're all his. He still dreams about you every night and believes you're his present and his future. While another man still believes you are his, I just can't be near you or else you and I both know things will slowly spiral out of control." He gave me a sheepish expression. "You and I are not so good at that whole self-control thing when we're together."

"Really?" I said around a groan before rolling onto my back in defeat. "Are you serious, Cole? We can't see, touch, or have mind-blowing, world-rocking sex until next weekend?" The thought was too much; how was actually living it going to work?

"Unfortunately, yes. I am serious," he said, trying to hide his smile as he inspected me pouting like a child. "How's that phone call sounding right about now? Because from where I'm lying . . ." his voice dropped a few notes, and his legs tangled through mine.

I closed my eyes and put my proverbial foot down. Of course I wasn't looking forward to a week of celibacy from Cole, but Logan deserved better than an over-the-phone break up. I wouldn't let my need for the man above me, sucking on my neck like it was keeping him alive, totally derail me from doing the right thing when it came to breaking it off with Logan.

"You'd better stop doing that then," I said, wanting to bite my tongue to silence it. Even now, I could feel my body start the upward spiral to that downward one that had me screaming his name last night. "Because it doesn't look like you'll be getting any satisfaction from me until next weekend."

Cole groaned against my neck, but his mouth didn't pull back right away. Then his hips flexed against me and I felt his erection hard against my hip.

I joined in the groaning game. "You don't play fair."

He flexed again. "Neither do you."

If I didn't get out of this bed and a few feet away from this naked and ready-to-go man, I'd never be able to resist him. Just as I was trying and failing to scoot away from him, a thundering set of footsteps pounded inside the quiet room.

"Everyone up!" someone shouted. "Suit up and be ready to go in T minus fifteen. We're headed to Chelan!"

The silent room exploded with noise and movement, but me, I froze in panic.

"Elle?" Cole looked down at my face with confusion before understanding. "This is what I do. This is what we all do. I'll be safe and back before you know it."

I nodded, but panic still sat heavy in my stomach. Cole was going to get in a plane, jump out of it, and fight a forest fire today. This wasn't the kind of career field someone got used to easily.

"I suppose it's a good thing I'll be stuck in the middle of some middle-of-nowhere forest because I highly doubt I could have stayed away from you this week." He grinned and sat up.

"You're a good bluffer," I said as he grabbed his boxers at the end of the mattress and tugged them on.

"I know," he chuckled.

215

"What the hell, Carson?" Suddenly, a familiar face popped above the mattress. "You had a hot girl in bed with you this whole time and didn't even let me know so I could jack-off knowing a sweet naked ass was hanging four feet above my head?" Matt slid me a sly smile before reaching up and shoving Cole's arm. "I thought we were friends, man."

"If I knew you were even thinking about jacking off to my girl, Matt," Cole leveled him with a serious look, "I'd consider removing your parachute and shoving you out of the plane."

"Two words, Carson," Matt said, making an unimpressed face. "Idle. Threat."

"You've got one of two correct, that's for sure."

Matt waved off Cole's comment before turning his attention back to me. I slid the sheet up to my chin and tried not to squirm as he smiled stupidly at my face.

"You've got one second to take that smile off your face and look away before I make you," Cole warned, tossing a pillow at Matt's face.

"Wait. Hold up." Matt's face changed. "Holy shit, man! This is the girl from that thin pancake place. And you nailed her?" Matt continued on, like he was recapping a sports game. "Wasn't she with another guy? Some local? And didn't I also hear that she is . . ." Matt's eyes amplified. "Correction, *was* a virgin?"

Could my face have gotten any more red?

No. No, it could not have.

"Why don't you go find someone else to irritate?" Cole said, leaning over me and shoving Matt's face back.

Matt lowered back down, but he was still chuckling evilly a whole minute later. "You de-virginizer, you," he said after he'd dressed and starting heading out of the room. "You are officially my hero, Carson. Higher up on the totem pole than Superman."

Cole motioned him to keep moving.

"See you on the plane, virgin snatcher."

"Remind me next time he sets foot in the diner to drop his crepe into his lap," I said as Cole leapt down from the bunk.

"I'll do it for you," he said, sliding into a pair of pants. "Happily."

All the other guys had already exited the room by the time Cole finished tying his boots. Standing up on Matt's bed, his face was level with mine.

"I'll be all right. I promise," he said, guessing the reason I was gnawing my lip to pieces. "Now get over here and give me something to think about while I'm off saving trees and bunnies."

After a second or two more of worrying my lip, I rolled over, covered his mouth with mine, and made sure he had plenty to think about while he was saving trees and bunnies.

TEN

This wasn't going to end well. It wasn't going to start well, either. Dad's form had been shadowing his office window when I pulled in the driveway and nothing about his expression gave away that he was happy to see his missing daughter had made it home.

He hadn't been worried that some sort of bad found me to make me go missing; he'd been worried I was out searching for the bad.

He was right and he was wrong.

No bad thing had happened upon me last night, but I hadn't found a bad thing either. From the time Cole found me until I pulled into the driveway, it had all been good. One giant mess of good.

I knew dad wouldn't feel the same when I explained where I'd been last night and who I'd been with.

After Cole and his fellow smokejumpers had suited up and

flown off in the direction of Chelan, I crawled out of bed, dressed, and grudgingly checked my phone. I cringed when I saw the number of missed calls and voicemails. I didn't listen to a single one because I was about to get the full, unedited version the moment I walked through that front door.

Sucking in a deep breath, I slid out of the Jeep and headed to meet the inevitable. I had to suck in one more before I could force myself to open the door.

Three, two, one . . .

"Where the hell have you been, Elle?" Dad shouted, charging into the entryway. "What were you thinking not coming home last night, or in the very least calling to let me know you weren't planning on coming home?"

"I'm sorry, Dad," I said, not able to look at him. His face was red, the crescents under his eyes were black, and his entire body was nearly trembling as he boiled over.

"You're sorry?" He crossed his arms. "Sorry for what? Not coming home? Not calling? Sorry your Grandma M, your uncle, and I didn't sleep a wink last night? Sorry for getting caught? Or are you sorry for what you were up to last night?" Pinching the bridge of his nose, he exhaled.

"I'm sorry for not calling," I replied, forcing myself to keep looking him in the eye. "And I'm sorry you and Grandma M and Uncle Ben didn't get any sleep last night because you were up worrying about me. But I'm not sorry about anything else."

Dad's brows came together. He wasn't used to seeing me stand up for myself or talk back to him. "You're *not* sorry for not coming home last night when you're a young woman who has a boyfriend who isn't, at present, in town?"

I didn't like the accusation in his voice.

"You might be naive, Elle, but you're not stupid, so you should know better than to try to treat me like I am."

This conversation was going nowhere. "What do you want from me, Dad?"

"For starters . . . what were you doing last night?"

I didn't want to lie, but I didn't want to give a full disclosure. "Figuring some things out." Vague, honest answer.

"Figuring exactly what out?"

In keeping with the vague, honest answer theme, I said, "My life."

"How very specific of you. Thank you, Elle."

Times like these, when my dad was so much more of a tyrant than a parent, I wondered what my mom had ever seen in him. Sure, Biggie wasn't exactly a golden boy, but I doubted he would have looked at his own daughter like he was disgusted by her.

"And who—while you were out figuring your life out—were you with?"

"I'm not going to answer that," I said, my voice not wavering once.

Dad's eyes widened before they narrowed. "Why not?"

"Because I'm not a little girl anymore whose life you get to know everything about," I said, almost shouting. "I'm eighteen, Dad. I'm entitled to some privacy and some secrets and some god damned mutual respect!"

I had a knee-jerk reaction to cover my mouth, but I didn't. Dad's eyes widened again and this time, they stayed this way.

Finally, when I was sure he was about to blow a gasket, he sighed. "You're still living under my roof, Elle. Therefore, my rules, too. I don't know what you were doing or who you were doing it with, and I can't force you to tell me if you refuse, but I can order you never to do that again, you hear me?"

I breathed faster as I neared my blow-a-gasket stage. "Yeah, I hear you," I said, heading for the stairs. "Your house, your rules? Fine. Consider me no longer a tenant in about ten minutes." Without another word or glance, I lunged up the stairs and flew into my room. I even slammed the door, which was a first.

Now that I was locked away, I let my brave act crumble a little. I sat on the edge of my bed, took a few deep breaths, then popped back up and stormed over to the closet. After rummaging through a heap of clothes and shoes, I managed to find my old duffel bag. It hadn't been used in a while.

I threw the first few tops and bottoms my hands fell on into the bag. When the bag was almost full, I marched into the bathroom adjoining my bedroom and tossed my toiletry bag inside. I couldn't think about what all this meant or the long-term repercussions. If I did, the fear of the unknown would have paralyzed me. So I let myself focus on what I needed to pack for a few nights away and where I could crash tonight.

Grandma M was the obvious choice. Dani's place was the second runner up, and the swimming hole was the third. My backpacking bag was fully stocked with a tent, sleeping bag, a few dehydrated meals, and even a pack of iodine tablets to purify the water.

As much as I loved being in the great outdoors, when it came to day-to-day life, I preferred a warm shower and electricity.

Just as I stormed over to my nightstand to grab the jar I kept a chunk of my tips in, a soft knock sounded at my door.

Squaring myself, I crossed my arms and waited.

And waited.

"Dad?" I called out after a good thirty seconds had gone by. "Can I come in?"

My face twisted with confusion. Dad's standard approach when entering my room was a quick warning knock before coming inside. He didn't wait for an invitation. It had become such a pattern I hadn't ever thought to give an invitation.

"Sure?"

My door opened slowly as Dad made his way inside. When he saw the stuffed bag in my hands, he frowned. In ten minutes, he had transformed into a different man. Instead of red, his face was more an ashen white. The hollows under his eyes were now purple instead of black, and instead of trembling, his whole body sagged. Like he was defeated.

"Dad?" I took a step towards him. He looked like he might topple over any minute.

"I never told you about the day your mom died, did I?" His voice had also changed. It was so quiet I had to crane my head closer to hear him.

I swallowed. Dad and I never talked about Mom anymore.

"Yeah . . ." I started. "You've told me how she died."

Dad nodded and leaned against my wall. "But I've never told you why she died," he said, pausing. Almost like he was choking on the words. "Or about how I failed to keep her safe."

No, this part of the encounter I'd never heard before. I wasn't sure I wanted to hear it now.

Taking my silence as my answer, Dad pinched the bridge of his nose and continued, "Your mom was wild in her youth. I was wilder." My eyes narrowed; this didn't fit with the man I'd known as my father. "We loved any and every chance to test ourselves against the great outdoors, and when we weren't working or sleeping, we were doing something outside that put us an inch or two above death. Once you came along, we toned down and pulled back a lot. As much as we loved putting ourselves to the test, we loved you more and we didn't want you to be raised without a mom, a dad, or both."

I had to take a seat on the edge of my bed. I already knew from the tone of things this was going to drain me.

"That day your mom went out kayaking, I was with her. It was during spring run-off and we'd had an especially snowy winter and an unseasonably warm spring. Your mom and I had kayaked that river dozens of times, probably even hundreds, but when I saw the rapids that day before dropping in, I knew those conditions, even for experienced river kayakers, could get sketchy. Your mom reassured me she felt up to it and I was so excited to have an afternoon off with her, I was careless." Closing his eyes, his face went a shade paler. "As soon as we shoved off, I knew it was bad. I knew we never should have attempted it. We hadn't been in for a minute before your mom's kayak rolled. She couldn't get it rolled back and no matter how hard I paddled toward her, the rapids I was in seemed to steer me farther away from her."

I didn't realize I was crying until I felt tears hit my legs.

"She'd been under a long time, but she was still fighting. I caught glimpses of her oar bobbing to the surface, trying to right herself . . . and then her kayak crashed into a boulder and your mom's paddle stopped breaking through the surface." Dad rubbed his eyes and took a slow, tortured breath. "Your mom died there at Haven Rock, but her body washed up on shore a few miles downstream. She died because I was careless. She died because I wasn't strong enough to save her. She died because of my weakness."

"Dad," I whispered, shaking my head. I'd never guessed he'd carried this kind of baggage around with him for so long.

"No, no. I know what you're going to say. I've heard it a million times before," he said, staring at the carpet unseeingly. "It's not my fault. There was nothing I could have done. It was God's plan." His voice took on a bitter hue. "And maybe that's what others believe, but the point I'm trying and probably failing to make with you is that's not what I believe. I believe I failed your mother . . . and I swore to myself I would never fail you."

I felt emotionally drained already, and Dad was just getting to the point.

"I thought that if I kept you close, didn't give you a long lead, and plotted out your life, I could keep you safe. Keep from failing you. And it seemed to work according to plan—you never expressed any resistance to the strict rules and lifestyle I expected of you—until lately."

I suppose "lately" could have been defined as the last month.

"I don't know who or what is to blame for this newfound asserting yourself thing you have going on . . ." Dad's face lightened, ever so slightly, "but I guess I don't really care who or what is responsible because, at the end of the day, I'm proud of you, Elle."

Say what? When I pulled up to the house, I knew the forthcoming exchange between dad and me would be epic. I didn't expect it to be epically good.

"You've got so much of your mom in you, sweetie, so much spirit. I hated watching you repress that. I hated knowing I was to blame even more. I'm sorry I didn't do a better job raising you. I was so busy running from the ghosts of the past that I ignored I was suffocating the life out of the living. I was suffocating you by not encouraging you to be the vibrant, tenacious young lady I know you are." Dad smiled at me. It wasn't an ear-to-ear grin, it couldn't even be considered a wide one, but it was as big and as genuine a smile I'd seen on his face in a while. "But you're also that sweet, thoughtful girl you've been leading with. You're two different people living in one body like we all are. Most of us just choose to show one of those sides to the world and strangle the other until, eventually, it dies off. But you, Elle, you've found the courage to let both sides show. Whatever's responsible for this change . . ." Dad shoved off the wall and nodded, "don't let it get away from you."

I wondered if Dad would still feel the same way if he knew the "something" responsible for my change was a young smoke-jumper with a checkered past and a day-by-day style approach to life. Maybe he wouldn't care; this man standing before me spilling his guts was an alien life form in a kind of way. But it was an alien life form I hoped was here to stay.

"And, Elle?" he said, clearing his throat. "I don't know where this leaves you and Logan, and you don't need to tell me. But I can make an educated guess. You might not want him to be your husband anymore, but don't forget he was your friend first. One of your best friends. Just be honest with him. Win, lose, or draw, Logan will be okay."

Dad might have been right, but he wasn't the one who would have to look Logan in the eyes, call it off, and hand him back a ring. Just thinking about it made me sick to my stomach.

"I'm sorry, Elle," he said. "I know my reasons don't excuse my actions, but all I wanted was the best for you and to keep you safe. I hope one day you'll be able to find a man who can do a better job of it than I did."

I was up and across the room before either one of us could say something else. Wrapping my arms tightly around Dad, I buried my head into his chest and let a few more tears fall. He hugged me back, quite possibly as hard as I'd ever been hugged before.

"You did a good job, Dad," I said. "You raised a happy,

healthy, mostly well-adjusted daughter. In case you haven't seen the statistics, that's quite the challenge these days."

Dad's chuckle rolled through his body, vibrating against mine. "I love you, Elle."

I closed my eyes and believed everything was going to be all right. I'd talk with Logan, Cole would be back hopefully in a few days, and now that I'd had this unexpected heart-to-heart with Dad, I could figure out what I wanted to do after summer was over.

"I love you, too, Dad."

He kissed the top of my head. "And that's all that matters."

ELEVEN

The Fourth of July Festival was the same every year. I should know since I've been to it every year since I was born. I might not have had the brain capacity to recall the first few, but I knew what they were like. Exactly like last year's, and the year before that, and the year before that.

Tonight though, the Festival would be different. At least for me and one boy who'd attended just as many of these things as I had.

Logan had rolled back into town earlier in the day. I'd really hoped to sneak in some time with him before the Festival, but when we talked, he said he was beat and in desperate need of a few hours of sleep before we met up. The Festival wasn't exactly the ideal place for calling it quits with your lifelong friend and once-upon-a-time future husband, but I'd have to make do.

I'd been anxious all week, working out in my head what I

would say to Logan, how much I would tell him. I was almost shaking from the adrenaline of knowing I was mere hours, if not minutes, away from giving the speech I was dreading.

But I had to do it. There was no way around it. I chose Cole. I had to let Logan go so he could hopefully one day find his female Cole equivalent.

Cole had been gone all week fighting the big fire down in Chelan. It was an area notorious for wildfires, and from the news, the smokejumpers and everyone else working the fire were having one heck of a time trying to keep it from spreading. I'd never been much of a news person up until that week. I don't think I missed a newscast or article. Anything that had anything to do with the Chelan fire, I was glued to. From the sounds of it, the fire was mostly under control as of yesterday afternoon and the efforts were now concentrated on putting out hot spots.

I hadn't heard from Cole since he took off with his crew last weekend—cell phones and wi-fi weren't exactly readily available at the core of a wildfire—but I kept my phone close by at all times. I turned the ringer up to full volume at night just so I knew it would wake me up if he called.

By the time I pulled into the grassy lot, a little after eight that night, the Festival was already in full swing. I had to park at the very edge of the lot, but even from there, I could smell the tell-tale Festival smells. Corn dogs, elephant ears, and something that wasn't quite as pleasant tangled in the air, creating a potpourri that was familiar, yet it was already starting to feel foreign.

Foreign because I knew I was leaving Winthrop behind.

Maybe not for good, but for a while. The day after Dad's and my heart-to-heart, I broke the news to him. I was leaving in the fall to go to college. The one I'd decided on a couple of weeks ago when this whole life altering path started. I don't know who was more anxious over the idea—me or Dad—but for the most part, I was anxious in a good way.

I had a couple more months left of summer and Winthrop before I'd spread my wings and leave. I had a couple more months of Cole. That was what I dreaded most. The end of the summer. Me going one direction. Cole going wherever the smoke and fire led him. I'd chosen him and I wanted him, but I'd learned my lesson. I wouldn't let the decisions I made that would affect my life be contingent on a man. Even a man like Cole.

We both knew what we had was special, something rare that took us both by surprise. If any couple had a chance of making a long distance thing work, it would be us. While I'd battle mid-terms and all night study sessions, Cole would be battling fires. Somewhere.

Even though I knew Cole and I had a fighting chance at giving this thing a go, no matter where life took each of us, I was a real-ist too. I knew the odds were more in favor of us not making it than in us riding into the sunset on a white horse. I got that. It twisted my stomach and made my breathing all panicky, but now that I'd figured out how to be honest with myself, I wasn't going to put that mindset on pause when it came to Cole's and my relationship.

So Logan and I had something to talk about, but so did Cole and I. Two intense conversations with two boys I cared for deeply. With Logan, it would break my heart, but with Cole, the possibility of my heart being ripped from my chest was very real. We'd been so busy just trying to be together, we hadn't worked out what happened next. That was a whole lot of gray area I needed to put a little color into. Was this a summer romance for Cole, or was he hoping for more? How much more? How much more was I hoping for?

The questions never ran out and as I started weaving through the bodies milling around the festival, I was tackled by an onslaught of even more questions. Maybe that's the reason I felt especially cynical about the festival that night.

My cynicism escalated as soon as I noticed a familiar, smiling face coming towards me.

"It's about time you showed your pretty little face," Mrs. Matthews said, wrapping her arms around me. "What do you think of the Festival? Best one yet, right?"

I surveyed the surrounding area. The same food vendors, the same dunk tank and carousel, the same white lights criss-crossing a few feet above our heads. The same people milling about. The only thing different this year was the cancelled firework display. Lack of rainfall and record high temperatures had a way of messing with a firework show.

"Hands down," I said, thankful when she finally released me. I'd been doing my best to avoid her and Mr. Matthews all week. Not because I didn't like them; they were great people, highly respected in the community, but the guilt I'd carried around like a one ton weight doubled when I was around them.

"Have you seen Logan yet?" she asked, waving at a family passing us.

"No," I said, my throat going a little dry just thinking about it. "I was just looking for him."

She smiled. "Last I saw him, he was hanging around the corn dog stand. About to tear into his fourth one."

"Didn't they feed him while he was gone?"

"I think he's eating because he's nervous," she said, leaning over like she was telling me a secret. "He's an emotional eater. Takes after me." She patted her flat stomach like it was anything but. Mrs. Matthews was twenty years older, but she and I could have shared clothes.

"Why's he nervous?" I wasn't sure if I wanted to know.

She bit her lip, chewing something out. Finally, she grabbed my hand and her eyes started to twinkle. "I think he wants to talk with you about something," she said in a hushed voice.

That made two of us.

Then, cocking an eyebrow, she patted my hand. "Or something to *ask* you."

Oh, boy. Not good. I got a little lightheaded thinking about it. She didn't need to say the exact words to get across what she was getting at. Logan was going to propose tonight. Officially. One promise ring to be replaced with an engagement ring.

I was going to break up with the guy who was planning on asking me to marry him tonight.

Life had a sick sense of humor. Or timing.

Or both.

"I already think of you as a daughter, Elle, but it will be wonderful when it's official."

Two ton weight of guilt . . . you've got nothing on what just busted my back.

"I'd better stop talking your ear off so you can go find Logan." She flashed me a knowing smile. "I want to be the first to know. I pummeled that into him earlier, but in case he's got the memory of his father, I'm telling you. Mother-in-law is the first to know," she said, sticking her thumb into her chest. "Okay?"

It took me a few moments before I could reply. "Okay," I said softly. "Logan or I will let you know what happens."

Just then, a small mercy popped up beside Mrs. Matthews. Mrs. Peterson, one of the fellow Festival planning committee members, had a stoic look on her face.

"Sorry to interrupt, Marny, but I just thought you should know that bunch of smokejumpers just showed up," she said, shaking her head.

My head whipped around instinctually, scanning for a familiar face.

"A few of them are pretty drunk already and the night is young. You know what happened last year . . ."

If I hadn't been so preoccupied looking for Cole, I might have grinned. Mrs. Peterson's and my definition of a tragedy were on opposite ends of the spectrum. My mom dying so young was a tragedy to me; to her, a few buzzed smokejumpers who'd held a contest to see who could climb to the top of the Ferris wheel first at last year's Festival was a tragedy.

If any sort of encore performance was planned for this year, I knew Cole would be at the front of the line.

Mrs. Matthews made a face. "I'll let Sheriff Montgomery know so he can keep tabs on them," she said, her eyes automatically drifting in the direction of the Ferris wheel. No band of death wish smokejumpers hanging from it yet. "Thanks for letting me know."

I waved at the two women before making my way through the crowd. I knew I needed to find Logan first. I had to talk with him before I could look for Cole because I knew if I found Cole first, I'm be consumed by him. All reason and restraint and better judgment would fly off with the fried food scented wind and I couldn't do that with Logan in the same vicinity.

Plus, I also knew Cole likely wouldn't touch me if he knew I hadn't broken things off with Logan. So, even though my eyes scanned the crowd for Cole, I went in search of Logan.

I'd almost made my way to the corn dog stand when a pair of arms wound around me from behind.

"Looking for someone?" Logan's familiar voice and the hint of hopefulness shot a stab of pain right through me. Just the tone of his voice was about to bring me to my knees. How was I going to make it through this?

I didn't have the answer to that. All I knew was that I had to do it.

I twisted in his arms, trying not to let those blue eyes of his I'd stared into thousands of times cripple me. "Not anymore," I answered him.

Logan studied my face and his forehead creased. I knew I looked almost as bad as I felt. I couldn't hide it. It would have been a wasted effort.

I might as well get this over with before I lost all control.

"I need to talk to you," I said quietly. "Alone." A handful of Logan's friends and teammates were scattered around us and the buzz of Festival noise made it hard to think, let alone tell a boy I'd loved for the past couple of years I wasn't in love with him anymore.

Logan's face fell, but not in worry. In nervousness.

Mrs. Matthews hadn't been exaggerating. He was really going to do this tonight.

"I need to talk to you, too," he said, shifting in place. "And I'd prefer to do it in privacy, too." He shifted again. He was crazy nervous.

"You want to get out of here?" I said, nodding for the parking lot. I wasn't eager to leave the Festival now that I knew Cole was likely wandering around, but right now, Logan was my priority.

"Yeah," he breathed, running a hand through his hair, "but not until you dance with me." He grabbed my hand and starting leading me towards the same band playing the same songs from the same stage to the same husbands and wives, boyfriends and girlfriends, lovers and ex-lovers, all moving on a dance floor of uneven earth.

I held back. I wasn't a dancing queen, nor was I a dancing fiend.

I was more a dancing dud.

"Come on, it's tradition," Logan said, pleading with his eyes. "We haven't missed a year of dancing to 'our' song since we were twelve years old." There might not have been a romantic spark between us back then, but our friendship was our bond. A lump formed in my throat when I realized I wasn't only breaking up with a boyfriend tonight, I was breaking up with a good friend.

"I can't let tonight be the year we miss our dance," he continued. "I'd never forgive myself." He smiled that Logan smile of his. "Come on. For me?"

It might have been the guilt. It might have been the way I cared for him. Or it might have been our history together. Whatever it was, I answered him with a single nod and let him lead me towards the stage.

Logan didn't stop until we were in front of center stage. Motioning up at the singer—a guy who was in the choir at church—Logan dropped his arms around me and drew me close.

The band stopped playing their upbeat rendition of an oldie and broke into something slow and familiar. And yet, just like so much of this town was becoming, it was a bit foreign too.

"Our song," Logan said, his face bright.

"Our song," I whispered, realizing this was a bad idea. A very bad idea.

Logan had worked out with the band that with a nod of his head, they'd stop what they were playing and break into our song. On the same night he was planning on asking me to marry him. Knowing this, along with the gleam in his eye and the set of his brow, I knew what was coming. Of a mere minute or two away.

"I love you, Elle," he began as a sheen of sweat surfaced on his forehead.

Crap. He was really going to do this thing. Right here and now.

So much for leading me to believe he wanted privacy for what he had to talk with me about tonight.

"I love you so, so much and I know you're the girl for me. I've known that from the first day I met you."

"Wait," I said, shaking my head. "Stop."

Logan's mouth clamped shut and he waited.

"Why do you love me, Logan? Do you know why? Can you list the reasons why?" My words bubbled to the surface faster than I could speak them. "Why are you with me? Do you know why you want to spend the rest of your life with me?"

Logan's face dropped. I could have just slapped him from the way he looked. "What?" he said after a while, sounding as baffled as he looked.

"Why are you with me, Logan? Why do you want to spend your life with me?" I asked, doing the best I could to make hard words sound soft.

Logan thought about this for a few moments while he held me close and moved in time to the slow song drifting around us. "Because I can't imagine anyone else I'd rather be with."

I tried to follow his lead as we danced, but I couldn't. I'd stopped following Logan's lead weeks ago and I suppose that even translated onto the dance floor. Eventually I just gave up and we wound up just standing in place, with his arms around me, staring at one another.

"So you can't think of anyone else you'd rather be with," I repeated. "But what does that have to do with *me*? Why do you love *me*?"

Logan's face couldn't have gotten more confused. "Because I do, Elle."

I inhaled and didn't back down. "Why?"

"What? You want a list or something? A spreadsheet of reasons why I love you?" he said, his voice going a little high.

I lifted my brows and waited.

"I don't have a list, Elle. Sorry." Then, with a sigh, Logan slid one hand into his jacket pocket. "But I do have something that I think will demonstrate just how much I do love you and how I want to be with you. Forever."

I shook my head and started backing away. "No, Logan," I whispered.

When he raised his eyes and saw me backing away from him, he froze. "Elle?"

I had to get away. Right now. "I'm sorry," I mouthed before turning and weaving through the obstacles of dancers and spectators.

So much for being strong tonight. So much for taking Logan aside and telling him it was over. So much for my whole plan.

I heard him call out my name as I sprinted away, but after I'd made it away from the stage and was halfway down food row,

I couldn't hear Logan anymore. People started to look at me curiously as I jogged. I suppose any crying, nearly hyperventilating person would attract some attention. So instead of heading for the Jeep so I could calm down and refigure how this whole night was going to go, I ducked inside a white canvas tent.

I was in luck because, not only was it dark and quiet, it was empty. It must have been some sort of storage area where the food vendors could stock their stuff because boxes and pallets of food and drink took up almost the entire tent.

I leaned into the closest tower of boxes and dropped my head below my knees. I needed to breathe. I'd never had one before, but I guessed what I was experiencing was very close to a panic attack. I wasn't sure what would kill me first: lack of oxygen or cardiac arrest. It didn't seem to matter how many breaths I took or how slow I tried to inhale and exhale them, I felt quite confident I was going to die or pass out if I didn't get myself together and calm down.

As soon as I started to feel like my heart was slowing down, I'd remember Logan reaching into his pocket and I'd be right back in heart thumping through my chest mode.

"Elle," a voice, as worried as it was relieved, broke through the tent right before a strong set of arms pulled me to him. "What's the matter?" Cole's fingers wove through my hair and drew my head to his chest. And just like that, I found the calm that had been evading me.

Or at least a margin of calm.

239

I slipped my arms around him and squeezed him hard. "How did you find me?"

"I just asked if anyone had seen the crying, frantic girl charging through the Festival like a madwoman and they pointed me this way," he said lightly, holding me a little tighter. "No, I was just getting here and saw you duck inside."

"I suppose I was kind of hard to miss," I said with a sigh. Everyone would be asking me what had happened the moment I left the tent. So maybe I just wouldn't leave it until everyone was gone.

"Yes, Elle. You most certainly are hard to miss." Cole's voice was so full of meaning and his body was so firm against mine, I kind of melted. I let myself go for a few seconds and pushed away everything but the here and now.

Just like that, I could breathe again.

"What happened?"

Just like that, breathing became hard again.

"Logan," I started. Cole's body tensed at the name alone. "He's planning on asking me to marry him tonight." His body went tenser still.

"And he's planning on asking you this, because he stills thinks you're planning on spending your life with him, because you haven't called it off yet?" Cole was better at it than Logan, but he couldn't totally mask the level of hurt in his voice.

"Yes."

Cole couldn't have tensed any more without snapping in half.

"Why haven't you told him yet? Has something changed?"

From hurting one boy to hurting another. I was on a real roll here.

"I haven't told him because he literally just got back into town, Cole. I was planning on telling Logan tonight, but then ..." I trailed off. I didn't want to repeat the word marry and Logan in the same sentence with Cole so rigid against me. "And no, nothing has changed." I bit my lip as I realized something might have changed for him. "At least, nothing's changed for me. I still choose you, Cole. I still want you."

His body softened a little then, but went rigid in other places. "Good," he said, lowering his mouth to my ear. "Because I want you, too."

Relief flooded my body. "Yeah?"

"Yeah," he said and the air around us changed. His hands grabbed my hips and he shoved me up against a wall of boxes. This wasn't helping my breathing problem.

"Here," he said in a low, rough voice, as his hand skimmed down to the hem of my skirt. A rush of air escaped my lips when he lifted my skirt all the way up and pressed his hips hard into me.

"Now." This time, he inhaled sharply when I covered his mouth with mine.

I kissed him like I wanted him to make me forget. I kissed him like I wanted him to make me remember. I kissed him like all we had was here and now.

I kissed him carpe diem.

When his mouth moved to my neck, I looped my legs around his waist and slid up and down him until he was more panting against my neck than sucking at it. He pressed me harder into the boxes, like we couldn't create enough friction between the two of us and really, at this rate, he was going to make me come before he even got inside.

When I heard his zipper lower, I moaned and lowered my mouth to the side of his neck to muffle the noise. It was noisy outside the tent, but it was noisy inside of it too and I didn't want to have anyone investigating if they heard my heady moans.

Cole smelled like his usual brand of scents. Soap, salt, and . . .

"You smell like soot," I said.

Cole chuckled. "Occupational hazard."

I buried my nose in his hair, where the scent was strongest, and inhaled. "It's kind of turning me on though."

"Benefits of the job, too," he said right as his finger slipped inside my panties.

My fingernails dug into his back as his finger trailed down. "Damn, Elle," he said, moving just barely inside of me. "You really must be all turned on." I arched my back and lowered my hips until his whole finger went inside. A stream of air hissed through his teeth as another finger moved inside of me. "I'm going to have to remember to keep a can of soot handy so I can sprinkle it on me before you come over."

"Sounds good to me," I managed to get out before his thumb started circling my clit.

"Elle?" He didn't sound like he was faring any better in getting words out.

"Cole," I breathed.

"I need to tell you something," he said, as my hand slipped inside his zipper. As soon as my hand wrapped around him, he groaned and his whole face creased with a mixture of pleasure and torture.

"What do you need to tell me that's so important it can't wait until we're . . . *done*?" I asked, sucking his earlobe into my mouth.

"You're going to need to calm your hand and your mouth down for one second or else I won't be able to get this out," he said as his fingers continued their lazy assault.

Instead of releasing him, my hand sped up and my mouth sucked harder at him. Stopping just long enough to whisper in his ear, I said, "You strike me as the kind of guy who likes a challenge."

A low growl vibrated up his chest as my pace picked up yet again. "Fine," he said, breathless. "Elle Montgomery. I—"

"Elle?" A new voice suddenly broke through Cole's and my haze. The last voice I wanted to hear right now. Lifting the flap of the tent so a stream of light came in, Logan's eyes bulged as he took in the scene. "Elle?" The first time he'd said my name, it was like he was searching for me. The second time he said my name was like he was wishing he hadn't found me.

"Fuck," Cole sighed, rearranging his hands and lowering my skirt.

I went numb and I couldn't seem to tear my eyes away from Logan's. I'd never seen them so . . . broken. So betrayed. I'd never seen him both so broken hearted and enraged that he looked like the intensity of his emotion was about to tear him down the middle.

Like he couldn't bear to look at Cole and me wrapped around each other for another second, his eyes flashed away right before the tent door flapped closed again.

Cole and I were alone again, but everything had changed in the span of a half minute's time.

"Logan!" I called after him, unwinding my legs from Cole's torso and charging for the exit.

"Wait, Elle." Cole grabbed my hand and spun me around. "What are you doing?"

"I'm going after him," I said, waving at the spot where Logan had just disappeared.

"I can see that," Cole replied. "But why right now? Give him a chance to cool down."

"He just walked in on us about two seconds away from having sex, Cole. A whole five minutes after he was about to ask me to marry him." I was so upset right now, I couldn't even cry. "I don't think he's going to be 'cooling down' anytime soon." I made a move towards the exit again only to be pulled back by Cole.

"No," he said. "Don't go. Stay with me and we'll find him tomorrow and explain together."

"Did you see his face, Cole?" I said, nearing a shout. "Logan is a few minutes from going nuclear and you want me to wait until tomorrow to explain to him what's been going on? To explain to him with you at my side?"

Cole's eyes flashed with something then. Hurt, I guessed.

"And what are we going to explain? That we hooked up multiple times behind his back because we couldn't seem to keep our hands off each other?" I wasn't thinking clearly. My words weren't coming out right, but I was past the point of frantic. My boyfriend had just seen me with another man and I was sure I'd just ripped his heart out of his chest and drove a dagger through it from the look on his face.

"Is that the way you feel about us?" Cole's eyes flashed again. This time there was no question what emotion it was. "That we were merely fuck buddies that went behind your precious Logan's back?"

I was hurting Cole now, too. I'd crushed Logan and was now in the process of doing the same to Cole. My life had become a soap opera and a Shakespeare tragedy rolled into one.

"No, that's not how I feel about us. Is that how . . . you feel?" I asked, torn between staying here with Cole and chasing after Logan.

"I don't know how I feel right now," he replied, dropping his eyes to the ground.

I tried to pretend that answer didn't cut me. I tried to pretend that his response wasn't breaking my heart for the one millionth time. I tried so hard, I think I might have fooled him.

This time, when I moved towards the exit, he released me. That hurt worse than his words. "Well, let me know if you ever figure that out."

As I reached for the tent flap, Cole let out a long sigh. "So this is it? You're choosing him over me? You're . . . . leaving me for him?"

For the first time ever, Cole sounded like a little boy. Like the little boy who'd been left behind so many times in his life. That voice stopped me in place.

"No, Cole," I said, glancing over my shoulder. He kind of looked like a little boy right now, too. "You're the one leaving me behind."

Before I could change my mind, I darted out of the tent and started weaving through the crowd again. One part of me searched for Logan's light head bouncing through the crowd, hoping I'd find him. Another part of me hoped I wouldn't be able to find him so I could go back to Cole and work out exactly what he felt for us. What he felt for *me*. Had I really imagined the way he'd look at me like if I was the only thing he could ever have in life, he'd be a happy man? Or had he been that talented a bluffer? I knew the way I felt about Cole. The confusion had cleared at last and I was confident in my feelings for him.

Just when my cloud of confusion had cleared, Cole's set in. Timing wasn't only a factor in love, it was the creator, keeper, and executioner.

Musings of my future with Cole would have to be put on hold because a familiar back marching towards the parking lot caught my eye.

Taking in a breath, I weaved through the crowd after Logan. He was a way off and wouldn't hear me if I called out to him, so I just continued snaking through the never ending stream of bodies until I finally broke free of the crowd, at the edge of the Festival grounds.

Logan's rigid form was storming away, likely ready to jump in his truck, peel the heck out of here, and who knows if I'd ever see him again. From the way he'd looked at me earlier, he never wanted to see me again.

"Logan!" I yelled after him, breaking into a run. He wove through the maze of cars at a breakneck pace.

"Logan! Wait!" I yelled louder and ran faster.

He didn't stop, slow, or pause. He just kept moving like he didn't hear me. Like I didn't exist anymore.

I was closing in on him and by the time he'd gotten to his truck at the edge of the parking lot, I'd reached him.

"Stop, Logan," I said, slowing down as I approached him. "Please."

His back was to me, but I didn't need to see his face to know he'd heard me and wasn't eager to see me. His entire body went stiff.

I rested my hand on the side of his arm, trying to turn him my way. He flinched like I'd just shocked him.

"Logan," I whispered. "I'm sorry. We never meant . . . I never meant . . ." I stopped and tried to collect myself, so I wouldn't sound like a blubbering, nonsensical mess. "I didn't want to hurt you. I never intended to . . ."

The way he wouldn't acknowledge me now was an indication of just how badly I had hurt him.

I blew out a rush of air. "Although I knew I would when I told you. Or when you found out."

Of course he couldn't have "found out" in a worse way. If only I told him sooner, even if I'd taken Cole's advice and just did it over the phone, Logan would have been saved from what he just walked in on.

He didn't move. He didn't say a word. Logan was a statue.

"Please, Logan. Say something," I pleaded. "Say *anything*." At that point, it felt like anything he could have said to me would have been better than cool silence.

Logan spun on me and now, instead of a mix of betrayal and heartbreak, he was nothing other than enflamed. His eyes were like two black coals glaring their hatred at me.

"You want me to say something, Elle?" he said, his voice trembling. "You want me to say all the things I want to say right now? All the cruel, mean things circling around in my mind? On the very tip of my tongue?" The sinews of his neck were popping to the surface. Logan was spilling over in a way I'd never seen him anywhere close to before. "You want me to tell you how I feel, what I think about you, what I think about . . . *him*?" he cursed the word before a full body shiver ran down him.

All I could do was nod and try not to cry.

"Well, there's a part of me that wants to do that, too. To say and do the things I'm feeling right now. But you know what?" His voice was lowering, although it still shook. "I'm better than that. I'm better than giving into my every emotion and my every whim. I'm better than hurting you the way you hurt me. I'm better than that." Looking away from me, he shook his head. "At least one of us is."

Logan's words drove the dagger of guilt in as far as it could possibly go. I couldn't have felt worse if I tried. The cruel words he refused to unleash on me couldn't have made me feel like any worse of a human being.

"Now if you'll just leave me alone already, I need to get out of here." Twisting back around, he threw open his truck door. "Tonight didn't go exactly according to plan."

Watching Logan turn away from me, for what could quite possibly be the last time, brought an onslaught of emotions and memories. The first day of kindergarten when the little boy in a blue polo shirt had sat next to me and told me he'd be my friend when I couldn't stop crying, after my dad had dropped me off. The boy who'd brought me a tray of brownies, a stack of movies, and sat with me on the couch all week after I broke my leg in fifth grade. The boy who'd blushed whenever I talked to him or looked his way when we became teenagers. The same boy who made it his business to make sure all the other boys treated me right. The boy who'd slipped a promise ring on my finger months ago.

The man who was leaving me, once and for all, because I'd crushed him.

"Forgive me, Logan," I said, starting to sob. The memories, the emotions, the night was just too much. I couldn't hold it back any longer. "Please, forgive me."

"Sorry, Elle," he said, crawling into his truck. "Forgiveness isn't something I'm up to right now." His voice was empty, with just a hint of sadness.

His voice and his words only made me cry harder. So hard, I couldn't take it anymore. I fell to my knees in a heap, the intensity of everything I was feeling about to tear me apart from the inside.

Logan paused before closing the truck door. I could feel his eyes on me as he sighed. "One day, Elle," he said. "One day I'll be able to forgive you. Just not today."

The door slammed shut before the truck's engine fired to life. As Logan drove away from me, I realized I hadn't only lost one good man that night. I might have lost two.

TWELVE

kneeled in that grass field for a while. Long enough to watch the Festival grounds empty of cars and people, but not nearly as long as I felt like I could stay in that defeated position.

I think some part of me was waiting for Logan to come back and yell at me. I needed to be yelled at; my remorse wouldn't settle for anything less. Some part of me waited in hope that Cole would come find me, hold me close, and tell me everything was going to be all right. Another part of me just was physically, emotionally, and mentally drained and couldn't work up enough strength to lift myself up.

When enough time had passed I knew neither boy was coming, I decided to take matters into my own hands. I needed to punish myself at the same time I needed to challenge myself. There was only one way I knew to achieve both.

I didn't care what time it was and I didn't care how crazy it was. I just needed ... something to channel the overwhelming emotions spilling from me into and I needed that something now.

After making my way back to my Jeep, I headed home to make a quick stopover. I was praying, hoping, crossing my fingers and my toes that Dad wouldn't be home when I arrived. When I pulled in the driveway, I discovered that finally one thing had gone my way that day.

Dad's car wasn't there and the house was dark save for the desk lamp he kept on in his office. He was probably still at the Festival, or maybe he'd made a quick stop by the diner to see how Dani and Paul were holding down the fort. I didn't know, but I didn't let my lack of knowing make me any less thankful for small mercies.

Rushing inside, I ran straight up to my bedroom. Even though Dad was gone, he'd be home any minute and I didn't want to be there whatever minute that was. Rifling through my closet, I tugged on my well-used hiking backpack. After a little encouragement, I managed to pull it free. I'd had the pack since I was twelve and used it a handful of times every summer. I hadn't used it this summer yet, but was about to make up for my neglect.

I did a quick check to make sure all my essentials were still packed inside and, not wasting another second, threw it over my shoulder and rushed back downstairs. Racing into the kitchen, I snatched my water bottle out of the dishwasher and filled it up at the sink.

There it was. I was done and ready. All I needed to do was get out the door and to the trailhead and I was golden. Just as I was about to sprint out the front door, I paused. Dad would be worried sick if I just disappeared on him again overnight. He would be frantic and worried and an all-around mess.

I couldn't do that to him again.

Grabbing the stack of sticky notes in his office, I scribbled down a quick note.

Gone hiking. You know the place. Will be back tomorrow night.

I considered adding "alone" to the "gone hiking" part, but I guessed Dad wouldn't be any more or less comforted knowing I was hiking at night, in the woods, alone. So I kept it open to interpretation.

By some other miracle, I made it out the front door, into the Jeep after heaving my pack into the passenger seat, and down the block before I caught sight of a pair of head lights rounding our street. I guessed they were Dad's, but if I couldn't make out his telltale classic Mustang from this distance, he couldn't make out my Jeep.

The trailhead wasn't all that far outside of town and I parked the Jeep less than thirty minutes after leaving town. The whole ride I'd been plagued with both Cole's and Logan's faces and how they'd fallen from things I'd said. From things I'd done.

Cole hadn't outright said we were done, and I clung to the hope that he felt the same thing I did: that we had something special. Something as confusing as it was combustible, but something worth fighting for. Something worth crushing a good man I'd known for over a decade.

What if Cole didn't want me anymore though? What if it was all about the chase for him? What if he was done with me now that he'd conquered me? What if, what if, what if?

I was suffocating in a sea of what ifs.

In a sea of the unknown that would remain that way until I had answers. But since Cole was ... somewhere, the unknown wouldn't be working itself out anytime soon.

So I slid out of the Jeep and did what I hoped would quiet my mind. It had always worked before and I hoped it would work for me now. After shouldering my pack and buckling the straps, I slid on my headlamp, tied on the hiking boots I kept stuffed in the back of the Jeep for emergency purposes, and set out on the trail. There were signs at the trailhead prohibiting campfires. It wasn't unheard of, but the no burn restriction didn't normally crop up until August. I couldn't remember a time it had happened in early July.

Trudging through a dark forest wasn't the first thing most people thought of when they thought of hiking, but it was hiking to me. True, most of my hikes had taken place during the daylights hours, but my most memorable ones had taken place at night.

I guess Mom had been into the whole night hiking scene, too. Dad had told me she used to say she felt more alive when she hiked at night, more in tune with herself and everything around her. That extra little sliver of fear derived from walking through a pitch black forest with nothing more than a stream of light coming off your head had a way of pumping the adrenaline to new heights. It had a way of making you forget everything but putting one foot in front of the other.

The night had been warm earlier, but as I got deeper into the woods, the chill in the air really started to bite. I had to stop to open my pack so I could slide into a fleece top. I even tugged on a light stocking cap just in case it got colder the farther I hiked in. The trail was windy, steep, and technical. It wasn't your everyday "backyard hiker" variety trail, and that, combined with the darkness and the night sounds, emptied me of everything.

Thinking about Cole and Logan was impossible when an animal snorted off to my right or when my toe caught on a jagged rock sticking out of the middle of the trail. I was in survival mode and would be until I hit the campsite I'd stayed at dozens of times as I'd hiked this trail. It was another mile off and, at this rate, I'd be there in record time.

Twenty minutes later, my legs were exhausted, my mind almost as much, and my backpack felt like it weighed a hundred pounds. Unbuckling it, I let it slide to the ground as I caught my breath. I took a few more sips from my water bottle, cleared a few twigs from the camp site, and dug deep into my pack until I felt the nylon bag containing my little tent.

I had the tent built, my sleeping pad blown up, and my sleeping bag tossed on top in another record-breaking time. After taking my hiking boots off at the tent door, I slid inside, zippered myself in, and checked my phone.

As expected, no reception.

The moment after I snapped my headlight off and zipped my

sleeping bag up, I hit that drifting-off-to-sleep stage. The hiking had done just the thing I'd hoped it would. It had cleared and emptied my mind. Cole and Logan and the whole mess swimming between and around the two was still there . . . it was just more manageable now.

Maybe thirty seconds later, my mind gave up and followed my body into sleep. That night marked the end of a phase of my life and I knew whatever waited for me the next morning would mark the beginning of a new one.

THIRTEEN

*S*omething was off.

That was the first thing I thought as I woke up the next morning. It was too hot. I was breaking out into a sweat at just past dawn in the middle of the Okanagon National Forest. Even in the middle of a hot summer day, I would have had to really be working to break out in a sweat thanks to the cover of the trees.

And it was too loud. Almost ear splittingly loud.

The sound was unfamiliar, but it didn't take too long to guess what was responsible for creating the hissing, cracking thunder getting louder with every second.

That menacing sound, combined with the stifling heat in the middle of a dry summer, could only mean one thing.

Fire.

I threw my sleeping bag off and unzipped the tent as fast as my fingers could. As soon as I stuck my head out, I met a blast of heat that almost took my breath away. I knew I was in trouble, but when I turned my head and saw the wall of flames engulfing trees and grass and everything that stood in its path instantly, terror set it.

The fire was like I'd never seen before. The footage I'd seen on TV of forest fires didn't do justice to what being on the ground, face to face with it, felt like. Cole flashed through my mind right then. That was what he did. He stared down fire without fear to life or limb.

At that moment, fear was the only thing I felt.

The fire was as tall as the trees, the flames licking the very top of the ponderosa pines that had been there for generations. One hundred year old trees went up in flames in less than ten seconds. And the noise. It was truly deafening.

When a tree that was just barely on the outskirts of my camp-site exploded from the heat and flames, I broke out of my hypnosis. I lunged from the tent and grabbed my boots, but there wasn't time. I didn't have a second to waste, let alone a minute to tie my hiking boots.

Leaving everything behind, I charged in the opposite direction of the fire, ignoring the stiffness in my legs from last night's killer hike, ignoring the sticks and rocks assaulting my bare feet, and ignoring the way my lungs burned from the heat engulfing me.

The only thing I didn't ignore was the fear. That I kept close in order to draw every last drop of adrenaline out of me. The fire kept me moving, but fear kept me flying.

After a couple of minutes, I'd put some space between the fire and me. Both the heat and sound had dimmed some, but not nearly as much as I hoped it would after running at breakneck speed. I had endurance, but how much? How long did I have before I ran out of energy and collapsed?

I could only hope that point was far enough away I could find safety before the fire found me.

Glancing over my shoulder to see just how far back the fire was, my foot fell into something as I continued my sprint. In a heartbeat's time, I was sprawled out face first on the ground, my ankle twisted precariously in the gopher hole I hadn't seen coming because I'd been too busy looking behind me.

Pain shot up my leg instantly. I'd sustained enough injuries in my eighteen years to know I'd either broken or sprained it. Right now, it didn't matter which one because either would be enough to keep me from running. I'd be lucky if I could manage a fast walk.

At a fast walk, there was no way I could outrun the fire. It was moving much too fast.

I was going to die here today. I was about to go up in flames.

The summer's figurative of this was about to take a very literal turn.

Grabbing my leg, I wrenched my foot free of the hole. I cried out so loudly I think I gave the fire a run for its money. I shoved myself off the ground and took a few steps. I *hobbled* a few steps. The pain firing up my leg was so intense I was tempted to keel over and let the fire have me. Surely the pain of burning wouldn't be as bad as the way my nerves felt like they were filled with acid.

259

Oddly enough, when I glanced back at the fire again, I saw Cole's face. I might not have known where his head was regarding the two of us, but I was confident enough to know he wouldn't want me to die out here this way. He'd at least want me to put up a good fight.

So I gritted my teeth, and took another step, and then another. By the time I'd taken ten, I was panting and breaking out into even more of a sweat from the pain. But I kept going, I kept fighting.

Shuffling past an enormous tree, my uninjured foot caught on a root. I didn't fall this time, I managed to get my other foot around in time to break my fall, but bracing a fall on my injured ankle easily caused more pain and damage than careening face first to the ground.

I fell to my knees after that, crying tears I couldn't have held back if I'd wanted to. The heat was growing so strong around me those tears evaporated before they rolled all the way down my face.

I was spent. I could barely kneel, let alone attempt to stand and keep crawling forward. This was the end, and although it wasn't a time in my life I would have chosen it to end, I was in the forest I loved, and I'd met and fallen in love with a boy that took me by surprise in every kind of way—the good ways and the bad.

I loved him. I loved Cole. I don't know why it took me so long to recognize it or admit it, but I suppose the point was that I had. Too bad I'd never be able to tell him.

The heat and noise from the fire had returned in all its overwhelmingness. The distance I'd put between me and it had been erased. I had a minute, maybe a bit more. That was all I had left of my life. A minute. A lot goes through your head when you realize you have a minute left. A lot that doesn't seem to matter and a lot that does.

Dropping my head back, I stared up at the sky. The smoke was so thick the sky was almost swallowed whole by it, but a dot of blue sky still peeked through. I stared at that small dot and didn't let it go. And then, that too was overtaken by something.

Something that wasn't smoke...

Something that was growing bigger as it got closer. Something I couldn't quite make out until the bottom of a pair of boots seemed to be staring me in the face. A pair of boots outlined by a ballooning piece of nylon.

He was an angel falling from the sky. He was *my* angel falling from the sky.

I experienced one moment of relief that Cole was here right before that faded into dread.

Cole was here.

With a forest fire practically licking at my neck hairs. Smokejumpers might fight forest fires, but they sure as heck didn't stand dead in their path when that fire was mere yards away.

As it was, Cole's parachute started burning around the edges. Snow flake sized pieces of parachute fluttered down on me right before Cole crashed to the ground. I made another move to stand, but I couldn't. I had nothing left.

"Elle!" he shouted, sliding out of his parachute harness as the rest of the parachute caught fire.

The tree just feet behind me started to catch fire when Cole kneeled in front of me. "Wrap your arms around my neck and hold on tight!" He had to yell over the fire screaming around us. I did as ordered, wincing when he grabbed my legs and wrapped them around his torso so he was carrying me piggy-back style. "What are you doing, Cole?"

He looked back at me with a mild smirk. "Doing what I do best," he said. "I'm saving the day, baby." Then, sucking in a heavy breath, Cole charged ahead. When I say charged, he ran like no man or beast I'd seen before. He ran like a forest fire was, indeed, nipping at our heels.

"What did you hurt?" he hollered back, ducking beneath a tree branch.

"My ankle," I replied, holding on to him tighter. He was moving faster with a one hundred plus pound weight on his back than I had.

"Broken?" he yelled.

"I don't know." I decided to go ahead and close my eyes because I was starting to get motion sick. The rough ride mixed with the heat and noise only exaggerated the feeling.

"How did you find me?" I peered back. Cole'd managed to put a respectable distance between the fire and us.

"Your dad!" he said, coming to a sudden stop. "Then a pair of binoculars came in handy once I was in the plane." He didn't need to scream anymore with the distance we'd put between the fire and us.

"Thank you," I said, twisting my forehead into his sweaty,

sooty neck. It was peaceful, this brief moment, this second stolen in time. For one beat of a heart, I experienced a peace I hadn't felt before.

That peace evaporated when Cole's body tensed as he studied the trees in front of us. Like he could see something in those trees I wasn't able to.

"Cole?" I said hesitantly. "What is it?"

He sighed. "The fire's in front of us, too," he said, glaring into the trees in front of us. Now, if I looked really hard, I could see the bright orange and red glow morphing and shifting in the distance.

I stopped breathing.

"We're trapped," he said.

Trapped. A fire in front of us. A fire behind us. We were up against a rock and a hard place. We had nowhere to go, no way to escape the blaze.

I looked up, I looked down. I looked to the right, I looked to the left.

I looked to the left . . .

"Cole!" I shouted, feeling hope take hold. "The river's not far from here. Maybe only a half mile."

Cole glanced back at me before looking in the direction I was pointing. He looked at the forest like I just had when I was trying to see something he could see that I couldn't. But I saw it. We were close to the river. So close I could almost feel it.

"The shoe tree!" I pointed a way's down to the left. "I can see it. My parents and I used to stop and take pictures of it before we went down to the river. If we can get there, the river is only a few hundred yards from there." I knew it was a good distance to cover considering the speed the fire was moving. I knew we'd need something of a miracle to do it, too, but I'd take running towards a river any day over waiting for the fire to reach us.

Cole didn't ask any questions. He didn't ask if I was sure or how I knew. All he did was nod, readjust his hold on me, and charge in the direction I'd pointed him.

"Damn," Cole panted, as we drew closer to the shoe tree, "that thing is downright freaky."

I smiled as he gave an over-exaggerated shudder. The fire that had been behind us was now creeping so close my side felt like it was on fire and the fire that had been almost invisible in front of us was now a wall of flames on our other side. We were in the Red Sea of fire and could still manage to smile and talk like it was any old day.

"Turn right here!" I shouted as we passed the familiar tree.

Over the years, I'd seen the sandals, sneakers, boots, and flip flops expand up the trunk of the old maple tree, until almost every branch that could be reached from standing up on the cab of a truck was also covered. I'd grown up with the tree, taking pictures of it and with it. It had become as familiar as the rest of my life and it was going to burn. I'd never have the shoe tree down by the river to look forward to again.

As Cole thundered down the trail leading down to the river, he didn't stumble once. He was so steady and sure footed over every obstacle of the technical trail you would have thought he was strolling around the park.

"How much farther, Elle?" He was back to screaming because the fire, once again at our backs, was closer than ever. I scooted my hair over my shoulder to keep it from catching on fire.

"Not far! Maybe another hundred feet!" I could tell because the bushes and grass were getting thick and started to slow us down. That didn't make for the best combination. The fire getting dangerously close to igniting our clothes and the brush we were charging through slowing us down. The sharp branches whipped across my face, drawing blood, but I couldn't feel the pain. I couldn't feel anything but Cole's body and the heat of the fire.

"Hold on tight, baby!" he yelled back before charging faster down towards the river. It was like Cole had a whole other gear. We'd just gone from insane fast to stupid fast, but still, it wasn't fast enough.

I could see the river, it was less than twenty feet away, but it might as well have been twenty miles because the flames ripped towards us. The brush on either side of us was consumed by a wave of fire and it was impossible to breathe. I don't know how Cole was able to keep moving without oxygen, but he'd already proven he could when he parachuted into the heart of a fire to save me. He was more superhero than man.

I felt the back of my fleece coat ignite and was just folding myself over Cole, trying to shield him from the relentless flames, when he lunged into the air. In the course of trying to outrun a fire, Cole had veered away from the trail and we'd ended up on a ledge above the river. It was a small ledge, only a couple body lengths, but it felt like we fell through the air so long we could have just leapt from the heavens.

The flames eating at my jacket intensified as we sailed through the air and I held my breath. Just in time too, because a moment later, Cole and I crashed through the surface of the river. Cole had leapt far enough that we landed in water above our necks.

I unwound myself from him and could have died a happy woman right there. The cool water rushing over my skin felt like a healing balm. Cole's hand grabbed mine, and he tugged me farther out into the river. I didn't have to surface for a breath yet and I knew that if ever all those sinking rituals in the swimming hole would pay off, now would be it. We swam sideways into the current, kicking hard. Cole seemed to be heading somewhere and I just let him lead me.

When we reached a large boulder sticking out of the middle of the water, we both surfaced. Just enough to take a breath and take in the scene around us. With one hand, Cole grabbed onto a handhold cut into the rock. With his other hand, he kept firm hold of me, drawing me close until his arm wound the entire way around my waist.

"Are you all right?" he shouted.

I nodded and dunked my head back into the water for a second. It was scorching hot around us. I don't know how Cole could continue to hold onto the rock. The heat alone radiating from it made me uncomfortable.

"Are you?" I asked, inspecting his face and arm since that

was all I could see. I could only imagine how torn up my face was from the sprint through the brush, but Cole's face had to be at least twice as bad. There were more red, open areas than tan skin.

"Yeah, I'm good!" he said, grimacing a bit as he adjusted his hold on the rock. "Just hold on to me, okay? Don't let go, Elle. We're going to be all right, we're going to make it."

I curled closer to him as I surveyed the fire storm around us. That's just what it was: a storm. The entire side of the river we'd just ran from was totally engulfed by the fire now, but the flames licking out from the brush and trees from that side were reaching out and extending across the river.

I'd heard of fires jumping rivers, but to hear about one and see one was an entirely different thing. As the fire continued to jump the river and spread, it was like being surrounded by a canopy of flames. It was on either side of us and above us. Those kinds of moments, one realized just how small and insignificant we really were.

When I couldn't look at the flames destroying the landscape I'd grown up with any longer, I glanced back at Cole. His head bobbed above the surface, watching me like he was afraid I'd disappear, and holding on to that rock like it was a lifeboat.

That rock...

Haven Rock.

My hands would have clamped over my mouth if I wasn't holding on to Cole for my dear life. In the course of veering off the trail and being towed a ways downstream after we'd jumped in the river, Cole and I wound up at Haven Rock. The place saving our lives was the place that had taken my mother's.

When Dad and I had hiked the shoe tree trail after Mom died, we were always careful to stay out of view of Haven Rock. It was like some silent agreement we'd struck. We didn't talk about it, we didn't look at it, and we stayed a few hundred yards upstream from it. Yet here I was, clinging to the man who was clinging to it.

It seemed the ironies of my life never ran out. This was the final and most heart-wrenching confirmation.

"What is it?" Cole's eyes filled with concern as he scanned my body as best he could.

I wanted to glare at the rock. I wanted to punch it, and hate it, and wanted it to catch on fire and be forever destroyed. Just as it had destroyed my mom. The knowledge that that rock would be all that remained of the landscape at the end of the day seemed impossibly unfair.

"This was where my mom died," I said. "This is the exact place where she died."

I would have cried if I hadn't run out of tears a ways back.

Cole's face softened before he nodded. "That explains it then."

"Explains what?" I asked, wanting to close my eyes so I wouldn't have to stare at it any longer.

"Why you and I are going to make it through this thing, Elle. I've been in some scary ass situations before, but even if you were to add all those up, they'd still look like a speck against what's going on around us."

A tree exploded on the other side of the shore, reminding me just what was going on around us. When I gazed back at Cole, he was watching me, waiting for me.

"Your mom is right here with us, Elle. Her spirit's here giving my exhausted arm strength to keep hanging on. She's keeping the current from whipping us all to hell. She's keeping the tree shrapnel from getting anywhere near us." A small smile formed. "She's keeping us alive."

So maybe I hadn't totally run out of tears. The lump in my throat was so big I could barely breathe and, as much as I wanted to say he was full of it, I knew he was right, too. Mom's spirit was right here with us. With me. The water gliding over me was as gentle as her arms were when pulling me into a hug. The rock shielding and protecting us was as strong and unwavering as she'd been. She was in everything. She was everywhere.

"I need to tell you something. You know, now that I've got you alone and you're not going anywhere," he said, winking. "Something I was trying to tell you earlier before I acted like a total asshole."

"Was this during the time I was acting like a total pain in the butt, too?" I replied.

His almost smile was enough of an answer.

"So what were you trying to tell me before we both behaved like idiots?"

Cole's eyes didn't leave mine. They looked like they never might. "I might kinda, sorta, really, truly love you."

Once I got past the shock of the word, I felt a million

different things at once. Every one of those things pointed towards one thing. Curling my fingers into the back of his neck, I kissed him lightly. "And I might kinda, sorta, really, truly love you, too."

Cole's grin spread. "Why don't you kinda get over here and kiss me then?" His eyes scanned the enflamed area around us. "Since it doesn't look like we'll be going anywhere for a while."

When I kissed him again, it was not light. In fact, it was so not light that somewhere in the midst of it, I forgot all about the storm circling us.

FOURTEEN

When you come literally a hair away from death, it gives life a whole new meaning. You stop anguishing over *what* you should and shouldn't do, *how* you should do it, *when* you should do it . . . and you just do it. It might be morbid, but holding hands with death gives almost an entirely new meaning to life.

I had a new perspective and I felt like I was a different person. Not wholly different, but different in the ways that counted.

My entire life had changed . . . and it had only been twenty-four hours since Cole and I escaped the fire that had already annihilated over one thousand acres of forest land. Thanks to the skill of the smokejumpers and the hotshot crews in the area, no homes had been burned and so far, no other hikers or campers seemed to have been in the path of the fire.

Once the fire had destroyed all that was left to consume along the riverbank, Cole and I made our way downstream, hanging close to the shore so we didn't get caught in the rapids. Thanks to my busted up ankle, which had turned out to be a nasty sprain, Cole basically carried, maneuvered, and helped me the entire way down the river until we finally passed shoreline that hadn't been affected by the fire. After dragging our wet, exhausted bodies out of the river, Cole carried me on his back another two miles until we hit the first road, and then he hoofed it another mile before we flagged down the first car we saw.

He'd been a machine that day. He'd saved my life more times than I could count on both hands. And feet. Cole hadn't only said he'd loved me that day, he'd proven it.

We hadn't been in the emergency room more than two minutes before my dad flew through those doors, screaming my name throughout the place until he finally found me. Dani and Grandma M were quick to follow and Logan had even called my dad for a quick check-in. After I'd assured everyone I was fine, I managed to get Grandma M and Dani to go home and get some rest, but Dad wasn't having any of it. He hadn't left my side.

Neither had Cole.

Even when Dad drove us both home after our cuts were bandaged and our burnt and torn clothes were exchanged for hospital scrubs. Even when we'd crashed on the couch and passed out for a good twelve hours.

Even when we sat at the kitchen table as Dad flipped a batch of huckleberry pancakes. Cole's hand gave mine a squeeze. "How are you feeling?"

There were about a hundred answers to that.

"Lucky," I settled on. That about summed it up.

"Yeah," he said, leaning in to give me a quick kiss. Even a tough guy like Cole was smart enough to be scared to kiss a girl for too long when her dad was in the room. "Me too."

Dad dropped a plate of pancakes in front of Cole and me. "More coffee?"

I shook my head and dived into the pancakes. I hadn't eaten in almost thirty-six hours and now that my appetite had finally kicked in, it kicked into overdrive.

"I can get it," Cole said, grabbing his cup and rising.

Dad cut him off. "No, no. Sit and eat. I've got the coffee." Grabbing the French press, Dad filled Cole's cup.

"This is really great of you, Mr. Montgomery," Cole said. "Thanks for letting me crash here last night and feeding me."

Dad grabbed his own cup of coffee and took a sip, studying me and Cole. His eyes lingered on where Cole's hand covered mine on the table. "It's the least I could do for the person responsible for saving my daughter's life," Dad said. "You risked your life for my baby, Cole. That's something I'll never forget or ever be able to repay. You ever need anything . . . anything at all, you call me, okay?" Dad tilted his cup at Cole before taking a sip.

I had yet to tell Dad where Cole and I had clung on for our lives in the river. I figured that might be a bit too much right now after he'd almost lost his daughter. Finding out he'd almost lost her in the same place he'd lost his wife could wait for another day.

"Actually, there is one thing," Cole said, setting his fork down. Looking over at me, he formed his hand over my face and stared at me like I'd never been stared at before. Like I was everything he needed and wanted without my even realizing what those things were. I melted under that look.

"I don't know how much you know about Elle and me. I'm not sure if you know when we met or how we met," Cole continued, turning his attention towards my dad. "But I'm guessing you know enough that you might be disappointed or disapprove of the way I pursued your daughter when she was with another guy. I don't regret meeting your daughter, I never will, and I sure as hell don't regret the feelings I have for her." Cole paused, shaking his head around a sigh. "But I do regret that our journey towards one another hurt someone. I owe Logan one hell of an apology, and who knows, maybe he'll try to kick my ass when I do, but I owe you one, too."

Dad set his cup down on the counter.

"I'm sorry, Mr. Montgomery. I know you want what's best for your daughter and I know the way I went about it wasn't that." Gazing back at me, he shot me a tilted smile. "I'm sorry to you, too, Elle."

I shook my head. There was nothing to forgive.

"It takes a big man to 'fess up when he's done something wrong. Most men never get there," Dad said, crossing his arms and leaning into the counter. "I don't know the details that make up your and Elle's story, and I don't want them, but I'm perceptive enough to fill in the blanks when I see my daughter changing before my eyes." Dad's face changed when he looked at me. It relaxed and softened instantly. "Since that change is for the better,

I can't fault the thing or the person responsible for that change"—Dad stared pointedly at Cole—"too much. Given you're a man who can admit when he's made a mistake, has made my daughter a better person, and risked his life to save hers . . . I'd say you earned yourself a forgive and forget from me."

Cole rose from his seat and headed for Dad with his hand extended. "Thank you," he said, sounding truly relieved when Dad shook his hand. "There's one more thing . . ." Cole rolled his head to the side and then the other side, like he was stretching or something.

Dad lifted his brows and waited.

"I know you're old fashioned and since I didn't exactly go about this the right way at first, I want to do my best to make up for that." Cole shifted and continued, "I'd like to ask for your approval to date your daughter."

I tried to hide my smile, but failed. As old fashioned as Logan was, he hadn't even requested my dad's permission when he took me on my first date. He did ask him before he'd given me the promise ring, but Cole wasn't asking my dad for my hand in marriage yet. He was talking about taking me out to dinner and a movie. Coming from the mouth of a man who didn't let anyone tell him what to do or how to behave, it was kind of adorable in the cute, ironic sort of way.

Dad didn't even try to hide his amused grin. "Yes, Cole," he said, clapping a hand over his shoulder. "You have my approval to date my daughter. Not that it makes any difference to me, but I don't think most guys ask for 'permission'."

Cole nodded. "I do have to ask someone's permission," he said, coming around the table towards me. "But not from you, Mr. Montgomery. I can only get permission to date your daughter from one person." He kneeled beside me and winked. "And that is from your daughter."

Running the backs of his fingers down my cheek, he took a breath. "So? Miss Elle Montgomery?" he said. "What do you say?"

I tried to hold out for a few seconds, to keep him on pins and needles, but it didn't work. I could barely keep my lips sealed a solid second. "Yeah, Cole Carson," I said, lifting a brow. "You have my permission to date me."

Cole wiped his brow and mouthed *phew* before settling back in his seat and diving into his pancakes. Dad went back to his coffee and I went back to finishing what was left of my pancakes. Just like that, we settled into a sort of routine, a kind of family. Dad sipping his coffee as he flipped through the newspaper. Cole chowing down on breakfast beside me. It was all kind of . . . perfect.

"When do you need to be back at camp?" I asked after I'd finished the last bite of pancake.

Cole stopped chewing mid-bite and exchanged a sheepish look with my dad. Rounding up his paper, Dad tucked it under his arm, grabbed his coffee, and headed out of the kitchen. "I'll give you two some time to talk. Alone," he added before disappearing into the living room.

"What was that about?" I asked, looking between Cole and the spot where Dad had disappeared.

Cole shoved his plate aside and turned in his seat towards me. "I won't be going back to smokejumper camp," he said, dropping his hands on my legs. "Since they kind of fired me."

My brows came together. From everything I'd heard, Cole was an invaluable asset to the team. From everything I'd experienced with him at ground level with a forest fire, he was an invaluable asset. Why in the world would they fire him?

"Why?"

Cole ran his hand through his hair. "I guess they consider bribing the pilot and commandeering the base plane 'grounds for termination,'" he said, making air quotes.

"Wait ..." I needed a few seconds to process what he'd said. "Are you saying ..."

"That I masterminded an unauthorized flight and drop into the middle of a forest fire?" he filled in.

All I could do was nod.

"Yep, that's what I did."

"Why?" I asked, still dumbfounded. Cole had to have known he was risking his career when he got in that plane and made that jump. Smokejumping was everything to him, his life.

"When I heard a fire nearby was so big and spreading so fast they weren't even flying the crew in right away to fight it, I got this feeling in my gut. I didn't know where you'd gone after the whole explosion at the festival, but I somehow knew that fire was heading your way." He studied my face that was only creasing more with confusion. "I know, I know. It doesn't make sense, but when I showed up at your doorstep early the next morning, asking if your dad knew where you were and he told me you'd gone hiking . . ." Cole blew out a rush of air. "I couldn't get back to base, in that plane, and then out of that plane fast enough. Your dad told me which trail you'd taken and where you'd likely be camped out and, like I said, the binoculars and my parachute figured out the rest."

So he hadn't only risked his life for me. He'd given up his career. Knowing Cole, he probably held his career to the same degree of importance as his life.

"Cole," I said, slumping down in my seat. "I'm so, so—"

"I'm not," he interrupted, shaking his head swiftly.

"But smokejumping was your life," I said, not sure whether to feel overwhelming guilt or overwhelming gratitude for what he'd given up for me.

Cole gave a small shrug. "It was," he said. "And then I met you and I wanted more out of life than just jumping out of planes for a quick rush. Because who in their right mind would settle for a quick rush when you could have a long, *long* rush?"

"But what are you going to do now?" I said, staring into my lap. He had no roots to keep him here in Winthrop. He had no roots to keep him anywhere in the state. Was I really about to lose the boy who'd given up everything for me?

One side of Cole's face pulled up. "I might kinda, sorta, maybe be going into Natural Resource Sciences at Wazzu this fall," he said, confessing it like a sin.

"Wazzu?" I said, dumbfounded. "Wazzu as in Washington State University? As in Pullman, Washington? As in a few hours away from here?"

Cole bit his lip to keep from smiling. "I believe that's the one, yeah."

"How long have you known?" I asked, scooting forward.

"Since this past winter," he answered. "I applied, not really expecting to get accepted, but then I received my acceptance letter right before I headed here this summer. Right before I met you."

"But the smokejumping? I thought you were going to be jumping out of planes until they forced retirement on you."

Cole chuckled. "I love it, don't get me wrong, but I gave it four years of my life. Now it's time for me to do something else. It's time to move on to the next great adventure."

"Why didn't you tell me?" I asked, trying to shake through the haze of surreal. It was pretty much impossible though, given the man who'd been a total stranger at the start of summer had turned into the man I loved weeks later, and now was attending a college I'd applied to myself in the fall.

"When I learned you'd applied and been accepted to a few different schools, I didn't want where I was going to affect your decision. I wanted you to make that on your own so neither of us would ever wonder if you'd only made your decision based on mine." Pausing just long enough to plant a kiss on my mouth, Cole's hands formed around my face. "I love you, Elle, but I don't want that love to inhibit you. I want it to make you feel like you can do anything you want. I want you to feel free to make your own decisions."

Resisting the overwhelming urge to kiss him again, I inhaled.

"I already made my decision," I said, about to lose the battle of resisting his mouth.

The way Cole stared at my mouth made my stomach flutter. "And what have you decided?" he whispered, just barely grazing his bottom lip against mine. My stomach wasn't only fluttering anymore.

"I've decided on you," I said before grabbing his shirt and tugging him closer. When his mouth was firmly crushed against mine, I leaned back just enough to add, "And Wazzu. Washington State University. Pullman, Washington. Three hours away. You ever heard of it?"

Cole was breathing heavily already from our almost kiss, but it picked up even more as his eyes widened.

"I sent in my acceptance papers a while ago," I said. "Go Cougs."

"You're telling me I get you to myself for the next four, possibly five, if we make like good slackers and take our sweet time, years?" He sounded like it was too good to be true.

I smiled and shrugged.

His hand wound behind my neck and he pulled me close again. "Sounds like one hell of an adventure."

"I wouldn't expect anything less from you."

Right before his mouth covered mine, he grinned. "From *us*," he said, "I wouldn't expect anything less from us."

Neither would I.